A SERIES OF SMALL MANEUVERS

Eliot Treichel

Ooligan
PRESS

A Series of Small Maneuvers
© 2015 Eliot Treichel

ISBN13: 978-1-932010-79-4

Ooligan Press
Portland State University
Post Office Box 751, Portland, Oregon 97207
503.725.9748
ooligan@ooliganpress.pdx.edu
http://ooligan.pdx.edu

Library of Congress Cataloging-in-Publication Data
Treichel, Eliot.
A series of small maneuvers / Eliot Treichel.
    pages cm
 Summary: "Fifteen-year-old Emma's growing up, and feels isolated from her friends and family. Things go from bad to unfathomably worse when Emma inadvertently causes an accident that kills her increasingly distant father on a spring break canoe trip meant to bring them closer together. Suddenly, Emma's efforts to reconcile with her father as a parent and a person have to happen without him, and she must confront her guilt and her grief to begin moving forward"-- Provided by publisher.
 ISBN 978-1-932010-79-4 (trade paper : alk. paper) -- ISBN 978-1-932010-80-0 (ebook)
[1. Fathers and daughters--Fiction. 2. Grief--Fiction.] I. Title.
 PZ7.1.T74Se 2015
 [Fic]--dc23
                        2015020922

Cover design by Stephanie Podmore

Interior design by Jessica Weber

Printed in the United States of America

Publisher certification awarded
by Green Press Initiative.

www.greenpressinitiative.org.

for BB

Prologue

My dad had just put on his daypack when I jumped onto his back. He stumbled forward a little, but then caught himself.

"Emma," he said.

I took hold of his pack's straps as if they were reins and clucked.

"Walk on," I said.

"Em, please." I was already slipping and trying to boost myself up again. "You're not your little sister."

The back of his neck smelled of sunscreen and campfire. He used to give me piggybacks all the time, and for some reason I was remembering them that morning, remembering what it used to be like before high school, a time that hardly seemed real anymore.

Once I'd gotten down, he grabbed my shoulders and acted like he was going to climb on. "Yeah, right," I said.

It was our fourth day on the river. We were leaving to go look for an old homesteader's cabin that my dad had read about on some online forum. The sun had pushed away the shade we'd been in all morning, and soon the heat would get oven-like. I'd wanted to spend the day by the water, laying out and swimming and pretending I was in Hawaii with Heidi and Tracy and all the other girls who'd come back from spring break bragging about their tan lines. I'd get tan lines, too, but they'd be from my personal flotation device. I'd have hard, calloused knees from kneeling in the bottom of the canoe, and blistered thumbs whose joints I could pop whenever I wanted.

"If we get back early enough," my dad said, "we can fish a little bit before dinner." His voice rose so that I'd be sure to know how awesome a deal it was.

Our hike was going to take longer than the half day he'd said it would, because they always did. I knew I was about to get sweaty and gross and scratched to crap by a hundred different kinds of cactus. Although it was a canoeing trip, there had been plenty of hiking already, plenty of kicking through the dust so we could check out some view, or some slot canyon, or some petroglyph, though those actually turned out to be pretty cool. My dad always wanted to go a little farther, always wanted to see what was around the next corner or over the next rise. We'd go until my legs were dead.

"We could be back right now," I said. I kung-fued my hands at him. It was another game we had. We did the same thing when we ran into each other in the hallway at home. "Then we'd have all sorts of time."

My dad kung-fued his hands back. "Seriously," he said. "Let's go check this out. This is our chance. When will we be here again?"

He was still posing, and I could sense the *Haiiii-ya!* about to come. He was probably right. I knew that we'd never be back there, and that it was important to seize opportunities, even if it only meant visiting the home of some crazy frontier guy from hundreds of years ago. I could see how much my dad wanted to go. His eyebrows were raised, and one side of his mouth kept breaking into a smile. It was the same look he got each week when he asked if I wanted to go to his kayak pool sessions—invitations I'd been saying no to more and more.

I jumped forward and chopped at his ribs, a blow he blocked with his elbow.

He tried a few of his fake-outs, but I knew them all. He'd taught me every trick he had. My dad was the reason I knew the J-stroke and how to light a camp stove and fillet panfish. The reason I could identify a blue-eyed darner, or a spotted towhee, or figwort. The reason I knew the word *geomorphology* and how to tell different sandstones apart, and why I was familiar with the biographies of John Wesley Powell and Tenzing Norgay. In my dad's home office, a whole wall of photographs documented his adventures—him rowing down the Grand Canyon, him kayaking some waterfall in Norway, him sitting on some snow-topped peak, his wraparound sunglasses reflecting the clear blue sky. In the oldest pictures, his hair is longer than mine.

My dad called time-out. "No, really," he said, when I wouldn't stop.

He bent down to retie a shoelace. The red bandana he wore around his neck slipped over his chin. He had on his favorite T-shirt, one so worn it was see-through in spots. A dragon curled around itself on the front of the shirt, and underneath the dragon's tail it read "Chinatown." Mom swore she was going to make him throw it out.

He'd finished with his shoe, but was still bent over when I tagged him on the back. "Sucker," I said, and took off in a sprint.

I could hear him clomping behind me, could tell he wasn't really chasing, but I kept running. When I got far enough ahead that I couldn't see him, I stopped. The streambed we were hiking up was completely dry. In front of me, the canyon walls squeezed together as they turned their first corner. On the outside of the curve, water had cut into the bank, forming a ten-foot-high overhang.

I was still catching my breath. I went a few steps more, looking farther up-canyon, where the walls grew even taller. Clusters of prickly pear clung to them. Sunlight cut through at an angle, and the air smelled of silt.

The rock was red—streaked in some spots with browns and blacks. I placed my cheek against it. It felt rough as sandpaper, but warm.

My dad had started whistling. He was trying to sound extra casual, but couldn't keep it up. I turned around and caught him grinning. He laughed, then I laughed, and then he laughed some more.

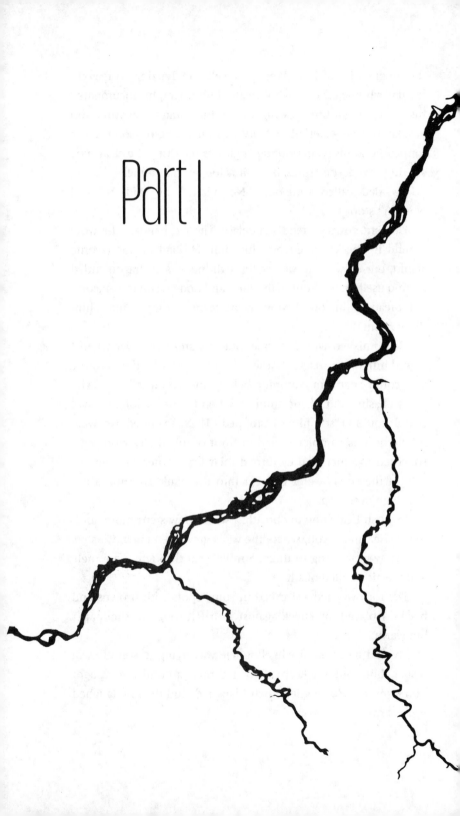

Part I

One

The sheriff first questioned me in the back of the ambulance. He sat on the bench next to the gurney, eating up the little space there was.

"I know you've been through quite a lot," he said. "I've talked to the other folks, and they've given me a pretty good idea of what happened, but I just wanted to see if you'd be willing to go over it with me a little yourself."

"Is my mom here yet?" I asked.

"She's on her way. My deputy just spoke with her."

"She knows?"

The sheriff shifted his legs, pulling on his pants so there was more room in the fabric. The leather of his utility belt creaked. "She knows you've been located, that you're safe."

"What about the other parts?"

"She understands there's been an accident. But we want to make sure we're clear on the situation so we don't give her any misinformation." He gave me a second to process that. "The other folks told me you were on a hike of some kind. Is that correct?"

I nodded.

"And can you tell me what happened?"

My feet and forearms and thumb all had clean white bandages on them. The IV bag was half-empty. I followed the tube as it snaked down and then ran into my arm, thinking that it was like a tiny river.

"We kept going to this other spot," I said. "It was a spring."

I thought about how we'd made it there, how we were resting before going back, and how my dad was climbing up on a log.

11

It was mostly saline in that IV, the same stuff as tears.

"I killed him," I said.

The next morning, the sheriff asked me to explain it all again at his office in Dixon. He sat across a metal table from me. The room was empty except for us and the table and chairs. Above the door was an EXIT sign, in case anyone got confused. The walls were made of cinderblocks, painted white, the ceiling a grid of foam panels. My mom was taking a break in the hallway. The sheriff had asked if we all wanted a break, but I'd said no. All I wanted to do was get it over with and go home.

"And this is the same day your father hurt himself?" the sheriff asked. I'd told him about the piggyback, the kung fu.

"The same day," I answered, "but earlier."

The sheriff had instructed me to call him Manny. Everyone else called him Sheriff Mendoza. His hair was dark black, but his beard had bits of gray in it. The sides of his crew cut were buzzed so short they were mostly skin. He said he just wanted to make sure he understood everything that'd happened. He told me that he had a daughter himself, one who was just a few years younger than me. He said my dad would've been proud.

The sheriff started playing with his hat on the table. You could still see the indentations it had made in his hair. The hat was clean and new looking, almost white, unlike the beat-up straw one my father always packed. The sheriff slid it back and forth between his hands. I felt like I was in trouble, or like I should be, no matter how much everyone had already said I wasn't. When his hat stopped moving, I knew another question was coming.

"How about we fast-forward a little bit. What can you tell me about later?" There was a legal pad beside him on the desk, a capped pen sitting on top. "Think back as best you can."

"I'm trying."

"I know, Honey." Maybe that was something he called his daughter. I didn't like it.

When they'd first brought me into the room, one of the sheriff's helpers had given me a Sprite. The can was cold from the vending machine. I took a long gulp, long enough so that the fizz climbed up into my nose when I swallowed.

The can was now empty, but I grabbed it anyway. I put it up to my lips and bit on the metal. Each time I exhaled, my breath echoed in the can. If I did it hard enough, it almost sounded like my horse, Magic, puffing those big nostrils of hers.

"Okay," the sheriff said. "Let's just focus on this. You told me before that your dad hit his head. Let's go back to that."

A deputy escorted my mom back in, even pulling out a chair for her. She sat next to me, her purse in her lap. It was bright orange canvas with funky wood handles. She had the handles in both hands, squeezing and un-squeezing, mashing the used tissues she also held.

The sheriff just let me talk. He'd let me keep going, however long I went, however off track, and then he'd go back and ask the original question again, sometimes in the exact same way.

"And you decided to go for help when?"

"I wanted to go right away," I said, "but I wasn't sure I would make it."

"It was smart of you to stick with the river," he said.

That really hit my mom. She pulled another tissue from the box and wiped her eyes with it, then wadded it with the others.

"I waited two days," I said.

"Two days after the accident?"

"After it was too late."

TWO

When we'd left home it was still dark, the streetlights shining. It was an eight-hour drive to the river, and my dad wanted to put on the water that afternoon. My mom kissed me on the forehead and told me to have fun as I trudged out the door. She was in her pajamas and looked half-asleep, like I was. Andrea, my little sister, hadn't even gotten up. "Don't drag your pillow," Mom said, but I was too tired to lift it, and she was too tired to press me.

My parents actually *believed* in camping, and my dad had been dreaming about the Rio Tinto for years, but there was another reason behind the trip: an email from Mrs. Meyers, the assistant principal, expressing some concern about my recent behaviors at school. Really it was just *one* recent behavior, though my dropping to a B minus in Spanish II didn't help any. I'd gotten caught with a cheat sheet in my Global Perspectives class—a cheat sheet I hadn't even been using. I was just passing it from Heidi to Tracy, but neither of them came to my defense.

"*I* wasn't cheating," I'd tried explaining to my parents. "I was just the mailman."

They were having none of it.

So that's why spring break was going to be off the grid. *Contemplative*. "So much needless drama," my dad had said while discussing the email with me.

It wasn't drama, I'd wanted to tell him. It was my life.

My dad nudged me when we crossed into New Mexico and pointed out the "Land of Enchantment" sign. I had the volume up on my iPod, but I could still hear the struggling engine of my dad's van. He drove a Westfalia that was almost twice as old as I was. The other cars flew past us.

"Yes. Enchanting," I said.

He moved his mouth, mimicking me. I could tell he hadn't really said anything. I gave him a thumbs-up and closed my eyes again.

For lunch, surprisingly, my dad pulled into a McDonald's. He was always lecturing us about fast food. About how evil it was because of the beef from factory farms, about the crappy wages, about how boring it was—the same food, the same décor, the same everything—and sometimes my mom and I would roll our eyes at the very same moment, cracking up because of how many times we'd heard it before.

"Laugh now," he'd say to us. "Go ahead and laugh now before your heart attack, and before everyone turns into diabetic blobs and the earth is some overgrazed hellscape. Get it out of the way."

The lunch stop was also a surprise because McDonald's was usually our *after*-trip ritual, an easy way to pay off Andrea and me. Sometimes, after camping, my dad would be so hungry he'd eat two or three burgers all by himself. That day, he just had coffee and stared out the window, not really talking. Using his thumbnail, he gouged lines into his cup. I sometimes still wonder what he was thinking about, if it was something about Mom, or if I'd said something to upset him. He kept checking his watch. Outside, the canoe hung over the ends of the van like an upside-down banana. I got fries and a milkshake and tried to see how long I could suck without taking a break.

"Oh, man," I said. "Ice-cream headache!"

"Happens," he said.

A few hours later, we turned off the highway and followed several smaller roads until we finally got to the gas station where my dad would set up and pay for the shuttle, which was how our van would get to the takeout at the end of the trip. He filled out some paperwork and gave the old lady behind the cash register an extra set of van keys. She had a whole system with tiny colored tags to keep the customers straight.

"It'll be there waiting for you," she said. She wore her gray hair in a bun and had on a big silver pendant. I learned later that her name was Ester. Her son was the one who did all the driving.

I grabbed a couple of Gatorades and a pack of gum, but my dad told me to pick just one. Ester smiled at me and then lowered her eyes. When I started to return the Gatorades, he told me to never mind and cracked one open before we were even out the door.

The last thirty miles followed a washboarded dirt road that zigzagged its way down to the river. My dad tried moving all over the road but it never really smoothed things out. The empty Gatorade bottles clunked around on the floor, and the sliding door sounded like it was disintegrating.

We arrived at the river just after three. Fine brown dust coated the canoe and the van, and I drew a happy face on one of the taillights. My dad wanted me to start unloading things while he untied the boat, but I lingered, trying to think of ways to improve my drawing. Maybe some big ears or something. I also wanted to lie down and take a nap and wake up back at home. He hadn't even gone and looked at the water—hadn't even taken a second to stand around and suck in a deep breath and make some comment about how good everything smelled—not the way he usually did. We'd been driving so long it was hard for him to stop moving.

Once we got the van unpacked, he relaxed. He stripped off his shirt and went through one of the dry bags to find the sunscreen, and had me rub some on his shoulders and back. He made himself a sandwich, which was the first thing he'd eaten all day, and he ate it standing up, staring at all our gear spread out on the ground. Our trip was Shotgun Creek to Piedra Gulch. We were going to be gone for seven days, eight counting the drive in. We had dry bags for our clothes, dry bags for our sleeping pads and sleeping bags, dry bags for the first-aid kit and the tent and everyday things like the Chap Stick and binoculars. We had a dry bag filled with empty dry bags. We had a cooler and a five-gallon water jug. We had spare paddles and throw ropes and old laundry jugs that my dad had modified into bailers. We had ammo cans—metal boxes that were once used to store ammunition and that he'd gotten from an army surplus store. They held our cooking gear and the water filter and the rest of the food. There was another ammo can, this one painted red, which was for our poop and toilet paper. It was called the groover because it would leave grooves on your butt when you used it, but then people figured out to also bring a toilet seat along. But that was the rule. Pack it in, pack it out.

I sat in the bottom of the empty canoe and listened to my iPod some more, trying to get in as much as I could because my dad wouldn't let me take it on the river. Part of the experience, he said, was to leave such things behind. It was about shedding the modern world. Life as it was meant to be. He wouldn't even pack a cell phone on the river, despite all of Mom's protests.

He wiped the crumbs off his hands and said something to me that I didn't catch. He took a deep breath through his nose. His cheeks were stuffed with food and he was chewing and smiling hard at the same time. Then he gave me a raise-the-roof move, raising it until I did one back, barely lifting my hands.

He lined up the canoe so that it was parallel to the shore, holding it steady while I got in the bow. The current looked slow, but I knew that it was probably faster than it seemed—that it was cold, which meant it was coming from way up in the mountains, and that so much distance meant a certain momentum.

"All set?" he asked, his paddle braced across the gunwales.

"Hang on," I answered. I took a deep breath. The canoe was pointed upstream so we could ferry out into the main current. My feelings of not really wanting to do the trip were suddenly ramming into the reality that this was about to happen. My dad had this ritual of getting himself wet right away—said you weren't as worried about tipping over and swimming once you had a little water on you. I leaned forward and reached down into the river and splashed some on my face, gasping from how icy it was.

That got him stoked. He splashed his own face and hooted and pushed us off, the boat's hull scraping across the gravel.

The river had us.

We didn't travel far, just a couple of miles for a warm-up. He had us go through all the strokes, practice all the different ways of steering and moving the canoe: pry, draw, back paddle, sweep. He made me hold my paddle out of the water and practice my balance while he rocked the boat back and forth underneath us. We went through high braces and low braces, those last-ditch strokes that could keep you from tipping over. We ran through some eddy turns and peel-outs and back ferries. My blade kept fluttering in the current or getting caught up against the boat, but then I remembered to loosen my grip, and that it wasn't how fast you pulled on the paddle, but how well.

After dinner, the first of so many planned pasta meals, I helped scrub the few dishes we had. I strained the dishwater to catch all the food scraps, and then I carried the strained water back to the river and poured it in. The river in front of me was wide and flat as a road, though I knew that in other spots it'd be narrower and steeper and crashing into itself. Even though we hadn't used any soap, when I poured the water a few soapy bubbles formed, and I watched as they drifted downstream. Sometimes you could use bubbles or bits of foam to tell which way the current was really going, or if there were different parts of the river moving at different speeds. My dad was good at reading rivers, but I could never see all the things he could. He'd once told me that I would just have to look at a lot of different rivers before I really got it, because every river looked and acted a little differently.

"It's all the same water," I remember him saying, "with a million personalities."

I once asked my dad what it was about the sound of water, why the sound of a river was so mesmerizing, so perfect.

"It all goes back to the womb," he'd answered. "Water is where we're born."

Across the river, a part of the bank sloughed into the water and startled me. A warm breeze ran upstream, swaying the salt-cedars. I noticed the three-part call of a red-winged blackbird.

When I returned with the dish tub, he'd just put some water on for hot chocolate. He had our mugs ready, an extra scoop of cocoa mix in mine. He leaned back in his packable chair and watched the blue flame on the stove. Before the water had even boiled he was conked out, his arms crossed over his chest, his head bent forward, snoring.

I stayed awake a long time after I finished my cocoa. A few coyotes howled to each other across the darkness. We didn't put up the tent that night, and I just watched the sky and listened to the river, because that's all there was. The sky didn't have the orange haze it had back at home, and the stars stood out sharply. If my dad had been up, he would've been quizzing me on the constellations, pressing me to move past easy ones like Cassiopeia and Orion. I was glad he was asleep and that I didn't have to answer his questions, but I also felt bad about that gladness, and I couldn't figure out which feeling was right. I pictured the numbers one through eight in front of me, one for each day of the trip. I crossed out the eight and told myself that in the morning I could cross out the seven, and then twenty-four hours after that the six, then the five, the four... until I was back sleeping in a real bed with a big comfy blanket, and the only coyotes around were the decorative tin ones in the living room.

A streak of light cut across the sky. "Zipper," I said to myself. It was the word my family used whenever we spotted a falling star.

"Zipper," I said again, already bored by how easy they were to catch.

Three

The day I'd gotten busted with the cheat sheet, Mr. O'Connor had the whole class stop what it was doing. "Pencils down," he said.

He'd been walking up and down the aisles, hands clasped behind his back, stopping here and there to look over our shoulders, especially those who seemed to be struggling. Tiffany Sanders had her head in her hands. When he paused next to her, she asked him if she was even doing it right at all, but Mr. O'Connor only smiled and shrugged, then moved on.

Mr. O'Connor's physique had a certain snowman quality to it. His hair was thin and white, and he had a white beard, parts of which seemed stained from the cigarettes he smoked. He was also fond of sweater-vests.

He'd started his rounds just as I got the note. I thought I'd hidden it under my thigh, but from where he stood it was visible.

Teachers are always saying things like, *Think before you speak. Choose your words carefully. Words have an impact.*

Mr. O'Connor should've listened to that advice. "Miss Wilson," he said. "May I see what's between your legs?"

The room erupted in a giant snort-laugh. Someone toward the back said, "Yeah, Emma. Show us what's between your legs."

After I handed it over, Mr. O'Connor held the folded paper in the air so everyone could see.

"That's it?" Eric Torres asked.

When I told Mr. O'Connor that it wasn't mine, he wanted to know whose it was.

"I don't know," I lied.

"You don't know?"

"I can't say."

Mr. O'Connor eyed the people sitting next to me—Heidi, Tracy, Kevin Strout, Colette Brown—but they just gave him the same shoulder shrug he'd given Tiffany Sanders.

"So far," he said, "I have no reason to believe you."

"Mr. O'Connor," I said, "this isn't mine. Honestly. You know me." I wondered if he really did. I'd only been in his classroom for a couple of months. He was mostly a PowerPointer, and if we didn't have any questions after his presentations, the lessons stopped there. I'd delivered exactly one three-minute oral report on Bolivia. Did that really count as knowing me?

If I'd been thinking faster, I would've had him compare the answers I'd filled in so far with the answers on the cheat sheet, because they wouldn't have matched up.

"One more chance for the truth," he said.

"It's what I told you," I said. He gave me an automatic F.

Four

The homestead turned out to be nothing more than a couple of knee-high stone walls. A fire ring and a pile of flattened, rusty cans plus some bullet casings from a .22. When I was little I used to bring the casings home from trips and fill them up with water and pretend they were vials of magic potions.

The spot was obviously a pretty bad place to have a home. It was too far from the river and too out in the unshaded open. My dad thought it probably used to be decent grazing land. If you were into dust and cactus spines, the place seemed ideal. I stood in what would've been the center of the building, wondering if there had at least been a few windows, or if it had been dark like a cave. My dad kicked through the yard with his eyes down, hoping for more relics. If I just let him look a while, he'd be satisfied and we could bail.

I went and sat down on the shady side of one of the walls, my back to him. The twigs and cactus spines spread out for miles—for forever—all the way to a dark band of mountains on the horizon. I stretched out my legs, my feet throbbing in my boots. My skin was so dry I could write messages on it. I pretended I could see an ocean. "Look," my dad said, coming over to show me a tarantula. "Check out our friend."

It was a young one. The tarantula's body was only about an inch wide, but with its legs spread out, the spider was nearly as big as the mouth of a coffee mug.

"Can I hold it?"

"Of course," he said.

The first time I ever held a tarantula, I freaked. Cried for like twenty minutes. I was eight, and even though I don't remember where we were—it was probably just in the backyard—I remember my dad pointing it out on the side of a boulder and then shooing it into his palm. The tarantula crawled round and round my dad's hands like it was on a spiderized treadmill. Whenever he played with one, my mom said she couldn't watch. She screamed at him when she found out he was showing me how to handle them too.

That first time, as soon as my dad guided the tarantula onto my hand, I panicked and flung it away. Then I started screaming and crying. After that, each time my dad saw one when my mom wasn't around, he'd ask me if I wanted to give it another try, but I never did—not until the Tinto.

He'd been feeding me fun facts for years: That tarantulas weren't mean, and that their bite wasn't anything worse than a bee sting, if one would ever bite you at all. That they have such soft bellies they can die if you drop them.

I'd already held one upstream. Part of it had to do with Heidi and Tracy, knowing that they'd never hold one, and knowing that there were a whole bunch of boys in my class and even teachers who wouldn't hold one, including Mr. O'Connor. Part of it had to do with an I-don't-know-what-this-is feeling that had been bothering me even before the trip.

The shade had lengthened at the base of the wall. I got up on my feet and wiped my palms on my shorts. The spider took cautious steps across the back of my father's hand. "Just hold your hand nice and flat," he said.

The tarantula paused for a second, testing with one of its legs, and then walked onto my palm. It weighed less than a cough drop. It stopped and bunched itself together, and from overhead it looked like a delicate black flower, each leg a petal. When it started walking again, I let it crawl from hand to hand, a long, steady journey to nowhere.

I looked up for a second and noticed my dad smiling. "Pretty cool," he said.

"It's totally cool. He's so weird looking, but also kind of perfect. He's almost cuddly."

"Weird is relative," my dad said. "What's weird?" *Weird* ranked up there with his least favorite words.

"I also said 'kind of perfect.'"

My dad reached into his daypack and got out his camera. He had me lift my hands higher so he could zoom in and still get my face in the shot. I made a fake terrified face, my eyes open as wide as they'd go. It wasn't much different from the silly face I made in almost every picture my parents foisted on me.

"One smile," he pleaded, "so we can show Mom."

I'm holding a tarantula, I thought. It almost didn't seem real. I flashed my dad a quick smile. It was quick, but he caught it.

"See?" he said. "I knew you could do it."

My dad, like I thought he would, wanted to keep hiking. The map hinted at a spring in the next side canyon, and he thought we could get to it from the plateau. But we didn't need spring water. We'd brought enough water for the hike, and once we got back to the river we didn't have to worry.

"It'll be awesome," my father said when I moaned about more walking. "Eden-like."

"Eden-like is relative," I said.

"You know how beautiful those springs can be." He was stretching his hamstrings, talking into his shins. "You know how geeked out I get by that."

I'd already indulged him with the trip to the homestead, had picked up a tarantula, and I was ready to go back to our own little Eden at the river. I didn't want any more practice shooting a bearing with a compass, and I didn't want to try and find anything else we weren't even sure was there in the first place.

"I knew this was going to happen," I said.

"What was?"

"That it was going to be longer than what you said."

"We're more than halfway there already." He said it as if that was reason enough to go the rest of the way.

"We never just go where you say we're going. Why don't you just say we're going for a twenty-million-mile hike before we start? Don't you always tell me to be honest?"

"Twenty million?"

"At least."

He stood up and tried not to laugh. "Em," he said, as I turned away. I hated how he sometimes laughed at me when I was mad.

He didn't say anything for a while, and neither did I. Without the constant noise of the river in the background, the quiet almost felt loud.

"If you want to go back," he finally said, "we can. It's just that I like to find things, things people don't always get to see, and you don't like to do that as much."

"That's not what I'm saying," I said. "That's not fair."

"But you're right," he pressed. "It's important to be honest. I said the hike was to here. Any hikes from here on out we'll decide how far we're going before we leave and stick to it. We'll go that far, and no more. No more, no less, just that exactly."

His mouth was clenched tight, his jaw flexing a little. His ethic was *epic*. It was a word some of the boys in class threw around, but they didn't mean it the same way. For them it was just slang, and it usually applied to parties, or hooking up with a girl, or some stupid YouTube video, but for my dad it meant getting lost in the rain or the snow, or in whatever miserable weather he could find. It meant scars and blisters and elevation gain. It meant surviving for days on tasteless oatmeal. He wanted me to believe in it, too.

I opened my mouth to speak, tears welling. I had no idea where to even start.

"Say it," he said. His voice turned quiet and soft, and he seemed to be decompressing. Sometimes the storms could be quick. When I didn't offer anything more, he said, "Either way, it's fine. But you have to decide. You're behind the wheel. This is what it's going to be like if you ever get your license."

He was talking about how I hadn't shown any initiative—his

25

word—in getting my learner's permit yet, which was such a crappy thing for him to bring up right then.

"I'm demoting myself," he finished. "You're leading. I'm following."

Sheriff Mendoza wanted to know if my dad had been right. Was I just going to the spring to satisfy him?

My dad kept telling me that I didn't have to say yes for his sake, and I kept insisting that I wasn't.

"I'm skeptical," he kept saying. He repeated it so much that I finally told him to shut up and leave me alone.

The sheriff wanted to know my dad's reaction, which was to do just as I asked: he stopped talking. He stopped talking, and we kept hiking, except I wasn't in front anymore. My dad took off and motored way ahead, so that there was a big gap between us and we were each kind of walking alone.

First I thought about hiking extra slow—so slow he'd lose sight of me and have to wait. The words *I'm sorry* echoed in my head, which started to make me pissed, because I didn't think I needed to be sorry. I was mad at my dad, and I was getting mad at myself, and so I put my head down and started walking as fast as I could, fast enough to snag him.

Except I couldn't.

I pushed until my thighs turned heavy and my lungs were burning, until I had sweat running down my face and dripping off my chin and nose, but I couldn't make up the difference. I'd caught his attention, could tell he was enjoying our little race, but I couldn't catch up.

What I didn't tell the sheriff, what I didn't tell anybody, was that I knew my dad had actually wanted to turn around and go back to camp more than he'd wanted to continue on to the spring. It was partially why I told him I wanted to keep going, just so I could contradict him and make it hurt a little. What my dad really wanted to do, even though he didn't always act like it, was make Andrea and me happy.

Five

Part of the way down the side canyon, we hit a roadblock. My dad pointed above us, to an uneven spot on the canyon wall. He thought a massive piece of rock must have sheared free and thundered to the ground at some point, leaving a mess of granite boulders for us to weave through, some of them bigger than his van.

In the cool shade of the canyon, our argument from before felt as if it had dissolved, or had at least dissolved enough. A half mile in the distance glowed a patch of green—the spring. Up where he was pointing, dirty yellows and reds and grays all marked the different layers of rock. He always said that geology was just another way of talking about time—much like rivers were just another way to talk about pretty much whatever you wanted to. "What's one day?" he would ask. What was one day of school, or one day of chores, or one day of something you didn't want to do? Was it anything to complain about? When you considered ten million, one hundred million, a billion years?

One day is one day, I always wanted to answer.

My dad would be probe. It was a phrase from the river and meant being the fool who would run the rapid first.

He'd go first, but I'd have to follow right behind.

We started squeezing through the boulders, the nylon of our backpacks *shrip*-ing against the rocks. For the most part it was easy enough to maze through. We had to crawl in the dirt a couple of times, backtrack once. At one point, my dad decided the better approach would be to just go up and over the boulders, spotting each other as we climbed. Some of the rocks were taller than I liked, but he didn't give me much time to think about them. Coming down the back side of one, I froze and couldn't find the next spot for my foot. When my legs started shaking, he had me jump into his arms.

"I got you," he said, and I let go.

It was something he'd told me ten million, one hundred million, a billion times.

The spring turned out to be little more than a trickle. Water dribbled from a crack in the ground and collected in a small pool that was only a few inches deep. At the bottom of the small pool, leaves decomposed, turning gray and mucky, while along the edge of the water a patch of puffy green moss survived. Cottonwood and honey locust spread their branches over us, shading us even more, and just that little bit of water from the spring was enough to make the air feel moist and refreshing, like my pores wanted to drink it.

My dad untied his handkerchief and then dipped it into the water, letting the fabric soak through. When he pulled the cloth from the water, he wrung out the excess and then rerolled the handkerchief and tied it around his neck, exhaling an "ahhh" when it first hit his skin. "Feels nice," he added. I could tell I was supposed to translate that as *you should try it.*

By dipping his handkerchief, he'd stirred up the water. It would've been impossible for me to not get leaves and pieces of gunk all over mine had I soaked it. I pulled out my water bottle instead and took a few long drinks, wiping my chin when I was done. I knew he'd have us fill one of our bottles from the spring before we left. It was a rule of his to take water when you found it.

"That homesteader-rancher dude should've built his place down here," I said.

My dad untied the laces of his boots, and then leaned back against a rock and closed his eyes. "It's definitely more inviting." A water strider skimmed across the surface of the pool. Along where the spring seeped out of the rock, I noticed a few tiny flowers blossoming. They were white and symmetrical and rimmed with purple, no bigger than a sesame seed.

"How come there's water right here?" I asked. "Why at this spot?"

I knew the answers in theory—that the water had probably come from the plateau and the mountains beyond, that it had seeped into the old volcanic rock, working its way to where we stood, where it had finally found a way back to the surface. He had told me all these things before, had even given me coloring books and picture books and chapter books about it. I knew that all rivers had a source—a melting glacier, an outflow from a lake, a spring. I also knew that these places, because they were the starting points of these long systems that connected everything together, should be treated with something close to sanctity.

Except reservoirs. Reservoirs didn't count. A reservoir is a river that has been drowned.

My dad answered with his eyes still closed. "Well," he said, and stalled there. I figured he was considering what kind of explanation to give me—a thorough and systematic one, or a quick and simple one that would allow him to keep resting. "I guess it's just the way things have come together," he said.

He was giving the quick version.

"But why was that the way things came together?"

"You sound a little like Andrea," he said. *"But why?"*

"I'm serious," I said.

"You want to know why this spring is right here?"

"Pretty much. Like what's the source of this water? Where does this water start?"

"I'm not sure I could tell you," he said. "'Start' is a tricky word in this context. Does it start with the water molecules in the atmosphere? The rain? The snowmelt?"

"That's what I'm asking."

"Well, what do you think? How could you figure out the answer?"

When one of us—Mom or me, or even sometimes Andrea—was trying to figure something out, Dad had this wonderful way of hovering in the background and then coming in and letting us know exactly how we were doing it wrong. And he had this other way of staying out of it and making you figure things out on your own when you went looking to him for an answer. Then once you'd gone through all that, once you thought you'd figured it out, he'd tell you the ways in which you hadn't.

"I could turn myself into a really, really tiny camera," I said. "Like the kind they use for surgeries."

"Yes, but beyond miraculously shrinking yourself, or some other unreal thing, how could you *actually* figure it out?"

I got up from where I was sitting. My dad opened an eye, squinting at me for a second, and then closed it. The cottonwood and the locust. If I spoke the trees' language, the roots could tell me. The rocks could tell me. The water could.

I gave him the answer I knew would drive him nuts. "I'll just Google it," I said.

I'd gone off to pee. You're supposed to make sure you're at least a hundred feet away from water sources like the spring when you pee, though down by the river you were just supposed to go right in it. My dad's siesta was over. He was up and walking around and checking out some of the animal tracks. He found mule deer, raccoon, some species of mouse. "Ours are the only boot prints I see."

There was an old tree that had fallen, its bleached-out trunk wedged at an angle between two boulders. My dad started walking up it. It was the kind of thing he always did. If he came upon a rope swing, he had to swing on it. If there was a body of water and rocks to skip, he had to skip them. A log ramp that ended ten or fifteen feet in the air, he had to climb it.

"I suppose we should fill up with water since we're here," he said. He'd made it about halfway up.

I'd just zipped my water bottle back in my pack. "I guess."

I walked over by his makeshift jungle gym, noticing his foot-prints in the dirt. I dragged a toe along the ground to make it look like a big snake had come through. I tried stepping onto the log, but I lost my balance right away and had to hop down.

"If you want to get it out, the UV filter is in the top compartment." He looked at me and then over at his pack.

"Not really," I said. All that sitting after all that walking had made me sleepy. My trail mix, most of which I'd eaten back at the homestead, was just peanut crumbs and raisins. I started kicking at the dried-out, bug-eaten bark on the log, as absent-mindedly as my dad had scratched those lines into his coffee cup at McDonald's. Most of the bark had already dropped off, but there was something satisfying about making the last chunks pop away. I actually started feeling glad that we hadn't turned back earlier, happy that I'd gotten to see the spring, the micro-scopic flowers, and everything else.

He'd almost reached the top. "Think you can get this high?"

"*Puh-lease.*" I kicked one last piece of bark free and then got up on the tree trunk. "Ladies and gentlemen," I said, spreading my arms extravagantly. I tried hanging on, but by the third step, my balance became a lost cause. I spun sideways, arms windmilling.

After I fell off, I kicked at the log in frustration. That's when it shifted.

Six

The sound of it. I can still hear the sound now, the icky hollow-ness of it, despite how hard I've worked to forget it. The way there were two sounds—the sledgehammer *thunk* of my dad's skull hitting the rock, and then how his head bounced a little and fell again, a lighter sound. Then a third: the air rushing out of him as he landed. How he lay there on his back, one hand reaching up to his head but suddenly frozen, unmoving. How there was a slackness to him that terrified me.

"Daddy."

I was supposed to go to him, kneel down beside him, but I stood a few feet away, unable to make myself get closer.

He'd made sure I knew basic first aid—that I knew how to clean and dress a wound, how to make a splint out of duct tape and branches, how to assess a person's ABCs. I'd even taken a CPR class with him one year, where I learned that the first thing to do is have someone call 911. But that had all been pretend. That had been saving mannequin lives.

"Dad, wake up."

One of his feet was turned inward and began twitching. The arm that had started to reach for his head unfroze and swatted the air. He opened his eyes a little and began rolling to his side, groaning, trying to get up, but then seeming to get stuck.

"Stay still," I said. My mouth tasted coppery, and suddenly I had too much spit. I forced myself to move. "I think you're hurt."

His leg and foot were still shaking. His eyelids fluttered. I grabbed his hand, which was completely stiff.

My dad took a big, deep breath. A big, sighing breath. And then he was back. Or sort of. "Huh," my dad said. His left eye opened wide for a second. I knew he wasn't winking at me, but that's what it looked like.

I repeated myself, only louder. "Are you okay?"

Both eyes were closed again. He mumbled a yes.

"You hit your head," I said.

"Huh."

"You hit your head."

He didn't say anything more, but just stayed like that for a bit, smacking his lips. It made me think of the time when my dad's best friend, Ron, got drunk at our house and passed out on the deck, and how when my dad woke him up to bring him inside, Ron moved slow and wobbled when he walked, like the commands from his brain to his muscles were moving at light speed negative. When my dad was ready, I helped him sit up.

I put my hand on the back of his neck and waited with him, each second bringing him back a little bit more. On the back of his head, darkening blood matted a patch of hair. The bump had already swollen to the size of a golf ball.

"I think the log moved," he said, after a few minutes.

"I think you're right." I don't know why I said, "think." I knew. I'd moved it. "You fell."

"Did I hit my head?" he asked. He'd looked a little white before, but now his color had come back.

"You did."

My dad reached both hands up to his head. He exhaled long and slow. "Wow," he said. "This really, really hurts."

I could tell the pain was coming in waves, in peaks and troughs, because he'd hunch over and moan in regular intervals and then go quiet again. I'd seen my father hurt before—seen him smash a thumb, tweak his back, or even come home bloody after a mountain-bike wreck—but I'd never seen him like this, where he wasn't hopping around and cursing, or totally spazzing out about how cool the wound looked.

I started searching through my dad's pack, removing stuff. He halfheartedly asked what I was doing, but I didn't answer. I pulled out his headlamp and a little Ziploc that had a box of matches and a squashed-down roll of toilet paper inside. There were a couple of granola bars and a stick of beef jerky. He had a raincoat and a small stuff sack with a few extra clothes. The first-aid kit was at the very bottom. He'd always told me to pack it at the very top.

Bandages and sterile pads and gauze and tape—all things that were white, or that came in white packaging—filled one half of the kit. The other half held orange prescription bottles my dad had filled with over-the-counter medicines. There was a Ziploc bag stuffed with latex gloves. Scissors, a thermometer, big pieces of cloth for making slings, a small flexible splint. We'd done the inventorying together while sitting at the kitchen table one night before the trip.

"Should you take one of these?" I asked, getting out the bottle of ibuprofen. "Or what about this?" I showed him the Certi-Cool pack, which was like an instant ice pack, one that had chemicals inside that got cold when they were mixed together.

My dad pointed at the Certi-Cool. You had to smash it with your fist and then shake it to get all the ingredients to mix. I had to hit it a few times to get the compartments inside it to actually break. Once it turned cool, I started placing the pack against his head, but I think I did it too roughly, because he snatched it away from me.

"What about the ibuprofen?" I asked. "Should you take some? Those are for headaches."

"I'm pretty sure I'm suffering from one of those."

I pushed down on the cap and twisted it open. I started shaking out a few pills, but my dad told me to stop.

"Save them," he said.

"You just said you have a headache."

"I do," he said, "but I can't take those right now." Ibuprofen was an anti-inflammatory, he said, which thinned your blood and could make you bleed worse. What we needed was some Tylenol, some acetaminophen.

"I don't see any of that," I said, searching through the containers again.

"We usually have some Children's Tylenol if your sister is along, but I probably didn't think to refresh it." *What had the checklist even been for, then?*

"But your head isn't really bleeding anymore," I said. "How can it make the bleeding worse if there's no bleeding? It's all dried up."

"On the inside," he said. "The bleeding on the inside."

Seven

We left the spring late that afternoon. He had me go first, made me promise I wouldn't walk too fast. I tried to remember the route we'd taken through the boulder heap, while he kept trying to remember the part about hitting his head. Going uphill, some of the route was harder than before, and one time my dad had to get down on his knees so that I could stand on his shoulders and pull myself up a big rock. Once I was up, he had trouble following.

That he couldn't recall all of the accident—that there was a blankness where he knew something should be—had him irritated already, irritation that only got worse as he struggled to climb the rock.

"I *am* grabbing you," I said, when he snapped at me.

"Do it *before* I start sliding back down."

He tried again, this time with a little bit of a running start. I locked both hands around his right forearm and pulled so hard I gave him a snakebite. He'd almost made it, had almost flopped his way over the lip, when he told me to let go and he dropped back down, swearing as he landed.

The skin on his forearm throbbed bright pink. He pulled up his T-shirt, revealing red slashes and dimples from where he'd scraped against the rock. "This is ridiculous," he said. "This isn't going to work."

"You got this," I said. It was a phrase he was always using on me when I struggled with something, even when it was completely obvious that things weren't going to be gotten. He'd even said it earlier in the trip—trying to show me how to flip pancakes without a spatula. I'd slammed the pan back onto the stove and told him it was hopeless, pancake batter dripping from my forearm. "Just keep trying," he'd said. "You got this." When I'd gone through almost all the mix and still hadn't landed one, he cut in and made a couple of perfect flapjacks. "Just so we don't starve."

Now my dad scanned the area, looking for a different route. From where I was standing, it was clear we had no other choice, not unless we wanted to do a whole bunch of backtracking.

"That last time we almost had it," I said. I'd never really had to pump him up before. "I think we've got it figured out. We'll totally get it this time."

"I just feel really weak."

"Come on," I said.

He stood motionless, silent, staring at the rock in front of him. I got the sense that he was about to sit down. After a minute or two, he said, "Okay." He reached out and brushed some of the dead lichen from the rock. He took a deep breath and backed up. "Okay," he said again. He said it quietly, as if it were something he didn't really want me to hear.

We were just past the homesteader's place when he started throwing up. He stood bent over with his hands on his knees, puke splashing on the ground. I turned away, gagging a little.

"It's the heat," he said, when he could finally talk. His skin was splotchy, and his hands trembled a bit. A line of drool hung from his mouth. He kept trying to spit it away, but couldn't get it. He wiped it off with his hand.

I'd gotten out my water bottle and unscrewed the top. He took it and swirled some water in his mouth, then spit again.

"Sorry about that." He kicked some dirt over his mess. I didn't want to look, but I did.

"It's okay," I said. What I meant was that he didn't have to say he was sorry, but the way it came out sounded more like I was accepting his apology. "I'm the one who's sorry," I said. "You're the one who's in pain."

"A little barfing isn't such a big deal," he said. "It's not the first time." He grimaced and cleared his throat, gave his mouth another rinsing. What I should've known, what I should've admitted I knew, and what he should have told me, was that in this case it *was* a big deal. In this case, it meant his body was starting to shut down.

My dad once showed me how to measure the amount of time left until sunset. You faced west and held your hand at arm's length, turned it sideways, and set it on the horizon. Each hand-width that you could measure above that—stacking them one on top of the other until you reached the sun—represented a half hour. It wasn't exact, but it was close, and I always thought it was so unique, like a smart feature of the human body. When I measured, we had just over one hand.

"Time to saddle up?" he asked.

"We've got about half an hour. Maybe a little more." He'd handed back the water bottle, most of it drained. The bottle was made of clear blue plastic, and I held it over my eyes like a pair of sunglasses. My dad seemed far away, almost like I was under-water while he was standing on the edge of a pool, like maybe an infinity pool in Hawaii, at some big resort. You could almost pretend there were palm trees.

"How long did it take us to get here this morning?" he asked, and then went ahead and answered himself, saying that an hour sounded about right, even though it had taken longer.

"I don't know," I said, "it seemed like it took forever."

My dad retched again as soon as we made it to camp. He stood over a creosote bush not far from the tent. I'd dropped my pack and was refilling my water bottle from the big jug, trying as hard as possible not to hear him. I couldn't help but look again—saw another string of saliva hanging from his bottom lip.

During one of the first aid practice nights that my dad insisted we do before the trip, he told me a story about a woman who'd been struck by lightning while she was hiking near her house with her son and the family dog. I interrupted my dad's story to ask what the name of the dog was, but he didn't know. He didn't even know what kind it was. "It's not the dog that's important in this one," he said. "I know—hard to believe."

Because the son had been walking way ahead, chasing the dog, the lightning missed him, though it bowled him over. The boy, a Boy Scout, knew CPR. He ran back to his mom. The air smelled like ozone and charcoal. Her clothes had holes burned through them and her hair had been almost entirely singed off. She had a smoldering burn on her leg in the exact shape of her cell phone, right where her front pocket had been. Her phone, blackened and smoking, sat on the ground twenty feet away. She was not breathing. Her heart was not beating.

The boy did what he'd been trained to do by his scoutmaster, and he went through the steps of CPR and restarted his mother's heart. They waited there until his dad came looking for them.

The boy made the news as a hero, and he got to be on all the morning talk shows, which is where my dad had heard about it. The boy, my dad had said, recounted how he'd heard the lightning before it struck. He'd heard a crackling noise, as if he'd suddenly become a radio and was casting off static. His ears started ringing and he got a really bad headache. And then— flash-*boom!* Like a bomb.

"In an emergency," my dad had said, "you can't let yourself get scared. Especially when you're in the backcountry." Frontcountry was civilization: houses, hospitals, malls, flushable toilets, microwave ovens, school cafeterias. Backcountry was where all that stuff wasn't. "You just have to do what you've practiced, as you've practiced it."

"What if you don't practice?" I asked. The point that I took away from the story was to be terrified of lightning.

"That's why you practice," he said.

My dad straightened up and stepped away from the bush. He frowned and reached up and shaded his eyes, although there was no sun. The sky was an unbroken, watered-down purple. I held out the refilled bottle for him, but he waved it away.

"Not yet," he said.

We went down to the river, took off our boots and socks, and soaked our feet in the cold water. The light had turned the surface dull, and the river looked like melted gray crayon. Our canoe—the paddles tucked inside, the life jackets clipped to the thwarts—sat pulled all the way up on dry land, both the bow and stern tied off to a stand of tamarisk.

My dad rinsed his face and poured handfuls of river over his head. The wet sand felt nice and smooth on the back of my legs, even felt good on the backs of my tender heels. On the first day in camp we'd sunk a piece of driftwood into the beach, right at the waterline, so we'd be able to tell if the river level was changing. For the whole trip the water had been dropping, and that day it was down another two or three inches. The more the river dropped, the less trouble the big rapids would give us.

I moved the stick to the new spot, something my dad insisted we always do. "If you don't move the marker," I remember him telling me, "you're looking at it and guessing exactly how much the waterline has shifted. You keep moving the stick and you know for sure." It made sense, but as much as anything, I think it was also because my dad sometimes got antsy, and when he got antsy he was good at finding things to do, could make up projects out of nothing, like a cactus pulling water from the desert air.

"Where do you think the level will be in the morning?" I asked, screwing the stick into the sand a little more.

My dad sat with his arms wrapped over his knees. He pivoted his head my direction. "Down," he said. "That's been the trend. That's probably a pretty good bet."

"I thought you didn't follow trends," I said. He'd told me not to be a sucker for trends about as many times as he'd warned our family about fast food.

My dad smiled. When he tried to tell me this was different, I asked him why.

"I'm not so much following," he said, attempting to pull in his amusement. "This is more like paralleling. Like I'm a trend paralleler." He was back to his wise-guy self, the self that got giddy when I pushed back a little. "You can be a trend paralleler," he said, "just don't be a trend follower. Instead of walking behind, it's like walking side by side."

"What if you have to walk single file?" I asked. "Like if the trail isn't wide enough?"

"That's one of those exceptions," he said.

"Oh," I said, "one of those."

A bat had shown up, and it flew overhead in erratic circles. Then there were two bats. Then three.

I reached down and scooped up some sand, using my palm like a panning dish. I isolated a few small pebbles and stood up. My dad was good at talking his way out of things, and had a way of judo-flipping my questions right back at me. It was like when he took me hiking, how he always wanted to go a little farther, or around the next bend, except that in conversation he wanted me to approach things from another angle or a new perspective, and he was always giving one more tidbit of history or science or whatever, and then asking me to reconsider it all—even if his point was now the exact opposite as before. "I'm not arguing," he'd say. "I'm just being passionate. It's good to be passionate."

When a bat flitted close enough, I flung one of the little rocks as high as I could. Sometimes you could fool them into thinking it was a bug and get them to swoop after. My dad hadn't been watching. He felt around the back of his head, prodding the tender spots. I tried to trick the bats some more, but could never tell if I actually did. The pebbles went *ploop* with the tiniest of splashes.

I scrubbed my hands in the river, bits of sand sticking to the folds between my fingers. Soon it'd be dark enough that we'd need our headlamps. We should've been getting dinner going, but I really just wanted to burrow into my sleeping bag and wake up to a new day with everything all better. Once my hands were clean, I flicked the water from them at my dad. He didn't seem to notice, and just kept rubbing his head and staring at the river.

I looked around for another stick, but I couldn't find one. Instead, I snapped off the top of our marker.

"I'll make a bet," I said. My dad loved little wagers, and I had his attention again. "I'll bet you a Snickers. When we wake up in the morning—" I placed my stick an inch inland from our marker. "—the water is going to be right here."

"Right there?" he asked.

"Right here exactly."

"A Snickers?"

"I've got two left."

"And what if I lose?" he asked. "Then what?"

"I'd take money. Or cash. Or even cash money."

"I'm sure."

"Just a couple of bucks."

"Two bucks?"

"Two dollars."

"Little Emma," he said, limply shaking my hand. "I'm going to enjoy the heck out of that candy bar."

Eight

I turned off my headlamp so I could change in the dark. My dad was already in his sleeping bag, in the same shirt and shorts he'd worn all day. I always tried to keep one set of clothes that were only for bed—clean clothes that wouldn't start smelling like vinegar, or that weren't all stiffened with salt. It was something my mom had taught me. With my back to him, I slid off my shirt and sports bra, then felt around for my other shirt—an oversized T-shirt I'd gotten from the animal shelter the summer before, when my parents instituted a mandatory, once-a-week volunteering thing. Once I was dressed, I flipped on my headlamp so I could find my lotion. My dad winced from the brightness.

"Sorry." I quickly squirted a dot of lotion into my palm and then cut the light.

"It just surprised me. You can leave it on if you want. My eyes were adjusting."

"That was a pretty ugly face you made."

"I can probably do uglier."

I left the light off and massaged the lotion into my elbows and along my forearms, rubbing some on my cheeks and eyebrows, which almost felt singed at the ends. The cream was my mom's and smelled of lavender, and it felt as refreshing on my skin as the air near the spring.

"You're so good at taking care of yourself," my dad said. His throat sounded dry, and he swallowed loudly. He'd meant the lotion, and how I brought skin cleaner, and how I usually took some time each night to scrub my face. "Women are so much

43

better than men. I brush my teeth, jump in the river, and that's about it. I don't even think any of the dirt comes off."

The compliment made me laugh a little. I sometimes didn't know what else to do when adults said stuff like that. I wondered if my dad was smiling, but I couldn't tell. I heard the sincerity in his voice, but I also knew there was another part of him that wished Mom and I didn't bring things like facial cleaner and special night-time clothes, and I knew this because he got crabby about it sometimes, complaining about all the room it took up, even though those things barely took up any space or weighed anything at all. He'd get grumpy with me at home, too—would see my eyeliner or mascara, or my disposable razor, and then would deliver a lecture about subscribing to outdated notions of womanhood.

I started to get in my bag. My dad sniffled. At first I thought it was just a running nose, but then I realized he was crying.

"Dad," I said. I started to pad around for him, but stopped. I sat still, listening to how hard he was trying to hold everything in.

After a while, he said, "You have to help me tonight. Just a little bit." His voice was shaky. "Every couple of hours. Every few hours, I need you to wake me up. You can use the alarm on my watch."

"Why can't you use it?"

"Emma, listen. Just tonight."

"Every couple of hours?"

"Wake me up and tell me I was snoring or something."

"What if you aren't snoring?"

"It doesn't matter," he said. "Just wake me up and check on me."

It was only nine o'clock, which feels late when you're camping. I took my dad's watch and pushed the button for the green background light. I set the alarm for eleven, realizing I was going to have to reset it each time.

"Okay," I said.

"Yeah?"

"It'll go off in two hours."

"Thank you," he said. It came out like a whisper.

I snuggled the rest of the way into my sleeping bag and stared at the tent ceiling. For a while it was just the darkness and the rustling of our bags and the sound of us breathing. The lullaby of the river outside. The sense of waiting for something.

"Dad—"

When I didn't say anything more, he asked, "What's up?"

"You're going to be alright, right?"

"Yeah," he said, "I'll be okay."

"Are you sure? You're not just saying that because it's what you're supposed to say?"

"No," he said, "I mean it. I'll be okay." I made him promise, because promises were important to him, and I thought if I made him promise, he'd have to keep it. "I promise," he said.

I told him goodnight. I said I'd see him in two hours.

"Goodnight, Emma-bean." When I was really little he'd sometimes just call me Bean. He still sometimes called Andrea Panda-bean. "I love you very much," he said.

"I love you, too."

He reached over and nudged me, his hand still inside his sleeping bag. I left my hand inside my bag too, but reached over to find his, fist-bumping softly through the down filling.

"I wish you could know how much," he said. "I wish all of you guys could." He'd turned his head and was facing me, his breath sour. He kept his knuckles touching mine.

"I know," I said. It wasn't supposed to sound so breezy. "We do."

I thought he was going to say something about how Mom and Andrea and I couldn't know, that none of us could ever know how much we loved one another, or if we were even talking about love in the same way, because we couldn't be inside someone else's mind.

He was crying again, but more openly than before, and it took a moment before he could get the words out. "I know you do."

Before the alarm even went off, my dad began seizing. At first, still halfway in a dream, I thought he was just moving around and trying to get comfortable—that maybe he'd woken himself up so I wouldn't have to. Then he started making gagging noises and his legs, completely inflexible, began kicking.

I found my headlamp and turned it on. His eyes were half-open and rolled back into his head. His back was arched and his muscles all seemed to be fighting each other—all of them pulling equally, but in opposite directions. Spit bubbled out of his mouth, and his cheeks looked blue.

"Dad, stop! Please! Wake up! Get up!"

After a long last sputter, his seizure finally ended. His body started to relax back to its natural shape, much as it had when he was coming around at the spring. His eyes fluttered a few times and then closed all the way. He breathed deeply, and then he almost seemed to be snoring.

I unzipped and loosened his bag, which had twisted around him. No matter what I did, I couldn't get him to wake up. I poked and shook him, slapped his cheeks, rubbed my knuckles into his chest. His eyelids would only stay up if I held them like that. Even when I shined my headlamp at his pupils, there was nothing—no change.

"Please," I kept saying.

Please.

Please.

Please.

When the alarm rang, the surprise of it made me cry. I thought maybe the alarm would be the thing to finally wake him, so I kept setting it to go off, but its awful beeping never did anything, no matter how close I held it to his ears.

Outside my bag, the cold started to get to me. I grabbed my clothes sack and dug for my fleece sweater. I had to keep him warm. That was one thing I could do. I straightened out his sleeping bag, and zipped it as far as I could. I found his jacket and spread it over his torso, pulled the collar up to his chin. I got out his beanie, but then didn't know if it was a good idea. His forehead felt warm and dry, though it looked waxy with sweat.

"Just for a one second," I tried again. "Just wake up for one second and say one thing and then you can go back to sleep."

Days later, Sheriff Mendoza told me how even if we'd had a cell phone, it was unlikely that we would've gotten any service where we were. But that was all I could think about that night— how if my dad had brought his phone, or if he'd let me bring mine, then I could've called or texted someone for help. What would they have said back, though? Sit tight and wait? That what I really needed to do was drill a hole in my dad's head to relieve the swelling, so I should probably get going with figuring out how to do that?

I unzipped the tent door and crawled outside, shouting for help. The beam from my headlamp cut across the campsite and faded out in the distance. Animals watched me, their green eyes glowing. I shouted again, but the river swallowed my voice. Overhead, mixed in with all the stars, an airplane blinked its way home. It was the only other manmade light I could see. I thought I might throw up.

His breathing was slow and labored. According to my father's watch, it was nearly three in the morning. He'd had two more seizures, but after the last his breathing began to race, almost as if he was panting, and then it abruptly switched, and the spaces between each inhale and exhale grew farther and farther apart, and I knew. His eyes were still closed, but slivers of white showed where his eyelids didn't quite meet, and I wanted to believe he could see me. I had to believe it. "I'm here," I said. I straightened his jacket one more time and then reached down and placed my hand on his arm. Once you begin CPR you're supposed to keep going until you get to a doctor, or the paramedics arrive, or you succumb to exhaustion, which would've been the case with me. "I'm here," I said again. It was all I could do, and it was nothing.

He breathed in, and then he was gone. I kept waiting—waiting for him to breathe out, to finish, but he didn't. *That's where you're going to stop?* His mouth hung open, and suddenly I was remembering a Thanksgiving when he'd fallen asleep on the couch, his mouth open like that, and Andrea and I watched Mom squirt whipped cream into it, the three of us in hysterics when he woke up and spit it all over. In my mind's next flash, I heard her voice—*Emma?*—and I could sense her there in the tent with me. "Mom!"

I yanked off his jacket and straightened his torso as best as I could. I found the center of his breastbone and stacked one hand on top of the other, but then remembered I was supposed to start with two breaths. It was two breaths, thirty compressions, two breaths. I tilted his head to open the airway, lifting under his chin. I squeezed his nose shut and put my mouth over his, but stopped right away, sobbing.

It was the prickle from his whiskers.

I can still feel it.

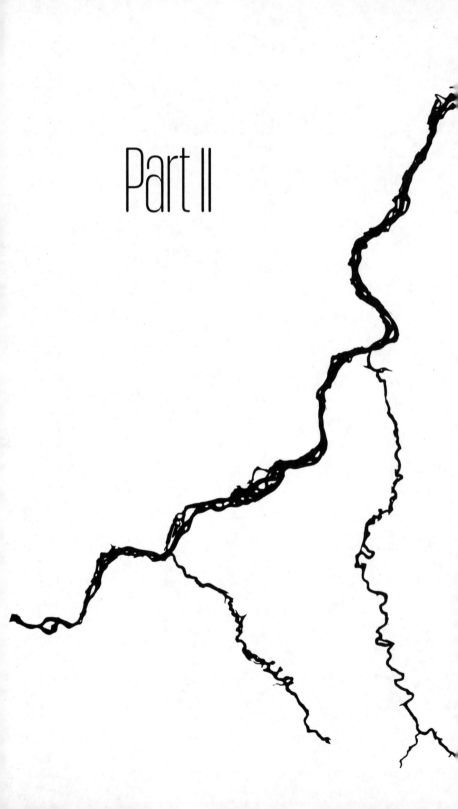

Part II

Nine

They'd closed the screen door, but had left open the window overlooking the deck. They were sitting in Adirondack chairs, both turned to face the yard. My mom still had on her running clothes, her tank top darkened with sweat. Her shoes sat at the base of her chair, socks stuffed inside. It was maybe a month before spring break.

I didn't hear the first part, but then my dad asked, "What kind of space do you mean? Do I need to find an apartment and get out of here? Is it that kind of thing?"

"I'm trying for it not to be that."

"Well, if I'm making you unhappy," he said. "I mean, if your first thought when you see me is *What is he going to criticize me for now?*, then we have to do something differently, where you don't think that way."

"So it's my fault for thinking that way?"

"Those weren't my words."

"You just remind me of all the things I already hate about myself anyway. So, yeah. You're right. I suck. I know."

"You don't suck."

"I'm just trying to keep track of all the things I'm supposed to remember to do: Turn off the AC in the car before I shut it off, make sure I pick up all my gum wrappers, don't mow the lawn in my nice shoes, leave a note if I go running. Any time I don't do one of these, look out for Parker."

"That's not what I want."

My mom wiped her eyes with the bottom of her tank top,

and my dad reached out to rub her back, but she didn't let him. "It's what you're getting, though."

I should've stopped listening. I should've walked away from the window as quietly as I'd snuck to it, but I stayed. I told myself I was staying for information, and that I needed information, since apparently my dad was moving out or something.

"I've just come to expect it," she said. "I know you're going to be how you are, so I just try and be ready for it. When you come home from work, or from a trip, I've just learned to get out of the way and let you be angry at everything. I just tell myself that you're being you."

"I'm not angry," he said. I could tell he didn't believe it. He even told us sometimes that we weren't angry enough, that we needed to get a little more pissed.

Next to the window was a repurposed school desk. A pair of my mom's old stirrup irons sat on it, half hidden by the spider plant. They'd been sitting there for I don't know how long. Grandma had sent them, and my mom was going to clean them up. The chrome polish and a rag were already right next to them.

"I guess what I don't understand," she said, "is how come I don't get to be me when I come home, or when I'm annoyed with you? How come I don't get to be who I am?"

"You do," he said. "You just have to be her."

My mom scoffed at that. I picked up the stirrups and clanked them together. It didn't seem to get their attention, so I clanked them again.

My mom and dad both looked over their shoulders, though my dad quickly turned back to the yard. "What is it, Em?" he asked.

"Can Mom help me clean these?"

"What are 'these'?" she asked.

"The stirrups Grandma sent. I wanted to get them cleaned up."

"I thought we said they were going to be too narrow."

"I still want to try."

When she asked if we could deal with it later, I tried to sound disappointed.

"If you want to do it yourself," she said, "you know how."

"I know," I said. "I'll just wait."

My mom turned all the way around in her chair. I doubt she could even see me through the window screen. "Give me ten minutes, okay?" She looked at my dad, but he stayed fixated on the yard.

"Should we do it in here?" I asked. "I've already got all the stuff."

"How about you do it in the garage," he said. "Take the stuff now, and she'll meet you out there."

"That sounds good," she said. "You start, and I'll be out there in a little bit."

"Ten minutes," I said.

"In a little bit," she repeated.

I tucked the polish and the rag under my armpit. I clanked the stirrups again, nice and clear. I kept clinking them as I walked away so they could hear when I was gone.

My mom and I sat in a booth near the front of a diner the sheriff had recommended. "Biscuits and Gravy Always $1.99" was painted across the window. Most of the tables were empty. A few men sat at the counter, quietly speaking Spanish. A group of old ladies were having pie and coffee, and I kept catching them glance over at us. Or maybe it was that I couldn't take my eyes off the unbelievable height of their perms, and it only seemed like they kept looking at us. Back home, after all the TV reports had aired and after everyone at school suddenly knew who I was, I'd feel like everyone was watching me all the time. Watching, judging, talking.

Our waitress smiled as she handed us the menus. She didn't have a name tag, nor did she say her name. She was probably only college aged, but she had bags under her eyes and her hair had started to pull out from her ponytail. She poured us both glasses of water thick with ice.

"Can I start you with some coffee?" she asked. "Coke? Diet Coke?"

I wasn't hungry, but my mom insisted that I get something, that I at least try. When our waitress came back with her coffee, my mom ordered for both of us—a cup of chicken dumpling soup for her, a grilled cheese for me.

"Fries or chips?" the waitress asked.

My mom looked my way. She also had bags under her eyes. For some reason I expected her to just answer, but she was waiting for me, and the waitress was waiting for me, and I was supposed to decide which style of potato I wanted, which at that moment seemed like an impossible decision.

"Can I get neither?"

"Just a grilled cheese?" the waitress asked.

"You don't want some fries?" my mom said.

"Just a plain grilled cheese and ketchup."

The waitress headed for the kitchen. My mom added cream and sugar to her coffee, which was the only way I thought I could ever understand drinking it. She asked me again if I was sure that I didn't want anything else, maybe a salad or some milk. "It's not too late," she said. She slid a little toward the end of the booth. I thought she was about to wave someone down.

"Mom," I said, "I already told you." It came out sharper than I'd meant. "I'm already eating the sandwich. I'm not even really hungry."

"Okay," she said. "Understood."

She wrapped both hands around her cup and stared down into it. I noticed that her nails, which she hardly ever painted, had bits of green polish on them. She and Andrea must have done each other's while Dad and I were gone, a tradition Mom had started with me. The last trip he went on, the three of us sat in the backyard on a picnic blanket and painted our nails and drank lemonade. Mom put some tequila in hers and garnished all our glasses with paper umbrellas, and we stayed out so long all of us got a little sunburned.

"What color did Andrea pick?" As soon as I said her name, all I could think about was how she wasn't there, and I couldn't believe that Mom hadn't brought her. Mom later confessed to me that she also hated that she'd left her home—said she didn't exactly feel mad at herself, just more like "a horrible mother."

"The color she picked?"

"For her nails," I said. "What color did you paint hers?"

My mom smiled. "She picked blue. Blue for her, and green for me. We did our toes opposite, though."

My mom unfolded her hands and laid them flat, her rings clinking on the tabletop. I think I was supposed to be looking at whatever was left of Andrea's work, but all I could focus on were those rings. Dad had given her all of them. The clear glass one he brought home from Montana. The wide silver one he got in Mexico City and gave her as an engagement ring. The curved golden one with the small diamond was their wedding ring, and had once been his grandma's.

"She did pretty good," my mom said, picking at one of her cuticles. "Relatively. She wanted blue because she noticed you wearing it once. But this wasn't the right one."

"Which one was she looking for?"

"That kind of electric blue, the really bright stuff. Where did that come from? Was that me, or did you buy it?"

When I didn't answer, she noticed that I was looking at her rings. She picked her hands off the table and looked at them with me, but then she curled them into fists and dropped them to her lap.

"I got it at the mall one time with Tracy," I said. I was supposed to have gotten rid of it, because my dad had checked the label when I brought it home and saw how it was made in China and that it contained formaldehyde or something. "I used to like it more."

Our food waited in the pass-through. One of the old ladies was spying on us again, her hair like a cumulus cloud. It was ridiculous and beautiful. Out on the sidewalk, a kid on his skateboard rolled past and reached down to pull up his sagging pants. A car honked, its brakes squeaking badly.

I didn't want my mom to think about whatever she was thinking. I reached for her coffee and slid it across the table. She often let me have some of hers, but she would just as often say no, saying that it'd stunt my growth or that I'd get hooked or something. Sometimes she'd slap at my hand and say no and then let me have some anyway. This time she just sat there fiddling with her wedding ring.

"I think a Coke sounds better," I said, pushing the cup back. "Will you go tell her?"

"She'll come back," my mom said, glancing toward the kitchen.

"But she's right over there," I said. "Will you get her attention?"

"Really?"

I replied by making a face, a face that was supposed to communicate *Yes, really.*

My mom shook her head a little and then got up from the booth, setting her eyes on our waitress and following her as she walked back to the kitchen. I only had a bite of my grilled cheese. The ketchup on the plate made me queasy, and I had to cover it up with a paper napkin. Instead, I just drank my Coke and chewed on the end of my straw. When the Coke was gone, I tumbled ice around in my mouth.

My mom poked at her dumplings. The saltines in her soup had bloated so much they'd started to fall apart. Now she was the one staring at people—the older guy with the slicked-back hair and leather vest who sat at the counter, the pimply kid with glasses a few stools down, the young mom cooing at her baby in the booth right across from ours.

"Did you ride Magic while we were gone?" I asked. I'd told her she could, as if she needed my permission.

Something came across her face, and I wondered if it was the "we" I'd used. I couldn't tell if it would've sounded worse had I just said I—while *I* was gone.

"I went out once," she said. "She rode pretty well, but was a little bit of a stink." She took a slurp of soup. She didn't seem to be any hungrier than me, but she didn't give up on it. "We'll get it figured out."

"What was she doing? Was she being bad?"

56

Magic was a quarter horse, which is like the most common breed there is. Her coat was a gorgeous dark black, and a white blaze ran along her face. Quarter horses could pretty much be used for anything—ranching, rodeos, eventing—but Magic had only been schooled in English a little bit.

"Not being bad," my mom said. "She just didn't want to work too hard. But I don't know that I wanted to work too hard, either."

My mom was my age when she got her first horse, a palomino named Tank. She had saved up her babysitting money and bought him from a family down the road. She talked her parents into letting her keep him by just bringing him home one day and simply tying him up in their backyard. After Tank, her parents helped her buy a more competitive horse, and she started riding seriously. First it was dressage, but then she started jumping, and from there she moved on to three-day eventing. She earned so many blue and red ribbons that the extras filled a shoebox.

When my mom chose an out-of-state college, her parents actually bought another horse, one for themselves. But then just after a year, when my mom said she wasn't going to come home the next summer, they asked her if it was okay to sell the horses. She wanted to say no. She thought about moving them to where she was, but knew she couldn't afford it. That it was unrealistic. That she was too busy with school. The horses were trailered off, and the next semester she met my dad. She hadn't really ridden since—not until I'd started high school and she asked me if I was serious all those times I'd asked if I could have a pony.

"What were you doing with her?" I asked. "How was her trot?" Magic had a tendency to not really push off her hind legs.

"We didn't work on that. I had her do some twenty-meter circles, some leg yields. She'll get there. She just needs some time and consistency."

My dad was always saying *follow your bliss* and stuff like that, but with Magic it was different. He wasn't *not* on board, but he was never totally *on* board, either. He'd always ask about Magic and would say how proud of me he was—how I was being responsible, how I was taking care of another living being, just like I'd learned that summer at the animal shelter. But he also didn't really come out to Peg's, which is where Magic lived. And a few times I overheard him talking with Mom about the cost of it all, about how much time and gas it took to drive back and forth. Once in a while at the dinner table, he'd start in about animal rights and about how horses should just be roaming free, and then he'd ask me what my moral stance was. If Mom and I really got going about dressage stuff, he'd get annoyed and tell us he felt like he was being left out of the conversation, like we were speaking a language he didn't understand—which is pretty much exactly how I felt sometimes when he was talking about kayaking and climbing. Then he'd tell us how if he ever got a horse, he was going to ride Western and wear chaps and learn how to rope—because that was *real* riding.

"She's a good horse," I said. It sounded so simplistic, but what a good horse was—strong, supple, loyal—that wasn't simple at all.

"She is," my mom said.

"When I was walking—" I hesitated until I remembered that she'd already heard most of the story. "When I was walking, I kept pretending I was her. That's how I kept going."

My mom set her spoon in the bowl then slid the bowl to the side. She'd folded and unfolded her napkin about a million times, like the Kleenex before. She unfolded it again and bits of paper dust spread into the air. Her eyes were rimmed with red.

"You were a good horse, too," she said. "You made it all the way."

"I want to go see her," I said. "Like before even going home. No—we'll go home and get Andrea, and then we'll go."

"Is that what you want?"

It was, but as I started to think about it more, I wasn't sure. I was going to tell her that we could wait and at least see what time it was when we got home, that Andrea mattered more. I passed her my napkin, which was dotted with grease but structurally sound.

"We'll do whatever you want," she said. "That's what I want to do for you."

Strong, loyal. My mom was the real horse.

Ten

The sheriff called me "Honey" again. We were sitting in his office, which was just as white as the other room. "Honey, I'm sorry," he said. He told me he knew he had put me through a lot by asking all those questions. Told me I'd been very brave. My mom nodded in agreement.

That may also have been the second time he called me brave. For a while, everyone would call me that. Only one person ever asked what I thought—if *I* thought I was brave. That was Aunt Mel, my mom's sister. "Not exactly," I told her.

The sheriff had closed the blinds—which were also white. Flourescent lights hummed above us. On the walls hung certificates and diplomas, all with "Manny J. Mendoza" calligraphied at the bottom. A nameplate was centered on the edge of his desk. The backs of several picture frames, with their flimsy cardboard kickstands, were turned my way. I guessed they held photos of his wife and daughter, but I couldn't see. Behind his desk stood a tan filing cabinet—one that would've been perfectly camouflaged along the Tinto—and on top of the cabinet were big three-ring binders. I kept wondering what the cabinet and binders were holding. Records of traffic violations? Mugshots? More forms like the one my mom had just signed? Pictures from crime scenes, with chalk outlines where the bodies had been?

The sheriff waited for a response from me. He'd asked for my story, and what I told him had seemed to satisfy him—seemed to have gone along with what they'd found at camp and how they understood everything to have happened. I didn't know what else to say, even though there was much more to it—like how delicious the peanut butter and honey sandwiches tasted one lunch, or how I'd finally beaten my dad in a can-opening race, or how we'd painted ourselves in mud one day and then let the sun bake it dry, giggling as the clay shrank and cracked and curled away from our skin, the tickling almost too much to take. How we drew designs on each other. How I painted bolts and stripes on his cheeks, and how he gave me spirals that radiated out from a dot in the middle of my forehead.

We used the mirror on the compass so we could see each other's work. As my dad was checking out his face, he mimicked a woman who was checking out her makeup, puckering his lips, batting his eyelashes—a performance he'd done with me before when he was annoyed again about the makeup I was wearing to school.

When it was my turn with the compass, he told me that I was a water sprite. A sprite of the river. He also said that he could tell I didn't totally love his design, even though I'd said I did. He said he could see it in my face, even though he didn't know what I was really thinking about, which was that the day he'd mimicked me on the way to school, my complexion was really bad, and I pretty much thought I was basically just a giant pimple, and totally gross, and I was sure someone was going to say something shitty to me—something he took care of before I'd even left the house.

Talking to the sheriff, I'd left out things that were no big deal, but also everything.

How my reaction to my dad's design had bothered my dad, which was something he tried to deny, as if he didn't also have a face for me to see things in. How when we'd rinsed the mud off in the river, parts of our skin were stained brown, like henna.

The sheriff slid back his chair and rose to his feet. "Well," he said. He nodded and smiled. His smile then shifted to my mom, and he took in and let out a deep, relieved breath. "I know you have a long drive. I'm guessing you both are ready to get underway."

"I am," my mom said, also standing. "It'll be a relief to get back."

The sheriff walked around his desk and shook my mom's hand. He grabbed one of his cards and passed it to her, even though he'd already given us one. "Thank you so much," she said.

"My cell number is listed there, too," he said, pointing at the card. "Doesn't much matter when you call."

I was still sitting down, unsure if my legs would lift me. In the café, all I'd wanted was to get back home to see Andrea and Magic, but now I felt differently—felt that once I started moving there'd be no stopping, not even when we got back to our house, because where we really needed to go was much further than any of us thought.

My mom put her hands on my shoulders. "What do you say, Em? You ready to start for home?"

How is it that sometimes when a parent touches or holds you it feels so comforting, so relaxing, and other times it feels like the most annoying thing ever? I squirmed out of her grip and sat forward in my chair. I started turning around one of the picture frames on the sheriff's desk, almost knocking it over.

"Is that your daughter?" I asked.

It was a photo of a sleeping baby wrapped in a yellow blanket. The baby had a head of thick black hair. Even its forehead was fuzzy with black.

"No," Sheriff Mendoza said. "That's Sophie, my niece." He stepped toward his desk, leaning past me, almost stepping on my foot. He grabbed another picture frame and held it out for me. "This is her," he said. "Abigail."

I took the photo from the sheriff. In it, he and Abigail were on a motorcycle—Abigail in front of him and sitting on the gas tank. The sheriff was dressed in blue jeans and a leather jacket, and Abigail looked like she could've been in the same first grade class as Andrea. A motorcycle helmet rested on the blacktop.

"She's got her own bike now," the sheriff said. I recognized the look of pride, the way he kind of stood a little straighter. "Not a Harley like that. Just a dirt bike she scoots around on."

My mom leaned over my shoulder to see. "That's neat," she said.

I looked at the picture again, at the squint in Abigail's eyes, at her strange smile—how the corners of her mouth didn't really curl up at all, but still seemed to flash all her teeth. "She's cute," I said. I wondered what she was like now—if the girls in her school made fun of her, or laughed at her haircut, or because she didn't have the right kind of clothes. Maybe she was the one being cruel.

"She certainly was back then," the sheriff said.

"Was?" I set the photo back.

"No, she still is. She's beautiful. But she's a few years older now and—"

"How old?" I asked.

"Thirteen," he said. "She gets a little annoyed when I call her 'cute' now. She wants to be something else."

My mom and the sheriff passed knowing glances between one another, and then tried really hard not to look at me— though neither of them could help it.

I don't know what I'd expected to happen, what I'd expected this moment to equal, but it felt different than I thought it should. I suddenly felt echoes from before, from when the sheriff kept telling me that I wasn't in trouble, but I kept feeling like I should be.

"I'm ready," I said, getting up. I was trapped on one side by the chair, another by his desk, and another by the sheriff himself. Leaving here was supposed to mean the emergency was somehow finally over, that no one needed anymore rescuing, but that's hardly how it seemed.

"Well," the sheriff said, again, reaching out to shake my mom's hand.

"Thank you," my mom said, again.

He held out his hand for me. "Emma."

I couldn't meet his eyes. "Thank you," I said. His big hand just sort of shook my fingers and then let go.

Even though my mom already had two, I picked up one of

his business cards, cupping it in my hand, bending it a little. There was a sheriff's badge on the card, and inside it was the flag of New Mexico—the yellow background and the red sun symbol—the same flag that my dad had pointed out when we crossed the border. The symbol was supposed to be sacred, was meant to represent the four directions, the four seasons. I lifted up the card like they'd just called my ticket in a raffle drawing.

"There you go," the sheriff said. "Now you know how to reach me, too."

"But I don't have to, right? It's not required or anything?"

"Calling?" he asked. I nodded. "No," he said, "of course not. Only if you feel like it." He smiled.

"Okay," I said. "I'm not sure if I will, then. I mean, I might. But I don't know. I don't think I'll really want to."

"I don't know if I'd want to, either," he said. He hooked a thumb inside his utility belt and pulled it up a little. "Just remember you can."

"I won't forget."

Eleven

Except for a few red taillights far in the distance, the highway was empty and dark. My mom had the radio playing so low I couldn't tell what she was listening to. I'd been sleeping in the back seat, but now I was sitting up and watching—my eyes focused on the hazy spot where the headlights ended and the blackness took over. I asked where we were.

She wasn't sure. "Still east of Arizona, I think." Her words sounded slow. She looked over her shoulder and gave a half smile.

"What time is it?" The clock on the dashboard wasn't digital, and it was hard to read the glowing arms from so far away. "Is it tomorrow yet?"

My mom was wearing her glasses, which she hardly ever wore. She rarely drove at night. Mostly, whenever my family was in a car, it was my dad driving.

I could tell she was having trouble with the clock, too, that she had to pull her eyes away from the road in order to read it. For a moment, I was the only one watching the highway. I imagined something popping out of the dark, pictured a tumbleweed or a jackrabbit streaking in front of us. My throat tightened. I could feel the words crawling to my lips, could feel myself getting ready to shout to my mom, telling her to steer left or right, the same way I did with my dad on the river.

"You've got an hour," she said. "In an hour, today will be yesterday."

I rested my chin on top of the front seat. My mom's glasses had chunky, tortoiseshell frames. She looked good in them.

Smart, like she was. But wearing her glasses also meant that her eyes were dry and tired and bloodshot. Sometimes at home I'd put on her glasses and stand in front of the bathroom mirror and try to recognize myself. Her prescription wasn't very strong, not enough to really blur things. I'd take her glasses off, then put them back on, entertained by how they made me feel like someone else, though also someone familiar, like someone I could see myself becoming. Other times it wouldn't work. Glasses on or off, I'd stare at myself and my skin and my body, and all I would see was a stranger.

"How far are we going tonight?"

"I'm not sure," she said. "I'm wide awake right now. Want to keep me company?" She patted the front seat.

"If you want," I said. The thrum of the tires on the pavement, the soft radio, the darkness—I was having trouble keeping my eyes open myself.

"Sure," she said, "Crawl on up."

I didn't move.

Earlier, when I'd first lain down, I tried listening to my iPod. My mom had been allowed to get a few things out of the Westfalia, which would be towed home later. She grabbed my iPod and my shoulder bag. She took my dad's cell phone and the set of clean clothes he'd left for the ride home, which was something he always did. She grabbed his good flip-flops, the ones he called his "dress-up shoes," which he tried to keep as clean and unstinky as he could.

I'd looked for the right music, but all of it seemed too loud and too close, like it was filling up too much of my head, instead of emptying it out like I wanted. Even the slow stuff felt wrong. I searched through all my songs, my face lit up by the screen's crisp glow. Hundreds of titles, yet nothing.

"You should do something with the radio," I said to my mom. "Like turn up the volume, or turn it off."

"Sorry." She reached over and switched off the power. "I wasn't really listening. Unless you want it on. I just needed noise."

"Off is good."

All the nights I'd been alone on the river, I'd never really slept. No matter how exhausted I'd felt, every little flutter of wind or crackling of wood would snap me awake and set my mind racing with what-ifs. But in the backseat, as the unlit roadside passed by at seventy miles per hour, I'd finally slept so soundly that I dreamed—a dream in which I was telling my dad that I was going to cancel my flight and stay one more day. We were in some kind of lobby. It didn't make any sense, but it seemed so real. I wanted to go back and figure it out.

"Mom," I said.

She waited for a long time. Up ahead, a semi was pulling onto the highway. My mom changed lanes to make room. As we passed, the truck's headlights flared in the rearview mirror and then faded just as fast. "What is it?" she finally asked.

It was hard to see what kind of land was off to the side of the road, but most likely it was brown and dry. Sometimes a darker shape rose up, some hint of a rock formation or hill. They could've been almost anything—maybe. For some reason, I felt glad not to be able to see them.

"Are you sure you don't need to stop for coffee or something?" I asked.

That wasn't what I was going to ask. I was going to ask her about Dad. I knew the Westfalia was in a parking lot next to the sheriff's office. There was a chain-link fence with curly razor wire on top. I'd seen it as we drove away. What I didn't understand was where my dad's body was, or how it was going to get home—though later I would learn that he'd been inside a refrigerator and was essentially FedExed back to us. It wasn't just his body. I was having a difficult time placing *him*. Where was that part?

"I stopped at a drive-through while you were sleeping," she said. "You might have had your headphones on."

"So you're not tired, you're awake?"

"I'm wide awake."

What my dad thought was that you came back reincarnated as something, and what that something turned out to be depended on how compassionately you'd lived your life. My mom thought that she wasn't exactly sure. She'd grown up going to church, so maybe she did believe in a heaven and a hell, but also maybe she didn't.

"Will you be okay without me?" I asked. "If I lie back down, you won't fall asleep?"

"If I get tired, I'll stop somewhere."

"What if you don't notice?"

"Sleep," she said. "It's past your bedtime anyway." I was like the only fifteen-year-old still with a bedtime. She took a hand from the wheel and reached back and awkwardly touched the top my head. She pointed to her cheek and told me to give her a kiss, which I did. Her hand smelled like industrial soap.

I stretched out again and stared at the ceiling. The tires went *tump-tump, tump-tump,* signaling each crack in the concrete. I tried to picture a lobby. I was telling my dad to wait for a little while longer, that I'd get a new ticket. I was trying to find my way back to the ticket counter, but I couldn't.

My mom clicked the radio back on, the notes coming through the speakers soft and liquidy. Outside, the road and the things along the side of the road stayed put. The juniper, the billboards, the gas station signs: they were all fixed in place. My mom and I were the ones in motion—a car flying down the interstate, streaking past the mile markers—but as I fell asleep again, as I drifted off to somewhere, it felt exactly the opposite.

Yellow light seeped through the scrunched-up opening of my sleeping bag. The whole tent was warped because of how I'd rolled against one of the walls, trying to be as far away from him as I could. I had this feeling that if I moved, that if I pulled my head out of my bag, I'd disturb everything, causing it to fall apart, even though it already had.

Outside, a bird went *chee-chee chee-chee.* I didn't recognize the call, but the sound was the sound of a little bird—I knew that much—a vireo or a flycatcher, or maybe some kind of thrush. My dad knew them all, or at least it seemed that way. He would sit around and just listen for them, sit around and listen for as long as it took, way longer than I could stand. "It's seeing," he once told me, "without having to use your eyes."

The bird moved from tree to tree, *chee-chee chee-chee*, darting around camp and then flying off, its call lingering behind. Without the bird, I could hear my breathing and the always-sound of the river. I stretched out my legs and searched for him—jerked back right away, whimpering. His body was already rigid.

When I finally had to pee so bad that I almost couldn't hold it, I undid the top of my sleeping bag. Once the zipper was open, I just stayed there, facing the wall of the tent. I'd almost slept outside, but then had gotten frightened—frightened that he really did have a pulse, and that he really was breathing, that he'd wake up and need me and I wouldn't be there. I couldn't remember how much I'd covered him up. I had a picture of him in my mind. His cheeks sagging inward. His tongue piled at the back of his throat. His sunken eyes.

I slid halfway out of my bag and got onto my knees. I saw a glimpse of his sleeping bag and the rise of his feet at the end of it. If I wanted to, all I had to do was turn and look. I pulled my bag over my head instead, and crawled for the door.

I kept crawling once I got outside. Sharp little rocks pressed into my kneecaps. I dropped my bag and stood up and took a few strides toward the river. In some spots, because of the way the light was, the water looked almost golden, but when you got up close it turned clear blue. I looked back at the tent, which sat slightly uphill. A patch of sun spilled through the doorway, but where my dad lay was still in shadow. His arms were mummied inside his sleeping bag, his head obscured. His bag was lime green, just like mine.

Everything but my sleeping bag was still inside the tent—my extra clothes, my headlamp, my sleeping pad. *That lime-green bundle is your dad.* The words repeated over and over. I tried to pretend that I didn't know what any of them meant.

A dog was yipping outside the car. I heard a man shush it, and tell it to come. "Get over here," he said. He called the dog Burt. Burt only kept yipping.

The early morning light was the color of ripe peaches. I'd been awake for an hour or so, trying to keep down a growing panic. My mom slept in the driver's seat, which she'd reclined halfway. She'd been using the towel from my dad's set of clean clothes as a pillow, but it had fallen into the backseat with me. At almost regular intervals, she'd pretzel herself into a new sleeping position.

I tried to track Burt by his barking. He never seemed to follow his commands, never seemed to go toward the *here*. Pretty soon Burt had scampered over to our car, probably to pee on one of the tires.

When Burt's owner came over, his size surprised me. Not like scared-surprised me, but not-what-I-had-pictured surprised me. He was easily the size of three Mr. O'Connors put together. He wore a pair of light blue jean shorts and a Boston Red Sox T-shirt. His barely-there brown hair was combed to the side. My dad, in one of his moods, might have labeled the guy something like "Everything that's wrong with America."

Burt's owner bent down, and when he stood back up, he had Burt in his arms. Burt was a Pomeranian or something, a fluffy cotton ball of a thing. When he barked again, his owner playfully grabbed for his mouth and then roughed his fur a little bit. With one hand massaging the dog, the guy turned and peered into our car.

He didn't see me at first. He was watching my mom. Her hair was fanned across the headrest, the side of her face smooshed. Earlier, when I'd first woken, I'd sat up and stared at her, whispering for her to wake up and get us driving again. As I'd watched her, something about her kept seeming—

—the word I kept thinking, shamefully, was *pathetic*.

Burt's owner stood next to the car and looked so long that I thought maybe he couldn't really see through the window, that it was all glare and he was just gazing at his reflection. Across the parking lot, another car's door thudded shut, and Burt's owner looked in its direction. When he turned back, that's when he finally saw me lying in the backseat.

I don't know how long our eyes stayed fixed on one another. Neither of us moved. He didn't seem dangerous, but I don't know what he was thinking. Here was this man and his little dog. This obese man with his round face and sympathetic eyes. I wanted to ask him where he'd come from, wanted to ask what cities, what turns. Wanted to ask what he'd left behind in order to get to wherever he was going.

I shut my eyes. Something about it felt accepting. I didn't open them until I heard my mom moving.

She ratcheted her seat forward. Burt and his owner were gone. She tried to stretch her arms, but the car was cramped. I thought I heard her crying a little.

"Em," she asked, "you up?"

I didn't answer. Earlier, when I'd been staring at my mom, when that word—*pathetic*—kept echoing in my head, what I eventually realized was that she actually looked vulnerable, and it was her vulnerability that made me feel scared and angry.

"Em," she said again. "Get up. I need to use the bathroom."

"Okay." I tried to sound sleepy. "I'll wait here."

"How about you come with me. I'm not sure I want to leave you alone."

"I don't have to go." I did have to go a little bit.

"Well, come anyway. It's good to travel in pairs."

"Mom," I said. I sat up and met her eyes in the rearview mirror.

"What?" She said that it was about keeping me safe, but I knew it was really more for her, that she didn't want to be alone, which I understood.

I leaned against the bathroom wall, near the hand dryers, and looked into the dirty mirror. Instead of glass, the mirror was metal. Maybe it had once been smooth and shiny, but now it was scratched and warped, and my reflection was blurry. My mom sat in one of the stalls. She told me to wait for her. I could see her shoes.

The restroom door was propped open with a broom, probably to let in some air. I slid along the wall until I was right next to the door. A woman came in, and I slipped out.

Instead of heading back to the car, I wrapped around the building and walked behind it. A coiled garden hose sat at the end of a cement pad. After that it was all rocky ground and scraggly junipers. A wind-shredded plastic bag fluttered from a branch. The semis and cars on the highway rumbled past, but things felt sheltered back there.

At the barbwire fence, I knew I should've turned back. I don't know why I had to see what it felt like on the other side. I was sure I heard my mother calling for me. She had probably already dialed 911.

I just wanted to go a little ways. The junipers, for as far as I could see, seemed to be spaced an equal distance apart—as if they'd been planted in a big grid. Something about them reminded me of gym class, when Mr. Mallon or one of the other teachers would tell us to spread out, and we'd all hold our arms out wide and measure the space between us, shifting when we needed to make more room.

The fence posts were made of round logs. The wood had turned gray and brittle, and as I climbed over I was sure it was going to snap. Something about climbing over made me want to run. I thought of Magic, the way she sometimes got hot and started bucking when I lunged her. Maybe this was close to what she was feeling. Sometimes you just had to work it out of her and then she'd settle down. You had to lunge her for an hour, run her round and round and round.

Out in the junipers, I faced the horizon, the restroom and highway behind me. I knew by their size—the fact that they had any real size at all—that the trees were old trees, that their roots had chiseled deep through the rocks in search of water. I took a breath and stretched out my arms, making sure everyone had enough room, just like in gym. I scooched left a little—a little more. Stop.

My mom was standing behind our car when I came around

the side of the bathroom. She had both hands up on her head, her cell phone grasped in one of them. The phone stuck up like an antenna. She was looking across the parking lot, looking out to the highway and all the traffic rushing past.

I stopped at the edge of the pet exercise area. She would later tell me all the horrible things she'd been thinking—how I'd been abducted, how I was already being raped, how she would have to come identify my body like she'd had to do for Dad. That was something I hadn't considered, and I apologized.

When she started screaming my name, some people moved away, while others—including Burt's owner—came to see what was wrong. I sort of wished Burt had been sent out to track me. Instead, two elderly women were standing on the sidewalk in front of our car. They had their arms hooked together like a couple going to prom, though I think it was mostly to keep each other from tripping on the curb. The shorter one noticed me first. She visored her free hand over her eyes, and when she'd had a good long look, she pointed at me and said, "There."

Twelve

A sycamore's branches spread halfway across camp. I sat at its trunk, watching young leaves flutter overhead. Sycamores had a way of shedding their bark, a way of letting go of the dark and rough stuff to reveal something smooth and white beneath. Once my dad had asked me—because he was having these kinds of conversations with me all the time—what kind of tree would I be if I could be any tree.

I didn't hesitate. "Sycamore," I said. "Arizona Sycamore," I clarified, knowing he would ask.

My dad went with Bodhi, which is supposedly the kind of tree the Buddha sat under when he achieved enlightenment. I didn't believe him. I think my dad was just saying that because he thought it might drop a seed of spirituality within me. I knew his tree was really the Bristlecone Pine, which are usually pretty ugly and gnarled, but are one of the oldest living things in the world. In my dad's translation, the Bristlecone had soul.

Across camp sat our tent: the yellow North Face that my dad had upgraded to when Andrea was born, the corners staked perfectly and the door positioned to maximize the view. Inside the tent: what I didn't want to think about.

Downstream, the land looked wrinkled, creased by water and wind and time. The river slowly disappeared around a wide bend. I'd yelled my throat raw again, hoping someone was out there, but now everything was quiet. Or not so much quiet as absent of people sounds. There was the babbling of the river, the water-like sound of the rustling leaves, the crows that had started squawking—noises, but ones that didn't seem to count. They didn't seem to count because the only thing I could really hear, though it wasn't so much a noise as a kind of atmosphere, was how I was totally and completely on my own.

I looked at the canoe, knowing I was going to have to take it. A smooth line ran through the sand and marked where my dad and I had pulled it ashore. It'd take some time to figure out how to spread the gear around so the canoe stayed somewhat trim, but I could do it. The kitchen would be the heaviest. The plates from our breakfast before the hike to the homesteader's cabin hung in the netting below the table, air-dried. The food bag was still rolled up tight from that morning, too. I hadn't eaten since I'd tried some of the Snickers I'd bet my dad, the bet he would've won. I only managed a few bites before I started to retch it back up.

Besides the kitchen, I'd need my sleeping bag and some clothes. My sleeping bag was heaped in a pile in the dirt. Except for the shirt and shorts I had on, my fleece and the paddling jacket in the canoe, all my clothes were still in the tent.

I could leave the groover. I hated dealing with it. I could leave the groover, but then it would just be the tent and my dad and the groover. I thought about how I could wrap him up in the tent, or in his bag, and put him along the floor somehow, but I also knew that I'd hardly be able to lift him, and that maybe I'd even have to rig bags on top of him, which I couldn't see myself doing. That his weight would make the boat so much harder to steer. That he had to stay.

My dead dad and the poop bucket. I decided I'd take the groover.

By the time I actually willed myself to get up and move, it was dusk. I put my hand on the zipper pull, trying again to imagine a way where I didn't have to go in. My eyes watered from the smell. Why is it that your bowels and everything release when you die?

I searched around for my headlamp and found it in the corner of the tent. When I turned it on, I saw that I'd pulled the sleeping bag as high up as it would go, which was just over his nose. His skin had already started to turn gray. His jacket was lying nearby, and I opened it up and covered the rest of his face without looking.

I wanted to say something to him, but I didn't know what to say. I wanted to say something along the lines of goodbye, and that I was sorry, and that I wished he could give me one of his stupid pep talks, one where he would convince me to just jump right in. *Because it's never as bad as you imagine it's going be.* I wanted to ask him if he actually believed that part, about it never being as bad as you feared, or if that was just some kind of motivational fib. This seemed worse. This seemed way worse.

There was something else, too. Whenever I told him I didn't know what to say, he'd always respond—Mom sometimes, too—*to just try and find the words.* That I should just say it however it came out. That I shouldn't worry if I was saying it correctly.

I said, "I hate you right now."

Thirteen

My mom wouldn't talk to me. She sat erect, drove with both hands on the wheel, and stared straight down the interstate. I kept looking over at her—the dark profile, the blue sky and rust-red roadside a blur in the background—but she wouldn't turn my way. Every few miles she sighed. I don't think she noticed she was doing it. She had asked me what I'd been thinking when I wandered off, and when I told her that I just wanted to go and look, that I just felt some desire to walk, she told me that I wasn't thinking.

"I'm sorry," I'd said to her.

"You have to think," she said.

She was sounding a little bit like Dad. I apologized again, but she didn't acknowledge it. They could be so similar sometimes, both of them ganging up on me about the importance of being responsible, of having the basic discipline to put my homework in a folder and not just stuff it into my backpack. Usually, though, they were so different—my mom more patient, more willing to listen first and not stare over my shoulder.

I put in my earbuds so she'd think I was listening to my iPod, but I didn't turn on any music. The battery was almost dead, anyway. My dad hadn't let me bring a charger. It was his way of making sure I didn't listen to music the whole car ride, his way of making sure that we would talk. Or that he could talk.

With my earbuds in, the world seemed muted again. I could still hear the hum of the road and the wind pushing against the car, but the place where I heard those things seemed to shift from my ears to my body. In some ways it felt like being under-water, cut off from air. I started thinking back to the river, to the day I lost the canoe—the cold shock of going under, the burn of the water up my nose and the way my muscles cramped as I swam for shore, the way I just wanted to let go.

We switched lanes to pass a motorhome. It had a small, red moped strapped to the back and there was a bumper sticker that read "Happy Camper!" As we crawled alongside it, I looked over into the cab. A grandpa-looking guy with white hair was driving. He was looking straight ahead like my mom, but he only had a couple fingers on the steering wheel. He wore a lavender polo shirt, and a gold watch hung loosely from his wrist. Except for the jiggling hula dancer stuck to the dashboard, he appeared to be alone.

Our momentum had stalled, and for what seemed like a long time our car and the motorhome travelled side by side. The man turned and saw me staring. When he smiled, I half-smiled back and then looked away. I checked to see if my mom noticed him. She was in the car, but she was somewhere else, too. Where it was I didn't exactly know, though I was pretty sure I had a sense of what it was like to be there.

I peeked back at the motorhome guy. He was looking down at me, and he smiled when he saw that he had my attention again. He reached into the air and made the gesture you make to truckers to get them to blow their air horns. I laughed silently. He repeated the gesture until finally I shrugged, pretending that I didn't know what he was asking.

The guy frowned. I knew that frown. It meant *Come on, give me a break, you know.*

He reached up and pulled the imaginary cord again. Then he pointed at me. His mouth made the word *You.*

"Mom," I said, taking out one of my earbuds and turning toward her. "Honk the horn."

She gave me a quick, confused look, but then went back to the road.

"He wants us to honk our horn," I said, pushing back into my seat so she could see him.

My mom leaned forward to get a clear view. The guy was still smiling and making the honk signal. Our two vehicles veered a little closer together and then moved apart. "Who is that?" she asked.

"I don't know," I said. "Some guy."

"What's he doing?"

"He just wants us to honk."

"Why?" she asked, speeding up. "What's wrong?"

"Nothing," I said. I looked over at the steering wheel and thought of reaching out and tapping the horn. Soon we'd be ahead of him.

Here is another difference between my parents: My mom is actually more spontaneous than my dad. If he knew what he was doing or what he was getting into, he seemed fearless. But sometimes, like when Mom wanted to go to a new restaurant, or to hang out with people they didn't really know yet, he'd rear and fight against it.

"Are you going to honk?" I asked.

"Emma," she said, "forget it."

"Just once," I said. "One honk."

She flipped on her turn signal, sliding back over. "It's too late."

"He would've," I said. "Dad would've played along and done it."

I said it because I knew it was going to hurt. But what I couldn't really explain was why I wanted to hurt her like that—not in terms that made sense to me, not then. In pamphlet-speak, I was experiencing *wide emotional range*.

I could see the ripples from what I'd said. Her face went slack and drained of color, but then came back as red as could be. There was a hardness, too. A hardness she rarely had with me.

My mom punched the horn so hard that it sounded like something broke off inside it. The motorhome was lengths behind us, so far that I couldn't even make out the driver. But he must have heard. Maybe he smiled. Maybe he even honked back.

She kept the honk going, even as we approached the next car.

I tried to pull her hand free, but she swatted at me with her free hand, knocking my iPod to the floor, the headphones yanking out of the jack.

"Oh, look," she said, as we pulled alongside the car.

I sank down in my seat, hid my face behind by my hand.

"They look confused," my mom said. "They're wondering if something is wrong. *Is this an emergency? A game? What is this?* I don't know, either," my mom said, now leaning into the middle of the car, talking to whoever was driving the other vehicle. "I don't know what's going on, either," she shouted, though there's no way they could've heard her. "I have no idea."

We were right at the exit, the McDonald's "M" floating in the sky.

"Pull off," I said.

My mom lifted her foot off the gas for a second, the turn signal even blinked once, but it was too late.

"That was it," I said. "You missed it."

She steered the car back into the middle of our lane. "You can't just say turn at the last second, not when I'm going seventy miles an hour." She checked all her mirrors. "That was *you* missing that, whatever we missed."

I was sure it was the same place my dad and I had stopped. The parking lot was the same, the little playground out front with the brightly colored equipment, the same gas station on the other side of the road. I told her we had to turn around.

"Can't we just stop at the next one?"

"I don't know if I can make it," I said.

"Really?"

"Really. I'm starving. And I think I have to go to the bathroom. This is a real situation."

"I'll stop at the next exit. We can't turn around until then, anyway."

We moved farther and farther away.

"Use one of those spots in the middle of the road," I said. "Those spots where cops or construction crews turn around."

"We can't use those. They'll give you a ticket for that. And it's dangerous. There are on-ramps so you can build up speed. Slow can be worse than fast. It's different than driving in town."

I already knew all that. I'd known all that when I told her to use one of the turnarounds.

"That makes sense," I said. I tried to make it sound like I was really considering it.

"You really have to go?" she asked.

"Bad."

We exited at the next off-ramp. We went right and then left and then right again, cutting into the parking lot of a Burger King. My mom pulled right up to the door. I had this crazy thought that maybe she was just turning around—that for some reason she'd pulled into the parking spot as the first part of a three-point turn. She put the car in park, and then the engine was off, and then my mom was dropping the keys into her purse, and a whole bunch of feelings I didn't want to feel started coming back.

My mom unbuckled her seatbelt and reached for the door. She unlatched it and the dome light popped on. She pushed the door open an inch and asked if I was ready.

I didn't say anything. Words passed by in my head, but for some reason I couldn't grab hold of them. The feelings, the way they actually felt in my body—as a tingling in my arms, a queasiness—that was one thing. But having to explain them, and not being able to—that only made them worse.

"Em," she asked, "what's wrong?" Her door softly clicked shut.

"Nothing," I said. Tears started, but I dammed them up. "I don't have to go anymore."

"You don't have to pee anymore?"

"We don't have to stop," I said.

"But we're stopped. What's going on, Em?"

I stared at the people inside the Burger King. A family—two little boys and a mom, I think—sat in a booth near the window. One of the boys was standing on the seat and the mom kept reaching for him, trying to get him to sit. The other boy kept dragging a french fry back and forth through his ketchup. A hamburger sat in front of the woman, still wrapped.

"It's going to be fine," she said. "We have extra clothes, right? It's nothing to be embarrassed about, Em. Everyone has accidents. I didn't know how serious you were."

Inside the Burger King, a man stood with his tray and scanned the room for a seat. He looked at the boys, both now standing in the booth, and walked in the opposite direction.

"That's not it," I said.

"I didn't—"

"Andrea doesn't even do that anymore."

"Do you want me to go in and get something for you?"

I told her it wasn't that. I wasn't even really hungry. I told her it was nothing.

"I know that's not true."

Inside, the mom had finally started to eat her burger. She took another bite. As she chewed, she bulged her eyes out at her kids, which made them both smile, which made her smile a little, too. Then the kids went back to goofing around with each other and her smile dropped away and I could see how exhausted she was.

"It's something," my mom said. "You can tell me. Whatever it is, you can tell me." She looked down at the cup holder between our seats. "If you want to."

As soon as we got there, I knew it was the wrong McDonald's.

"Look familiar?" she asked.

"It does," I said.

After I'd told her about why I wanted to stop, about how Dad and I had stopped there, about the tradition, which she should've remembered, she reached over and held the back of my head and started going on about how I should've just said all that right away, because if I didn't communicate those things there's no way she could know, and of course we could turn around and go back. She started thanking me for telling her. She said this was going to be the kind of thing we were going to have to do more from now on.

Inside, she ordered for us both. When the food was ready, she carried the trays, her purse dangling from her elbow. I had a fistful of napkins.

"Pick a seat," she said.

"I don't know. Anywhere is fine."

"That looks dirty," she said, nodding toward the nearest table. "Where did you sit last time? Let's sit there."

I led my mom to a booth near the window that looked out at the playground. "Either this one," I said, "or that one." I pointed at the other table. "It was one of these."

"You decide," she said.

I didn't want to choose. It didn't really matter anyway, because my dad and I hadn't sat in any of them. Maybe it did, though. If you tell yourself something matters, then I guess it does. Or if you say it doesn't, it doesn't.

My mom had this calm smile going, like turning around and coming back had given her a kind of peace, and I wondered if she had a sense that everything, despite everything, was going to be okay. Of course, maybe she was thinking something else. Maybe inside she was all different—nothing calm about her. You have to communicate these things if you want others to know.

"Thank you for this," I said.

My mom smiled wider. She lifted our tray a little, indicating that I should choose a seat. Whatever she was thinking, I knew I shouldn't ruin it. "How about we eat," she said.

I moved to a third booth. "Actually," I said, sliding in, "this was the one. We sat right here."

Fourteen

The fire smoldered. My sleeping bag was soaked with dew. The birds were up and making happy little chirps again, chirps that made my head hurt. A trail of pancake mix crisscrossed the ground. The food bag rested on its side with the opening undone. I must not have done a very good job closing things back up. I remembered the peanut butter sandwich from the night before, how I chomped it in a few bites and then chugged a bunch of water. How the ball of dough sat like a stone in my stomach. How that felt good somehow. I drank all that water, and I still didn't even have to pee.

It didn't take long for the crows to return and chase the chirpers away. A bag of granola had also been torn open. I sat up against the tree again, my sleeping bag bunched at my feet, dirt coating the fabric. I watched the scene as if I was watching someone else's life, in some other reality. Despite how pushy they could be, my dad loved crows, loved how clever they were. He once told me how he thought a crow's markings were as beautiful as any other bird's, and he showed me how if you looked close at the feathers there was more than just black—they shimmered blue, like deep, unpolluted water.

The crows were cautious at first, eyeing me between each bite of food. Sometimes one of them would fly up into a tree and peer down at me and caw before returning to the ground. I tried naming them, but there was only one I could tell apart from the others because of how its chest feathers were all messed up and missing. Each time I tried to name them all, I'd lose track of which one was which, except for Patchy. I could tell he was a male because of his size. My dad kept binoculars at the kitchen window so he could teach Andrea and me that kind of stuff. There was also a pad and a pen, and everyone in the family had their own page, and anytime we spotted a bird we'd never seen before, we got to add it to our list. Andrea's was the longest, but only because she'd written "BIRD" like a hundred times in a row while practicing her penmanship.

Patchy looked bad, but was probably just molting, which was natural and meant healthy feathers would grow in next. But I also worried that it could be something else, that maybe the spots where his skin showed through were bad, like it was some parasite, something that meant healthy feathers were definitely *not* on the way.

He moved over to the bottom of the food bag and started pecking at it. He waddled around the whole bag, stabbing at it with his beak, trying to find a way in. Every few jabs, he'd stop and swivel his head and squawk at the bag, like he was telling it to stop misbehaving.

"You're on the wrong end," I said to him. He'd gone right past the opening again, which was still partway folded over. "You walked right past it."

Squawk.

"I know," I said.

Squawk.

"Yep."

He didn't give up. He hopped on top of the bag and tried busting his way in from there. He returned to working the edges, nudging with his beak, digging with his claws.

"Are you going to figure it out, or do I have to help? Go to the top," I said. "Find the opening. The *o-pen-ing.*"

When I moved to help him, Patchy flew off into a cottonwood.

I repositioned the bag. "Here," I said. "Watch." I put my hand in and then pulled it out.

I expected him to come back as soon as I sat back down.

Instead, Patchy stared at me sideways and then started bobbing his head up and down. Whatever he was cawing made all the others caw with him.

"It's unfolded now. You can figure it out. It'll be way easier."

He didn't say anything back, but lifted off and went upriver. A few others followed. The rest stayed. A half hour later, when one of the crows actually did figure it out, nosing through the opening and pulling out a Ziploc of dehydrated beans, I jumped up and flapped my arms and shooed them all away.

The one with the dehydrated beans tried carrying the bag off, but it was too heavy. All you had to do was add water, and those flakes would become food. Or I should say that all you had to do was add *the right amount* of water—otherwise they became something closer to wet cement.

The river had broken its pattern and had come up a little overnight, the water dark with sediment. I'd have to move the marker. I could do that. I could put the dry bag away and move the marker. Find one thing, and then find another thing, and then keep going like that. *The right amount of water.* That's how you could solve it.

Some of the crows had moved over to the tent. One had perched itself on top. The others were poking at the walls, nipping the fabric.

My aim was a little off, but I scared them enough. The Ziploc skipped off the side of the tent, spilling open.

After I repacked the food bag and hung up my sleeping bag to dry, I grabbed a stick of driftwood from the pile and tried scrawling "HELP" into the beach, but the sand was too loose for it to really show, so I made the sign out of wood. At first the letters were thin, but I kept adding more wood until each line and each letter was at least a foot thick.

All along the shore, tangles of driftwood were plastered against the upstream side of boulders and trees. Almost all of the wood had been peeled of its bark—rough edges rounded off. Stick by stick, I took apart what past floods had deposited. It was hard work, and I was breathing heavy. The undersides of my fingernails were ringed with dirt, my hands and arms powdered brown. I'd dragged over a big log for the exclamation point, made the dot by piling up a bunch of smaller pieces. It felt good to pull and tug against something that I could actually move.

I looked at the letters and then the sky. A few planes criss-crossed above me, leaving behind trails of white. Later, after I was rescued—after they knew where my dad was and went to look for his body—they sent a helicopter. The pilot told the sheriff about the letters, about how easy they were to see when they knew to be looking for them.

How high were those other planes flying? When I asked the sheriff about that during our interview, he said he wasn't really sure.

"Twenty thousand, thirty thousand feet," he said. He looked at his deputy, who shrugged. "Something like that."

I asked the sheriff if he knew why the planes in the sky appeared so small, and before he could answer, I told him that I knew it was because of distance, that it had to do with angles of light. My dad had explained it all to me, though I still didn't totally understand. I realized, then, that was something my dad wouldn't have understood himself—how if he'd already explained something to someone, how it'd still be possible for them to not get it.

"I don't mean that," I said to the sheriff.

When he asked me what I meant, I told him I wasn't really sure.

I spread the map on the ground and found north on the compass, rotating the paper until its edges lined up with the needle—orienting it. I weighted each corner with a small stone so the wind wouldn't lift them. Now that the map was oriented it was aligned with the real world, which meant you were supposed to be able to translate from one to the other.

"Right here," I said, stabbing at the paper with a twig. Using a pointer was something my dad had taught me. It made it easier for everyone to see what you were talking about. "You're right here."

I mostly knew where we were because at every campsite—and even sometimes when we were floating down the river—my dad would get out the map and go over it with me, and we'd figure out where we were. The map was a topographical map, a bunch of squiggly brown lines and green splotches, shapes and patterns that often still confused me. The lingo was *topo map*, probably because topographical doesn't exactly roll off the tongue.

Unlike a street map, which was only a flat grid of roads, topo maps also showed the ups and downs of the land—the land's shape. The way they showed all this, the mountains and valleys and stuff, turning three dimensions into two, was by using contour lines, each of which represented an elevation. The space between the lines also meant something. Depending on the steepness or flatness of the land, the contour lines would either get closer together or farther apart. However much vegetation there was, the color of the map changed as well. Sometimes it was solid green, meaning there were lots of trees and plants, like it was along the river, and other times it was only dotted green, which meant something like scrubland. White and tan—the colors most of my map consisted of—indicated open land, sunburned rocks, and dirt—that kind of thing.

The blue line of the Rio Tinto squiggled across the bottom half of the map. I turned and looked at the real river as it flowed past. Downstream, the water was flat and calm, the shoreline open. Slowly the channel curved, until finally the river disappeared around a corner. The lines on the map for that section were spaced far apart.

When my dad was first teaching me about topos, he'd pick a hill or a pinnacle in the distance and ask me to find it on the map, and when I'd struggle, he'd say, "Okay, if we're here, and we're facing this direction…" and then he'd go on and on, asking me to try and picture this or that feature—not as I was looking at it then, but as if I was looking at it from the top down, like a bird might. Often he'd explain things faster than I could keep up with, pointing to nearby features and tracing them in the air with his hands.

"See how that works?" he'd ask.

Sometimes I could. But a lot of times I couldn't—not at all. Either way, I'd usually just say, "I think so."

If my dad wasn't already worked up about something, or wasn't all low blood sugar and needing to eat, he'd give me a thumbs-up and tell me how awesome I was doing, that I'd get it eventually. But if he was grumpy or if he was out of patience, he'd ask me what I meant.

"*Think* so, or *know* so? Either you can or you can't."

Depending on how out of patience I was, depending on how frustrated I already felt with him, I'd either lie or tell the truth, the truth being that I didn't know whether it made sense or not. Much of my life, especially recently, felt like a kind of half-sense situation, so I wasn't really sure I believed my dad's *either it does or it doesn't* way of dealing. I always wanted to tell him that.

My dad told me that reading maps was something I was just going to have to know how to do. He told me that's all life really was—trying to come up with a map of things.

For a while there, until I really did start to understand how to read them a little bit, almost all those map lessons ended at the same spot: me on the verge of tears, saying that I wanted to do something else, and my father, frowning, lying, saying, "That's fine. We can do something else now."

Below the hole I'd pierced into the paper to mark the spot, I traced the blue line south, where the contour lines wiggled closer together, squeezing in on the river. At one point all the contour lines seemed to blend into one, which meant vertical land, and I knew that stretch was where the biggest rapids would come, the ones big enough to have names. My dad had explained there'd be two fun ones: Big Sluice and Upset. I knew to be cautious when my dad used the word *fun*.

Past the rapids, the contour lines parted again. The river

turned east for a long while and then jagged back south. Just after that jag was Piedra Gulch, the takeout, which my dad had penciled with an "X," even though the landing was already indicated on the map. Winding away from Piedra Gulch were two broken but parallel lines, the symbol for an unimproved road.

For an exact measurement, I would've had to cut a piece of fishing line, or use one of the laces from my boots, and trace each curve of the river. Instead I just measured my twig against the map scale and used that, estimating for the curves. As best as I could tell, I had a little over thirty miles to go.

Months after the trip, when I went and bought a new map and then came home and spread it out on my bedroom floor and measured using a piece of dental floss, I found out the real answer: thirty-five and a quarter miles.

Earlier, my dad actually had us stop paddling so he could see how fast we were traveling when only floating. It was the second morning, not long after we'd left camp, and I was still tired. He told me an adult walked about three miles an hour. "Think we're going faster or slower than that?" he asked.

"I don't know," I said. "I guess."

He laughed at that. I'd been aiming for more of an *I'm-going-to-leave-you-alone-now* response. "Watch the shore going past," he said. "Gauge it by that."

"I don't think I'd be able to walk fast enough to keep up."

"What about me?"

"Maybe," I said. "Probably."

"Maybe?" He pushed us forward with a hard stroke. "Probably?" Sometimes it was hard to tell if he was acting, or if he really thought he was so cool. "Man, I can walk *backwards* this fast."

"Of course you can," I said.

Ten hours. If he was right, it'd be ten hours of floating. Plus the other parts, like stopping to scout, or stretch, or eat. But I could paddle and make up time. Two days. More like a day and a half. One big day, maybe. Leave early in the morning and just follow the river. If I followed the river, I couldn't get lost. It would lead me right there.

Fifteen

For my fourteenth birthday, I told my parents I wanted to have a sleepover—that I wanted to invite over Heidi, and Tracy, and Zoe Myers, and Alyson Stewart, and maybe some other girls from school. We'd walk down to Nib, which was this fancy dessert place nearby, so everyone could get whatever kind of cake or sweet thing they wanted, and then we'd come home and watch movies and open presents and stuff.

My mom thought it sounded fine, and my dad said the same thing, but less enthusiastically. Then he started asking me all kinds of questions, like where was everyone going to sleep, and was I expecting him and Mom to pay for all the desserts for everyone, and how were nine people all going to order individual things at Nib, where the layout was all wrong and it was always super busy and so hard to order, even when you were by yourself? And what did I mean by open presents *and stuff*?

"I named four people," I told him. "I said I'd maybe invite a couple of other friends."

"Plus your mom and me, and your sister."

I glanced at my mom. Her arms were crossed and I could see she wasn't really listening this time.

"But that's—"

Then the lesson I'd recently learned came back to me: let him say whatever he was going to say, nod like you understand and agree, and then escape back to your room.

My dad just had his concerns. He told me he wasn't saying no, but only wanted to make sure I'd thought about a few things.

He tried talking me into getting everyone to sleep outside, but I wanted everyone to be crammed into my room, which had electricity and a stereo and a solid roof. Entertainment possibilities. He didn't want me to get too excited about presents, didn't want me to forget how when they'd started leasing Magic for me, we'd already talked about how she was a big gift, one that'd also have to be my birthday present.

"I know," I said. *So what?*

In the end, instead of going to Nib, my dad just went there and bought us a cake, and then we had pizza delivered. Zoe was the only one who couldn't come. Heidi and Tracy texted one another almost the whole night, which drove my dad crazy, even though he was in the other room. The texting drove me a little crazy, too, especially since they both knew I couldn't get a phone until I was fifteen, but sometimes one of them would lean over and show me what they were writing, or I'd take the phone and add something, and then we'd laugh and hit send.

We stayed up until midnight watching a silly horror movie, and then went up to my room and spread out the foam mattresses my dad had pulled out of the basement. Heidi and Tracy kept texting, but weren't just texting themselves anymore, but also Elijah and Grant, two boys who had graduated from our school.

For a while, Grant was another of the boys that Heidi said she was going out with, and Tracy said she could've called Elijah her boyfriend, if she wanted to, but she didn't. Heidi and Tracy and I had all grown up on the same street, and we were always over at one another's houses. When their families moved, we still kept going to the same school and kept hanging out like we used to, except that in the past couple years things had been changing. They'd started hanging out together more, just the two of them, or with this group of friends who lived over near them, friends I didn't really like.

Elijah and Grant were skateboarding downtown, or were at least carrying their skateboards and walking around because they weren't actually any good at skating. Whatever they were texting was making Heidi and Tracy crack up and say things like "Oh my god" and "What a freak" before texting something right back.

"Grant thought you were Suzi Jenkowski," Heidi said to me. "With the boobs."

"Yikes," I said, not really knowing what it all meant. I did not have the boobs—not really. That was another way we'd all been changing. I had pads from old bras that I cut out and stuffed into my new ones, just so I had something.

Around one thirty, my mom knocked and asked us to quiet down. She tried coming in, but all the mattresses were in the way. "Girls," she whispered. "You have to start *speaking like this now.*" She reached through the crack and turned off the lights. She kept whispering *okay* until one of us finally acknowledged her.

Alyson and I fell asleep a little while later, but Heidi and Tracy stayed up texting till almost five in the morning. Our bathroom door didn't have a lock, and anytime one of them had to go, they both went together, one of them standing guard in the hallway. My dad told me this the next day and said that the whole time they kept talking to each other, right through the door, loud enough that he could hear them going on about how one of them was telling her mom this boy she knew was gay, because otherwise her mom wouldn't let her hang out with him, and how one of their other friends had gotten drunk and called them and how unfair it was that neither of their parents would let them hang out with that other friend anymore.

"I don't hang out with those friends," I said, before he could even ask.

In the morning, while Heidi and Tracy were still asleep, Alyson and I ate Belgian waffles and organic bacon while not really talking to one another. I liked her because she was nice, but we didn't have much in common outside of school. I had gotten out whipped cream and chocolate chips, neither of which she ate. My mom turned the oven down low and tried to keep the food for Heidi and Tracy warm. My dad had been remodeling the spare room for the past few weekends, trying to turn it into a library-slash-creativity room, and he kept running his saw and pounding on things.

While Alyson and I were eating breakfast, Heidi and Tracy called their parents to come and get them. When a car pulled into our driveway and honked, Tracy came running downstairs in her pajamas, holding her shoes in one hand and clutching her sleeping bag and pillow to her chest.

"Are you leaving already?" my mom asked.

"Bye, Mrs. Wilson."

I went with Tracy to the front door and gave her a half hug.

"I can't sleep," she said. *Bang bang bang* went my dad's hammer. "I'll call you later, okay?" I helped with her sleeping bag, which was spilling out of her arms. The car honked again. "Happy Birthday," she said.

Heidi was downstairs just a second later. She'd changed and had everything stuffed away in her backpack, which she always had with her. She was wearing knee-high pink socks and a pair of blue short-shorts with stars all over them. My dad had come out into the kitchen to refill his coffee. He had this way of clunking his mug down on the counter. He was sucking on some nails, rolling them around in his mouth. My mom kept asking Heidi if she was sure she wasn't hungry—the food was all ready, and it'd be easy to fix a plate. My mom told her not to be shy. Heidi said she was fine, kept having to say it over and over, until finally I ditched Alyson and took Heidi onto the front porch to wait for her ride.

Heidi had given me a sock monkey for my birthday. She'd made it herself. "I love the monkey," I said.

"Me, too," she said. Her backpack was making her sit all hunched over. She was clicking her phone screen on and off, like someone absentmindedly clicking a pen.

I wanted to ask why she was leaving so early, but I didn't. I could hear plates being cleared from the table. Someone rode by on a ten-speed with upturned handlebars. Maybe Heidi knew what I was thinking. "Is your dad scary?" she asked.

"I don't know," I said, "Maybe, I guess. Why?"

"He kind of yelled at us last night."

"When?"

"Tracy and I were going to the bathroom and we were talking, and your dad shushed us."

"Was I asleep?"

"You and Alyson both were. She was snoring. Your dad told us to shut up and go to bed."

"Did he shush you or tell you to shut up?"

"He shushed us like we were in the library. I don't know, it made us laugh. That's when he told us to shut up and go to bed."

Inside, the power tools started up again. Then Heidi's phone rang. It was her brother. Out on the street, a white SUV was crawling by. "I'm right here," Heidi said. "Here. I'm looking right at you."

Heidi made an exaggerated sad face and gave me an even limper hug than Tracy had. Her brother pulled over to the curb. "I swear I'm adopted," she said.

"Thanks for coming."

"Of course." She ran a hand along her socks, pulling them up tighter.

"I'll call you later," I said.

"Later," she said.

That afternoon, when I thought my parents were gone on a walk, I stumbled into them downstairs. I was on my way to get another glass of soda, which we'd gotten with the pizza. I hadn't heard what they were talking about, but the way they stopped when I walked in gave me the sense it was probably about me.

"There she is," my dad said, turning on his smile. There was sawdust on the knees of his pants. He was eating Heidi and Tracy's cold waffles and bacon from breakfast. There was a half-finished pint of beer next to him.

"Yep," I said. "She is."

My mom asked what I'd been up to. I'd been listening to music in my room. She slid out one of the chairs at the table. "Come and sit down a second," she said.

She asked me if I'd had a good time, and I said yeah, which was true. It'd been fun to stay up late and be stupid and hyper—even if I didn't really get that hyper, and actually didn't stay up that late.

"So, what's it feel like to be fourteen?" my dad asked.

"I don't know," I said. "Not any different, really."

Last year it had been versions of "How does it feel to be a teenager?" or "Does it feel different to be a teenager?" or just "Uh-oh, a teenager!" Tracy said her parents said all the same kind of stuff on her birthday, stuff about how they couldn't believe it, and Heidi said that her parents always asked her all sorts of unanswerable questions, questions that she'd have to answer twice—once at her mom's house, and then another time at her dad's.

"Well," my dad said, "It's only been a couple of hours. Give it some time. Things change."

"True," I said, thinking, *This feels pretty familiar.*

He started up again: "A couple more years, you know, and you'll be driving." I knew about this possibility. "You're getting to that age now where's it's going to be more and more freedom, which is the fun part, but that freedom means more and more maturity, which isn't always fun. And sometimes, socially... socially, you just really have to remember who you are and not get distracted or too influenced by what other people are doing."

"Okay," I said.

My dad wedged off a piece of waffle and pushed it through the syrup and melted whipped cream. "Do you know what I mean?" he asked, stuffing the food in his mouth. "Does that make sense?"

"I guess," I said.

"He's just making sure he says the stuff you're supposed to say as a parent," my mom cut in. "It's our job." She joked and made a scrunched-up face and shook her finger at me like she was telling me to stop. It was supposed to be funny.

Between bites of waffle, my dad was looking over at my mom and then looking over at me. He was trying to tell her something without saying it out loud, but she didn't seem to be getting it. I thought that, if I moved slow enough, maybe I could slip away without either of them noticing. Then I saw I was wrong.

My mom wasn't the one who didn't get it, it was my dad—she was trying to say something back, something he seemed to be misunderstanding.

"So, Emma," he finally said. "We can go buy you some new ones—I totally don't mind doing that—but those shorts, the ones like Heidi was wearing, those shorts have to go away."

"I just got those," I said. My mom was frowning at my dad, shaking her head. "Mom bought them."

We'd even gone shopping together. I helped her pick out a new dress, and we shared a fitting room. I remember her standing to the side so I could have the mirror. I'd told her that Heidi had a pair of shorts I liked, ones I'd wanted to get, and she asked if they were the right ones. She'd even told me they looked nice.

"Em," she said, "You're right. I did buy them, but I shouldn't have. It's okay. We'll get you some other ones, something just as cute."

"You said you liked them."

"I know," she said. Now my dad was frowning. "It's not that I don't like them."

"It's—" my dad said. He looked to my mom for help, but she wasn't going to offer any. "You can't blame the clothes, but…It's that you're not a kid anymore. Certain clothes have certain connotations now."

I didn't know what to do with that word: *connotations*. I had ideas about the things he was talking about—things like the old guy in the grocery store who just randomly told me how he liked my smell, or the guys at school asking girls for bra pics. I think I was supposed to feel a certain way about those things, at least in my dad's mind, though I'm not sure I did feel the way he wanted me to. Mostly, I was trying to figure it out because it was confusing as hell. And what I was figuring out—and what I wanted my dad to figure out, too—is that people will come up with whatever connotations they want to. People see what they want to see. You can't do anything about that.

"Didn't you once tell me that men weren't supposed to tell women what they should wear?" I asked him.

"Well—"

"This is both of us saying this," my mom said.

"And I reserve the right to contradict myself."

"Do we all get that right?" I asked.

"Sure," he said, "but I still get to tell you that you can't wear those shorts."

I'd hardly even worn them. Plus, I had board shorts that were just as short and those didn't seem to be a problem. Apparently faded denim held some magic power. "What am I supposed to do with them?"

"That's up to you," he said.

"It doesn't feel that way."

His eyes narrowed.

"There's a Goodwill box in the basement," my mom said. "Just throw them in there."

"Is that it?" I asked. I told them I'd been doing homework and wanted to get it done.

"What homework?" my dad asked.

I started to answer, but my mom jumped in, "Yes, that's it."

I was going to say Biology, but I didn't have any Biology homework. I actually didn't have homework at all, because I'd wanted to make sure I got it done before the sleepover.

"Thank you," my dad said as I walked away, soda-less.

Happy Birthday! I mouthed once I was around the corner, lifting my glass for a toast they couldn't see.

Afterward, I put the shorts in the Goodwill box, which is where they stayed for weeks. I left them there long enough for my dad to go check and make sure I'd told the truth, long enough for the whole episode to get replaced by some other episode, and then I went back downstairs and reclaimed them, stashing them in the bottom of my closet. He wasn't going to decide what clothes I could have. I even wore those shorts to school once, hidden under a skirt I'd planned to take off before first period, but then never did.

Sixteen

Mom and I crested Old Rabbit Ridge and began the long, steady descent into the valley. The road was the primary highway to and from the interstate, so I knew the hill well. Down below us was Dewey, a little town with a stoplight and a café and a farm that mostly grew melons and pumpkins and gourds, a farm we drove out to every Halloween. We still had another twenty minutes until we got home, but once you reached Dewey, you knew the trip was about over—that instead of the big open vistas, it was going to be more and more pavement and billboards and strip malls. If we were coming home from vacation, and not just a trip to Phoenix or somewhere, it was usually around Dewey that my dad would start to get grumpy, or if not exactly grumpy then profanity-friendly.

My mom dug into her purse and pushed things around until she found her cell. Once she got it out, she held it above the steering wheel and looked to see if she had a signal.

On either side of the road, it was mostly untouched juniper. The hillsides south of town had already been terraced by roads and planted with manufactured homes. The work was moving east now. We passed one of the work sites, which had shut down for the day. They'd already built to the first switchback.

Mom handed me the phone and told me to check again.

"Two bars."

"Okay, good," she said. "Find Mrs. Hayes's number and call her and tell her—"

"I don't want to talk," I said.

"—tell her that we're just outside of town and we'll be there in less than a half hour. Just let her know we're almost home."

I clicked on the phone's camera and held it up to the windshield, watching the road rush toward me.

"Emma," she said.

One time, in front of my dad, I said something was just like a movie, and he snapped at me and said life wasn't like a movie. "Movies might be like life," I remember him saying, "but life isn't like a movie. That's stupid."

Now I just wanted to watch the way the center lines—and the lines along the shoulders, and the lines of the road itself—and the way they stretched forward and converged up ahead. Sometimes, when we were coming home from a trip, my dad would tell us that he wasn't going to stop—that we should all just settle in, because we were only going to get some gas and roll right on through the other side of town. Joshua Tree? The Sea of Cortez? Bryce Canyon? The Alaska Highway? He'd tell us we could go anywhere—that we would just make one long trip to everywhere. It would be our jobs and our school and our everything. It would never end.

Other times, especially if we were getting home at night, my dad would stop at Albertson's and buy ice cream—one pint for him, and one for the rest of the family to share. He'd always come out of the store at a near run. "Scary," he'd say, meaning the bright lights, the music, the scanners.

Mom and I had gotten to the bottom of the hill and the last turn, a right that would take us all the way into town. The light switched from red to green. Mom held up her hands when the car in front of us didn't move fast enough.

I turned the phone to take a selfie. When the camera made its shutter sound, I glanced at my mom, but she didn't seem to hear. The picture was dark and out of focus. I took one of her, and it came out better. I deleted the one of me and saved hers, even though she still had trouble finding pictures on her phone once they were stored.

"Em," she said, "call already."

"Dialing."

People sometimes mistook me for my mom on the phone, even Dad. I think Mrs. Hayes probably just saw that it was my mom's number. "Robyn," she said.

"It's me," I said. "This is Emma."

"Emma," she said, "it's so wonderful to hear your voice."

"My mom wanted me to call." She was motioning at me, mouthing some words that I couldn't figure out.

"How's the drive going?"

"We're in Dewey," I said. "I'm supposed to tell you it'll be like half an hour."

"That's fine," Mrs. Hayes said. "Whenever you get here is fine."

I looked at my mom to see if there was anything else I was supposed to say. "What'd she say?" she asked.

"That it was fine."

"What else?"

"Is there anything else?" I asked Mrs. Hayes.

"No," Mrs. Hayes said, "everything is under control. We just finished up dinner." I heard Andrea laughing in the background. "There's been some negotiations with your sister about dessert."

My mom started waving a hand at me, motioning for the phone. I held up my finger as if I was struggling to hear what Mrs. Hayes was saying, though I could hear her perfectly well.

"Would you like to say hi?" she asked. "She's right here."

"I don't know," I said, "we're almost home." Andrea still wasn't very good at talking on the phone. She had this problem of speaking too fast and shouting into the receiver.

"She's been talking about you a lot," Mrs. Hayes said. "My big sister this, my big sister that."

"That's funny," I said.

My mom had gone from simply motioning for the phone to actively trying to take it out of my hand.

"What else?" I asked Mrs. Hayes.

There was a pause on her end. "She's happy that you two are on your way home."

I already knew that my mom hadn't told Andrea the real story. My mom hadn't even known the real story when she left to get me. She still didn't, not totally. Andrea was about to hear all sorts of things, and I had no idea how they were going to sound to her, or if they were going to be the kinds of things she could even understand. I knew that she would miss him, and that it would hurt, but I didn't know what she would do with ideas like *it was an accident*. I tried remembering what it was like when I was six, like when a bird flew into one of the windows and died, but I couldn't remember what it was like not to know about things like I knew about them now. I heard her laughing in the background again.

"She hasn't asked about him or anything?"

"Are you sure you don't want to say a quick hi?"

"I'm supposed to give the phone to my mom," I said. "Here she is."

"Hang on, dear," Mrs. Hayes said. As I passed the phone, she said something more, but I didn't catch what it was.

"Bonnie," my mom said. By my mom's response, I could tell no one was there. Then I heard a mumble coming through the speaker. A big smile washed over her face. She looked over at me and laughed, and I tried laughing back, though mostly I felt like crying. "Are you sure this is Mrs. Hayes?" she said. "You sound a lot like this silly girl I know."

Our car swung into the driveway, the headlights sweeping across the front of the house. Mrs. Hayes had turned on the porch light. My mom usually kept her car in the garage, but she parked in the driveway instead. My dad had already given me some driving lessons, and had explained how with Mom's car, an automatic, you didn't have to set the emergency break, but with the van, a manual, you did—or that you didn't have to, but that you should.

My mom unbuckled her seat belt and grabbed the keys.

"Here we are," she said. I couldn't tell if she meant something by it, or if she was just stating the obvious.

"We are here," I said.

She reached out for her door handle, but then just sat there. My seatbelt retracted slowly across my chest. We were staring at the garage door. When I was little, we didn't have an automatic garage door because my dad thought they were a waste of electricity, and that opening and closing a garage door by hand was one of the small things you could do to stay young.

"Do you remember the old garage door?" I asked.

"The gray one?" Two years ago my dad had painted the front door and the garage door red.

"No," I said, "the old door, the one you had to open by hand."

"The one that weighed about a million pounds?" she said. "Yes, I remember it. Why?"

"I don't know," I said. "It had windows, right?"

"That's part of why it was so heavy."

"Did I break one of them once or something?"

"Probably," she said. "They were always getting broken. Your dad broke like ten of them."

"I just remembered that for some reason."

The front door swung open and Andrea came bounding out. She jumped off the porch steps and into the yard. She was a pretty good runner already, and sometimes even went with Mom around the block. Dad had started calling her Lil' Ripper.

I watched Mom put on a different face. It's not that it was any less genuine, it's just that I saw it was conscious, that she chose it.

"There she is," she said, holding the car door open with her leg. Andrea fell into Mom's hug, and then Mom started kissing the top of her head all over, saying, "Oh, I missed you so much!"

As I got out of the car, Mrs. Hayes was just coming down the front steps. She gave me a little wave. I waved back, then tucked my hands in my pockets and walked around the front of the car. The engine radiated heat and smelled faintly of burnt rubber. Mom was still kissing Andrea all over. When she finally finished, she pointed at me. "Look who's home," she said.

Andrea looked at me like she did when she was being shy around someone new, like she needed time to decide about me. Like she already knew it was partly my fault.

"It's me," I said. I squatted down and held out my arms for a hug. She ran so hard she almost knocked me over.

Seventeen

I was sleeping outside the tent. Halfway through the night, the wind started howling. At first it was kind of exciting—how hard it was moving, how warm it felt, how loud. There was a charged energy to it. It'd swirl upriver and then gust through camp, whipping the tamarisks around and snapping at the fabric of my sleeping bag, pelting it with sand. The sky was cloudless, lit up with bright stars, but I knew that could change, that wind like this often brought other weather with it. If it rained, I'd have to get in with him, or hope for enough cover under the trees.

I slid down into the darkness of my bag, covering myself. Sand eddied out inside the opening above my head. I wanted to fall back asleep, but each time I got used to the wind and started to drift off, an even heavier gust would blow through and wake me up. There was no break to it, no tapering off to a whisper or anything gentle like that. It was just loud and then LOUDER. It even covered the sound of the river. Somewhere nearby, there was the creak and snap of a big tree branch. That's when the fun went away.

My dad once told me that if you're having trouble falling asleep, the best thing to do is just lie still. Don't toss around and try and get comfortable because you'll just wake yourself up more. Just lie there and be still and wait. But I couldn't do it. Hours went by with me trying to sleep on my back, then my side, then my stomach, then my other side—slowly twisting my sleeping bag around me. Maybe my dad also told me this, though I feel like it might've come from a book I read: there are winds that blow so hard and so long they make people go insane.

I tried to think of things to distract myself. Some of the gusts were so strong and sudden, I flinched, frightened that I was actually being swept into the air. My eardrums throbbed with pressure. Branches continued to snap off and crash through the underbrush, the big ones booming when they hit the ground. I kept waiting for one to smash the canoe, or land on the tent, or me. I kept worrying the canoe was going to get blown into the river and float off, but the bowline was banging against the side of the hull—*ta-tunk, ta-tunk, ta-tunk*—and as long as it did, I knew it was still there.

My mind wouldn't stop. Instead of distracting me from the wind, it created its own storm. There were all these voices. Some of the voices were talking about Heidi and Tracy and Hawaii, translating the wind into the sound of crashing surf, and instead of me being alone along the river, the three of us were on a perfect beach. I saw a photo of our bare legs, oiled, a photo of me that would actually get uploaded to the internet, a photo a boy would actually comment on. But there were also voices saying it wouldn't be like that at all—that in reality Heidi and Tracy were probably not even missing me. That instead they were probably having all sorts of fun, and that they were probably flirting with the local kid who ran the towel exchange, or at least telling each other that they *should* flirt with him and then chickening out. And there was also a voice that said they were the ones missing out—that they'd never have the experience of being out in wind like this. Or the experience of not having walls and a roof and a Tempur-Pedic mattress. The voice said there was no way they could've handled this, just like the tarantula. It said it didn't matter how both of them always had the newest phones or could wear whatever, or how they'd both had kind-of real boyfriends. It didn't matter how they liked to patronize me about lacking in all these departments. None of it mattered because they wouldn't survive here, which meant I was actually the one who should've been patronizing them for being so inept… and for not even knowing what the word *patronizing* meant.

But there were also voices telling me I shouldn't be so sure about surviving, either. Voices talking about the next part of the trip, recalling what they'd read in the guidebook about how to identify Big Sluice. Voices telling me how bad my strokes were and recalling times when I'd been paddling stern with my dad and crashed us into shore. Voices telling me just to breathe.

I heard Magic's whinny, heard her paw the ground, heard her snort and roll. Her stall needed to be cleaned. I heard my mother's voice, her comment about how you could tell a lot about a person by how they mucked a stall. That you needed to muck it every day, and you didn't just leave the horse in the stall and clean around them, you put them out to graze or let them loose in the arena. No skimping on fresh shavings because you were too lazy to go get more. Take the wheelbarrow right to the manure pile instead of letting it sit around. Put the wheelbarrow and the pitchfork and scoop shovel back where you'd found them.

One of the voices was talking to Andrea—saying *Yes, please tell me that knock-knock joke again*, and I'll laugh, even though *Cat who? Bless you!* isn't even funny. A voice saying that I'd read to her. That I'd snuggle. But please don't use my lip gloss. And I will never make you go camping, ever. And here are all the things our father wanted me to share with you, how he specifically said that night in the tent *You make sure you tell her—*

Some of the voices were wondering about the crows and where they slept when the wind got this bad. Some were just lyrics from songs, or jingles from commercials, especially commercials I couldn't stand. There was a voice that whispered *Here, pass this to Tracy*. A voice repeatedly insisting to my parents that I *was* telling them the truth. Another voice wondering what my dad was thinking, wondering if he really thought that by asking me if I was sure *one more time*, I'd finally break down and confess whatever it was I was supposedly withholding. A voice talking about the assignments in Spanish I'd never done, the ones largely responsible for that B minus, the ones I'd told my mom I had finished. "*Es verdad,*" the voice said.

I heard voices that sounded like my parents on the deck that day, wondering what they were supposed to do, wondering why exactly things between them had changed so much.

A voice that said, *You are guilty for so many things.*

A voice asking, *What if?* What if we hadn't even gone on this stupid trip, or if I hadn't been so stubborn and made us hike to the spring? Or if I'd hidden the note better, or had fatter legs? What if the rockslide had made the way impassable and we turned back there? Or if he'd just broken his arm or something, or someone had come along? What if he'd actually listened to Mom about the cell phone when she said, "It would just make *me* feel more comfortable?" What if I hadn't kicked the log that last time, or if it was me who'd fallen? What if it could've been me instead?

The voices all seemed to collide with each other, bouncing one way and then back, becoming a kind of white noise—sort of the way it got in the halls at school sometimes, especially in the mornings or after the last bell.

It was just the voices and the wind and my stuffy little cocoon. And at some point I fell asleep.

When I woke up and poked my head out of my bag, I scratched at all the sand in my hair. The wind was perfectly still. The sky was turning blue.

I stood shin-deep in the river, holding the gunwale. The canoe bobbed on the eddy currents, and the ups and downs were bumping the bow into the shoreline. Up in camp, the tent sagged a little after the windstorm. If the breeze shifted just the right way, it smelled rank.

I'd taken a few pieces of wood from the letters and made an arrow that pointed downstream. I'd also stabbed my dad's paddle into the sand and hung his lifejacket from it, hoping the bright red fabric would stand out. I'd left whatever was still in the tent in there, but packed up and rigged everything else—even the groover. Instead of rigging the canoe so most of the gear rode in the middle—which is where I needed to sit—I split everything between the bow and the stern. The spare paddle was tucked along the floor, right where I could reach it.

I must have counted down about a dozen times in my head. Then on the thirteenth time, or maybe the fourteenth or fifteenth, I got to zero and finally hopped into the boat. I pulled hard on a forward stroke, water swirling around the blade. The boat went nowhere.

Almost every maneuver in a canoe comes down to three things: angle, momentum, and lean. You have to have an angle to the current, have to be going a different speed than it, and have to always be leaning your boat with it—all the while realizing there are a million different currents in the river going a million different directions and speeds. If any of those three are off, paddling is more of a wrestling match, one you're probably going to lose. But if you have them dialed, the water will actually do most of the work for you. It can be effortless.

I set up for a peel out of the eddy. The boat felt huge and heavy. I angled myself to the eddyline and attempted to build some speed. Each forward stroke I took turned the boat, screwing up the angle I wanted, forcing me to pry and correct. Because my pry sucked, it often turned out to be more of a backstroke. I went: Forward stroke, backstroke. Forward stroke, backstroke.

I didn't remember it being so much work getting into the eddy before, but now I was trapped inside it. With no momentum, each time I tried to escape, the bow swung right back around, right back into the eddy—and there was the tent again. The sign. The arrow. The red lifejacket.

On my final try, my arms exhausted, I remembered something my dad had showed me earlier on the trip. I switched hands to paddle on the upstream side of the boat and studied the current a little closer. I took a couple of quick strokes to build up as much speed as I could, which was not much, and right as I hit the eddyline, I put in one last pry. The current jammed the paddle hard against the upstream gunwale, and I pulled on it with all I had left. The boat rocked violently, tipping so far that a bunch of water poured in.

My dad always said to never let go of your paddle—said if your hands weren't on the steering wheel, then you weren't steering—but as the canoe tipped, that's exactly what I did when I tried to catch my balance. I just let go. With both hands.

The paddle disappeared beneath the surface. I could feel it underneath me, banging along the hull.

A second later it popped up on the other side of the boat. I reached down and grabbed it, got the T-grip back in place. Through all of that, I'd somehow made it out of the eddy and was moving downstream.

I'd told myself I was just going to go and not look back. With all the water inside, the boat was even heavier than before. Unsteadily, I took a sweep stroke and turned so I was facing upstream.

"Stay out of trouble," I said. It's what he said to me every time I stayed home alone.

"I'll try," I always answered back.

"Try hard enough," he'd say.

I started bailing. "I will."

Eighteen

The four of us were still out in the front yard, even though it had gotten nearly too dark to see. Across the street, at the Dunlaps', the light popped on in one of the rooms, then Mr. Dunlap was standing in the window, pausing there and watching us for a second before pulling shut the drapes. Andrea was sitting in my lap, my arms wrapped around her like a blanket. Mom and Mrs. Hayes had been talking house stuff—about how there was some extra food in the fridge, a clean load of towels in the dryer—but all the information had been swapped and there wasn't much left to say. Mom reached over and put her hand on top of Andrea's head. "How about we get you in your jammies?"

Andrea groaned and bristled at that.

"Come on," I said, nudging her out of my lap. "I want to get my PJs on, too. Let's go get tucked in." I wasn't anywhere near sleep.

Mrs. Hayes grabbed hold of the porch railing and pulled herself up. "I should be calling Frank for a ride anyway."

Mom told Mrs. Hayes that she didn't need to do that: she'd be happy to give her a ride. Mrs. Hayes had been my babysitter since forever, and even babysat Heidi and Tracy before they moved. Sometimes Mr. and Mrs. Hayes came over just for dinner, like as my parent's friends, and sometimes Mrs. Hayes and my mom would go out for coffee, or they would go and volunteer at the library together. My mom said the ride was the least she could do.

Mrs. Hayes said not to fuss but relented pretty quickly. Mom could have her home in the time it took Frank just to get his shoes on. Mrs. Hayes's purse was in the kitchen, so Mom and Andrea followed her inside. I stayed on the porch for a second and looked through the doorway. I took in the coatrack, which never really had any coats on it, and the shoe rack, which was always overflowing with shoes. Just off the hallway was the living room, the couch, Mom's decorative coyotes.

Here were my last few steps, steps I couldn't seem to make. Almost everybody—teachers, classmates, Aunt Mel, my mom— all of them would tell me that I should take as long as I needed to take, even after it became obvious to me that some of them felt like I'd taken long enough. I didn't think there'd ever be enough time, not in this life.

I looked down at the doormat. It was made of natural fibers and had a picture of a house, a blossoming cherry tree, and a grazing horse. Mom had gotten it for Dad's birthday one year. I liked it—thought the picture was pretty—but I also thought a doormat was kind of a lame thing to get someone for their birthday. When he unwrapped it, despite how he tried to hide it, we could see Dad felt the same way. "Cool," he said flatly, holding it up. "It has a horse." He hated how we tracked in mud and hay and stall shavings when we came home from the barn, and hated how he was always having to remind us to take off our dirty boots *outside* the house, as he claimed to always do.

I wiped my feet carefully and went in, leaving the door open behind me.

"Sometimes," my mom had said when we were shopping for Dad at the home improvement store, "sometimes you give a person the gift that *you* need."

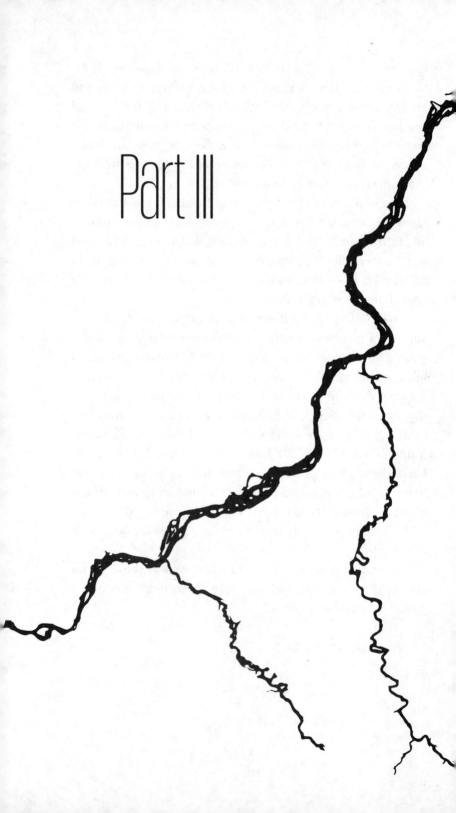

Part III

Nineteen

It took all day to reach Big Sluice. The guidebook described the long calm section preceding the rapid and noted to watch out for an old steel cable that stretched high above the river—a remnant from the days of copper mining. *Check. Check.* Then I could hear it: a muted booming, plus the sound of static. And then came the horizon line, the line across the river where the water just disappeared. Past that—mist in the air, rainbows when the sun hit just right.

The guidebook advised scouting from river right, so as soon as I saw a somewhat open spot of shoreline, I dug hard. So far I'd only had to deal with little riffles, wavelets that I could just rudder my way through. Big Sluice would require making deliberate moves.

I landed hard and bruised my shin as I jumped out of the boat. There wasn't much of a portage trail yet—not that far upstream—but I picked my way down the shoreline, which grew steeper and rockier the closer I got to the rapid.

You're supposed to scout from the bottom of a drop to the top. Scouting that way gives you a different perspective, one where you can often see things that are otherwise hidden by the water. Rocks disguised as waves. Holes disguised as waves. Stuff like that. Sometimes the waves are just waves.

I didn't have to go any further than the top to know. My heart sank. I stood on a wide, flat rock watching the water move past. Below me, the riverbanks pinched together, funneling the water into a big white mess that slammed right into a pair of very undisguised boulders. The guidebook said the move was a middle-left-middle move. You could also take a middle-right-middle route, but the right side featured even more boulders below the boulders. The one option you definitely *didn't* have was a middle-middle-middle move, which was about all I'd been able to manage in the rapids above.

There was an obvious portage trail, but it was narrow and twisty and not made for a tandem canoe. Even if I carried all the gear down first, piece by piece, I still didn't think I'd be able to drag the canoe the whole way. I'd have to line it. Lining meant using the painter lines to send an unmanned boat down along the edge of the rapid, where the water had less force. On rapids whose banks were straight and clear of obstacles, lining wasn't too bad. But Big Sluice had a jumble of boulders, which I'd have to scramble over—all the while trying to make sure the canoe didn't get stuck, or that I didn't slip and fall in, or that the ropes didn't get yanked out of my hands. Or all three at once.

I made camp right where I'd first beached, even though there were nicer spots downstream. The sky was sunny, but the river was shadowed, and I was shivering. I told myself to just do all the things you are supposed to do. I changed out of my wet clothes and put on my warm fleece. I started boiling water. I set up the tarp as a lean-to, used the paddles in two of the corners and weighted down the other two with rocks. If I'd tested it and shook too hard, the whole thing would've collapsed.

I got out some ramen noodles and peppermint tea. The hot chocolate had spilled out of its Ziploc and was all over the inside of the food bag. I unrolled my sleeping pad, set up my camp chair, and grabbed my headlamp and put it in my pocket. Then I watched the water on the stove, which is supposed to make it never boil, though it always still does.

I drank the tea first, using the travel mug to warm my hands. I ate the noodles with a fork, then drank some of the broth until my belly felt water-balloony again. When I was finished, I did the dishes and put away the cookstove. Draining the dishwater, I realized that I didn't have anything more to do. All the chores, all the day-to-day things of camping, had pretty much been done. What came next was the quiet.

I rolled up my pants, slipped out of my flip-flops, and stepped into the cold water. The river was shallow, the bottom sandy and soft, my feet sinking down unevenly. Out in the middle of the river, there was a kind of stillness, which I knew was the water backing up a little before it poured down the rapid. Closer to me, clouds of stoneflies hovered just above the surface. Other kids might just call them bugs. As nymphs they lived underwater, sometimes for years, shedding skins and growing until they were ready for one final change. Then the nymphs would crawl out of the water and stick themselves to a rock. There they would sit until it was time to hatch, until the temperature and moisture and angle of the earth was just right.

I couldn't stay in much longer. My shins already felt numb. I bent over and scooped up some water and splashed my face several times. I looked downstream at the horizon line, pretending to not remember what was on the other side of it.

You can find the split-open exoskeletons of stoneflies all along the river. Sometimes they are fresh, and almost look like a live bug, and when you smoosh them they smear black with goo.

Other times they are so old and worn they just turn to powder.

My parents went through these phases—phases where they swore they were just going to get rid of everything, all the knickknacks and electronics and useless things they'd accumulated over the years—and for a few days they'd weed through the house, boxing and bagging things for Goodwill. *Simplify! Simplify!* They made Andrea and I do it, too. Anything that no longer fit or I no longer wore or couldn't pass down to Andrea, I was supposed to get rid of. And all those papers from school, all those magazines, all that stuff heaped in my closet—recycle it, or it became garbage.

When they got really obsessed, they brought up their dream of selling the house and the cars and buying a nicer van, almost like a mini-motorhome, and just living like gypsies.

It was one of these phases that sent the photo of my dad out into the garage, where it hung above his workbench. The picture—a twelve-by-fourteen-inch of him kayaking down the Grand Canyon—used to be in the house, in the living room, sitting on a bookcase shelf. One of my chores was to dust that bookcase, and I hated having to lift up each knickknack and picture frame to wipe underneath, something my mom insisted I do. But then, during one of those phases, the photo moved to the garage, and the picture glass became coated with dust, the corners of the frame spanned by cobwebs.

In the photo, my dad's kayak is cresting the top of a huge wave, the bow cutting through a crash of dirty whitewater and angling into a popsicle-blue sky. Most of his body, all except part of his face and one hand, is buried by the wave. A sliver of paddle blade is also visible, but that's it. *Swallowed* is what he and his friends called that kind of moment.

When I asked him how big that wave was, my dad showed me how you could use the kayak in the picture as a kind of measuring stick, just like you used a scale line on a map: use your fingers to measure the kayak, and then measure how many kayaks fit down the face of the wave. It was as simple as that—and now I knew how to do it by myself. I was about twelve at the time. He said his kayak was eleven feet long, which is way longer than they are now. He also said he wished he still had that old boat, even though it was unstable and unsafe, because it was like a historical artifact now. "It'd just be so cool to have."

When I asked my dad how I was supposed to use the kayak, since you couldn't actually see much of it in the picture, he told me that this particular case might be more of a measuring-by-guessing thing.

He got the picture down and held it so we both could look. I counted about three kayak lengths. "Maybe two and a half," he said. "I think that wave was about twenty feet tall."

"How tall is that?" I asked, which made him laugh.

"Twenty feet," he said.

Later, after I'd wrestled the stepladder out of the garage and set it up in the middle of the driveway, just as I was about to get up on the very top of it, my father came running out the front door, telling me to freeze right where I was.

"Just don't move," he said. "Not up, or down."

My dad came and held the ladder, while I sat on it. He pointed out how the words "No Step" were molded into the top. When he asked what I'd been doing, I told him: "I wanted to see how high twenty feet was."

We just had the one ladder. Where I was sitting, that was only about fourteen feet. He asked me how I'd feel on that big of a wave.

I remember sitting there and looking down, how the world had a different shape to it from that height. How it was a little bit like the craziness of a swing set. "I think it'd be fun," I said.

"Yeah? You wouldn't feel scared?"

"Maybe. But fun scared."

For my dad, the thing that awed him the most about the Grand Canyon was how it messed with his sense of scale. Because it was so wide and so deep and so long, he told me, the Grand Canyon had a way of making everything else seem small. And he didn't just mean things like bosses, or slow traffic, or celebrities. He also meant actual things in the actual Grand Canyon. If you weren't careful, you could get tricked into thinking rapids were smaller than they actually were, because in comparison they were small, even when they were really big.

Most of those times when I was supposed to be dusting, I really wasn't. My philosophy was to do such a mediocre job that I'd get dismissed and put on something else. Often, instead of wiping things clean, I pretended the pictures were illustrations from textbooks.

Figure 1: American Family. Christmas. Color-coordinated outfits.

Figure 2: Active Mom. Trail Runner. First race completed, 2nd Place medallion.

Figure 3: Daredevil: subset, Whitewater Kayaker. Notice the unkempt facial hair. Also Known As: Water Cowboy, River Rat, River Scum, Kayak Bum.

That day I dragged out the ladder, I asked my dad if he'd been scared on that wave in the picture.

"Probably," he said. "My eyes look pretty round."

I asked my dad if that was the most scared he'd ever been.

"I don't know about that," he said. "Maybe it wasn't so much that I was scared. It was more that I just felt really wide awake. Really...alive."

"*Fun* scared," I said.

"Is that what that is?" he asked. "That's probably right."

Later, while my dad was straightening up the stuff that had crashed in the garage when I'd gotten out the ladder, he told me this: "The times on the river when I really got scared were usually when I was out of control. And I don't like being out of control. Panic isn't a nice feeling."

I was on my bike, like I was about to go somewhere, but I had the brake squeezed tight. "Then how come you and your friends are always talking about being ballsy?" I asked.

"Don't say 'ballsy'," he instructed.

"You guys do."

He grabbed the wide broom, and started pushing with short, quick motions—motions that somehow felt comforting. "We shouldn't," he said.

He began telling me about the idea of calculated risk. Running rivers, rock climbing, whatever—they weren't about being crazy, even the stuff that seemed crazy. You had to push past your fears, sure, had to be *ballsy*, but it was all in a calculated way. When he got nervous before a rapid, which was probably the case with the one in the photo, he'd ask himself all these questions: Did he, based on past experiences, have the skills to make the necessary moves through the rapid? If he answered yes, he'd ask himself why he was nervous. If he was nervous because he was tired or hungry or just having an off day, maybe he'd portage the rapid. If he didn't know why he was nervous, if he was nervous just because he was nervous, or he was letting doubt get the better of him, he'd hike up to the top of the rapid, get in his boat, and take two deep breaths before peeling out and running the thing. Of course, sometimes he misjudged and ended up getting his butt kicked. But that's how you learned.

"You just take two breaths then go?" I asked. I pushed my foot down on the bike pedal, testing the handbrake.

"Breathe, don't think, just go," he said. "Remember that. You can use it in life. Whenever you're nervous or scared—if you have to give a report at school, or there is a test, or all of a sudden everyone is doing karaoke—it's two deep breaths then go."

"You've done karaoke?" I asked.

"I've never done karaoke," he said.

He asked me if I got it—not the karaoke part so much, but the rest of it. I told him I did. The idea of calculated risk seemed sensible, and I was already practicing the two deep breaths thing, but what I didn't understand then was that there are all these different ways for doing the calculations, and sometimes the math wouldn't even be math you knew, particularly in high school. He said that finally you had to ask yourself this: What's the worst that could happen?

If you could live with the answer—go for it.

I'd taken my breaths (four, actually). The last exhale. My fingers uncurled from the brake. I stood up on the pedals and went.

"Faster," he said, as I shot past.

I woke up knowing that I was going to run it. As I ate breakfast and packed up, I kept telling myself to wait and see, that it wasn't a decision I needed make just yet, but I knew.

I walked to the bottom of the rapid. The run-out was fairly straightforward—a line of diminishing waves. The big boulders were fairly straightforward, too. I just had to avoid them. I watched the water pile into them and pillow up. The water was actually making a buffer around the rocks, so as long as I didn't go barreling into them or lean the wrong way, the current would actually guide me around them.

Kneeling in a canoe—or even more so, sitting in a kayak—means being down at the water's level, where everything looks different. A lot of times you can't really even see anything downstream, especially as you're entering a rapid. The key to not getting lost is to pick out landmarks along the shore: weird-looking trees or markings on rocks, or in the case of Big Sluice, the patch of prickly pear I chose.

After I scouted, I peed. After I walked back up to the canoe, I peed again. My dad said that's how you could tell if you were nervous: the bladder scale. He also once said that if you sent an empty canoe through a rapid, unless it was a really gnarly waterfall or something, the boat would usually make it through just fine. The problem was only when you added a human.

I coiled and stowed the painter line. I grabbed the paddle from the boat and pushed it all the way into the water, carefully lining it up with the shore. My blood felt whooshy, and my stomach leaky, like things were coming up. But here is how I knew that morning that I'd run Big Sluice: I could feel that some part of me had disengaged, or the opposite, that some part of me had engaged, locked into place, preventing the controls from being tampered with. And somehow, in my sleep, I'd set the controls to *Go*. There was no other voice.

On the day with the ladder in the driveway, after I cruised around on my bike for a bit, my dad told me that the most scared he'd been wasn't on a river or a mountain. "The most tired and cold and hungry," he said, "no doubt. But not the most scared." The most scared he'd ever been was the first time he held me. "You were so tiny," he said. "So totally defenseless, and now you were in my hands, and I couldn't drop you. Not that I was in the practice of dropping things," he said, "but I was convinced I was about to trip, or that my hands would just give out. The most scared I'll ever get is with you guys, with something happening to you or your mom or your sister."

I got in the canoe and seated myself, knees spread wide for

stability. I'd positioned the boat with the bow facing upstream so I could ferry out toward the left side of the river. I twisted around and looked for my prickly pear, which were suddenly lost among all the other prickly pear. The whooshiness whooshed more, and I started to have to pee again. Jamming my paddle into the sand, I shoved away from shore.

One.

Two.

Forward stroke.

Go.

Twenty

Partial list of things my father told me about rivers:

1. Rivers belong to river systems. Streams and creeks feed into other streams and creeks, growing in size. Branches merge with branches, growing again, and then they feed into a main stem, and then these main stems eventually flow into other main stems, growing until you have something like the Mississippi River, or the Colorado, or the Amazon.

2. Where these big rivers spill into the ocean, sometimes the fresh water pushes out into the sea for hundreds of miles before turning salty.

3. This is how my dad would talk to me about things like wanting *stuff* or being a good big sister, how he'd try to deal with me when I complained about not being allowed an Instagram profile. I tried explaining how frustrating it felt, how un-normal. That the other kids at school, the kids who were actually doing bad things, they didn't get hardly as many lectures as I got. But then he'd tell me about the many miles a single droplet of water might travel in its lifetime, or how it'd morph with other droplets of water and still be okay. How when scientists x-rayed them, they saw that water atoms had the same branching patterns as river systems. How it took millions of years for some rivers to carve their paths. How a river did all sorts of things without getting all hung up on itself.

"Comparatively speaking," my dad would say, addressing whatever it was that I was griping about, "it's trivial."

4. Where different river currents meet is called a seam. If these seams have to do with eddies, which are really just small

whirlpools, they are called eddylines. If it's a really violent eddyline, it's often called an eddy fence because of how they tend to either keep you out of the eddy or hold you in. My dad described seams as unstable water, as water that can't make up its mind. Water you don't want to spend a lot of time hanging out with.

5. Pour-overs and holes were like eddylines, but horizontal instead of vertical. When I didn't understand that, my dad took me to the park downtown to show me. Just one day during lunch in middle school, he came and got me, and we went. We walked around, him pushing Andrea in her stroller, and we ate Goldfish crackers and grapes and looked at the water. There was a big man-made pond in the middle of the park, and on one end was a spillway where the water dumped into a canal. My dad dug a little plastic ball out of the stroller. We stood on the bridge that went over the canal. He reminded me never to litter, and then he tossed the ball into the water, right where it was pouring out of the pond.

"Watch," he said.

The force of the falling water pushed the ball under, making it disappear. A second later, the ball popped up a few feet downstream.

"Keep watching."

The water was white, all bubbles, fizzing like a soda. Instead of floating downstream, the ball slowly started drifting back toward the spillway, as if it was being reeled in. When it reached the pour-over, the ball danced around a bit until the falling water pushed it back under again. It popped up in almost the same spot as before. And then it just kept repeating that cycle—getting sucked back, pushed under, and then popping to the surface—on and on. My dad told us that the ball would be stuck like that for days.

6. Almost every civilization in the world started on the banks of a river.

7. In some parts of the world, rivers are referred to as mothers.

8. After a big downpour one summer, he took me outside

and told me all about flash floods. We watched the rainwater run along the street gutters, sticks and trash being swept along. He told me how some soils suck water in, but others, like most of the soils in the Southwest, pushed water away. These were called *hydrophobic* soils. The absorbent kinds were *hydrophilic*.

9. He told me that Egyptians used to think floods were the tears of a god.

10. That anything worthwhile, he learned on a river. If he didn't learn it there, he usually had to go back to the river to learn it in a way that would make it stick. When I asked for an example, I stumped him for a bit. Then he lamely said, "Go with the flow."

11. There was an ancient Greek dude who'd philosophized that you could never step in the same river twice. It was a paradox about rivers. My dad said he never got tired of thinking about that—how if you stood on the bank of a river and watched the water, the water you were seeing was constantly new water, water that hadn't been there one second ago. Spend some time watching a wave on a river. The wave holds the same shape, and the water just flows through it.

"Dude's name was Heraclitus," he said. "Way, way, *way* ahead of his times."

Twenty-One

Here is something else you'll learn on a river: second-guessing yourself never works.

I was so afraid of those boulders, was so freaked out by how much bigger they seemed—by how much bigger and noisier and flashing all of it suddenly seemed—that I ditched my landmarks and set up farther left than I had planned. Waves peeled off the shoreline, and the bow rode up the first then crashed down into the second, splashing water in an arc. I pulled hard, but the next wave shoved the bow toward the center of the river, where waves breaking off the left bank were smashing into the waves breaking off the right. I began sweeping as hard as I could, but instead of turning, the boat only picked up speed.

The next wave lifted me, and for a brief moment it almost felt weightless, like maybe being up in space. That's how they trained astronauts on Earth, after all—how they got them to float. Fly them up and down in big waves in the sky.

As the canoe slapped back down, I fell off balance. The bow drove into the next wave. The wave peaked and hung then broke over the gunwales. Water inside the canoe rolled from side to side, forcing me to constantly counterbalance. On the river, you're always supposed to focus on where you want to go, not where you don't want to, and then you're just supposed to paddle yourself there—which is another life lesson, I guess. But all I could do was keep leaning on high braces and stare at the two big rocks headed my way and think about the pleasures of oxygen.

The canoe started to turn, until it was almost sideways. The boulders stood like towers—more towering every instant. The worst way you could hit them was sideways, where the canoe could get wrapped. Another wave drenched me. Another. I was right there. I could have extended my hand and touched that first rock. I would've barely had to reach. I went limp instead.

The pillow of water grabbed the canoe and flicked it river left. The bow was pushed into a shoreline eddy while the stern swung downstream, and then I was going backwards, and then I didn't even have my paddle and was instead just death-gripping the gunwales—*Never grab the gunwales!*—and crying. Before I'd even gotten to the bottom, I was crying. The boat kept spinning and pitching up on the waves, and all the while I just held on and cried. I'd cried *before* running a rapid, and I'd cried *after*, but I'd never actually cried *in* a rapid before, and I think that was maybe because my dad was always there to un-paralyze me, shouting: *Paddle! Paddle! Paddle!*

Past the boulders, in the long run-out, the waves calmed and the current slowed. I opened my eyes. Forty yards upstream, the tail end of Big Sluice flashed white. The canoe wobbled with all the water it had taken on. The current drifted me to shore and deposited me in an eddy. The boat came to rest gently against a cluster of sedge. The rapid was almost soundless from there.

I bailed and cried until I was out of tears and was left with just bailing. I couldn't match what I was looking at with what I'd just done. In thirty seconds of whitewater, there had been fear, then panic, then surrender, then anger, then relief. In one of my sessions with Roland, the counselor my mom would make me see for a while that summer, I actually told him about that moment after Big Sluice—about sitting there and bailing, and the sunlight, and the sky, and how I felt drained. I told him I was a pool, the above-ground kind, one whose side had split open, the water flooding out. A gush, then empty.

"In this weird way," I told him, "it felt really good. Like how I wish I could feel now."

"When they fix pools," he said, "they have to drain them before they can be repaired."

Downstream, low hills striped with yellows and grays and a kind of bone-white ran parallel to the water. Sixteen miles that-away was the next big rapid, Upset. I leaned over the side of the canoe and rinsed my face. My eyes felt both sunken and swollen. I drank some water and took one last look at what I'd just come through.

"And after they repair them?" I asked Roland, about the pools.

"I think you go swimming," he said.

Twenty-Two

Below Big Sluice, the valley widened and the way-off mountains turned hazy and blue. Without the cliffs and hillsides containing it, the river started to oxbow. I paddled near the middle of the channel, where the water was deepest. Between the oxbows were large stands of tall, dried-out reeds—reeds that were taller than I was. They were colored the same faded brown as the dirt. My dad and I were just going to take our time through this section, but it was already afternoon and I needed to keep moving. He'd thought it was going to make for good birding, and that we might even see some grebes, but all I'd spotted were a few mallards. They were totally common, though. *Ubiquitous* is the term.

Something rustled along the shoreline. The size of it startled me. The reeds snapped side to side.

I could tell by the line it cut that it was headed for the river. It's so easy to hear things on the wind sometimes: *Emma*.

"Here," I yelled, backstroking. "I'm here!"

They had figured it out and come. I paddled to keep from slipping downstream, and I noticed other areas of the reeds being walked through, and I could hear that it was more noise than just one person could make—that it had to be a whole search party.

"Hey!" I yelled, moving their way. "I'm here! It's Emma! I'm on the river!"

The other searchers were still headed toward the water, but the first one had stopped. He'd come right up to the edge and paused, hidden behind a curtain of reeds.

"You're almost there," I said.

When the first cow crashed through and saw me, she stopped and snorted and backed her butt into the reeds again. Others trampled past, right down to the river's edge, splashing into the water, peeing and drinking and mooing. The cows all had droopy ears, the left ones pierced with yellow tags. Their hides were dull gray and hung loosely on their necks. Some had nubs where their horns had been sawed off. They all looked a little wild. So much rib on some of them.

I quit paddling and let the current pull me back toward the other side of river, wondering how I could be so stupid.

My dad often ranted about grazing issues—about how cattle were allowed to graze on public land, how big cattle companies would lease the land for cheaper than it was worth, how the cows wandered all over, tearing up the native habitat and polluting the water. I should've known.

One of the cows had started following me and was trotting through the shallows.

"I'm not going to help you," I told it. "If that's what you want. It's not like I can fit you in here."

The cow mooed, but kept coming. Saliva ran from its mouth.

"That means what?" I asked. "I don't speak cow."

She pushed me a good ways from the herd when I finally figured it out.

"You're just trying to scare me off, aren't you? You don't want a ride. You're just trying to scare away the weird-looking thing on the river."

The cow stopped at that. She flared her nostrils and flicked her tail. She bent down and took some water. When she raised her head, more saliva drooled out, and she made a kind of baying noise. Her eyes were so big and black, her tongue as thick as my forearm.

"Well, you did it," I said. "That was a pretty good job of saving everyone."

Everyone except me.

I lifted my paddle high into the air, just like my dad and I did after a clean run through a rapid, then I smacked it down on the water, the clap as loud as a gunshot.

The cows started running the other way.

The current had picked up, and I was right against the bank. It wasn't even a rapid. Then there was some overgrowth, and I was leaning back and trying to do the limbo and not get all tangled up. Even ducking down, I couldn't slip underneath it. Branches started breaking and falling into the boat. As I hit the thickest part, the canoe started to drag, the water piling against the upstream side of the hull. I dropped the paddle again and punched and pulled my way through the vegetation, dried leaves and sticks showering down my neck. A piece of twig went up my nose, slicing it. It was only once I'd gotten through that I flipped.

Actually, what I really did was a slow-mo losing-my-balance roll combined with a lunge-for-my-paddle dive, all the while wondering, *What just happened?*

Dehydration. Sunburn. Mental error. Exhaustion.

The cold hit my eardrums first and then quickly seeped through my clothes. My feet were already a little frozen. I remember being surprised by how murky the water was, how there was only a thin layer of light right at the surface. Something brushed against my leg. When I popped up, I was just behind the canoe, which floated upside down. My paddle was there, too. It already seemed hard to breathe.

I pointed my head downstream and swam. After I grabbed the paddle, I had to do a sort of side-crawl. When I got to the boat, I reached under and found the grab loop. The thread of current was shifting away from shore, pulling me with it.

The way my dad did it was to hold both his paddle and the grab loop in one hand while he swam, but my hands were too small, and I had to try and swim with my paddle in one hand, the canoe in the other. I set an angle with my body so that the water would help ferry me toward shore, but it didn't really work. No matter how hard I kicked, I could feel the weight of the canoe dragging me downstream. My legs and back and ribs all began to ache. My throat burned.

Sometimes my dad had this other technique—one where he flipped the canoe back upright, so that instead of pulling it through the water, he could push it along the surface. I swam toward the center of the canoe. I kicked myself up out of the water as much as I could and reached over the hull. I'd use my body weight to pull the canoe back toward me. I was on the downstream side of the boat, meaning I was going to be rolling the canoe against the current. If I'd been on the upstream side, if I'd have thought about it, I would've been going with the current. It would've worked.

The canoe rolled, but only halfway. On its side, the hull flooded with water and sank even lower. I scissored my legs as hard as I could. One of my shoes slid halfway off, and when I slowed down to keep it from coming all the way off, I felt the canoe pull me backwards. My head went under, and I gagged on some water. My shoe came off all the way, disappearing.

When you tip over and keep your paddle and your boat and you swim yourself to shore, that's called a self-rescue. Or it's one version of a self-rescue. Some canoeists, in specially outfitted canoes, they can tip over and roll back upright, just like a kayaker's Eskimo roll. That's another version.

You were supposed to follow a sequence. If you were going to let go of something, you were actually supposed to let go of the canoe first, which seems backwards. But the thinking is that boats are bigger and move slower and eventually end up in some eddy. Let go of your paddle, and like a shoe, you might not ever see it again.

I did it backwards. My hand simply uncurled from the paddle shaft. I don't know if it was a conscious decision or not. But once the paddle was out of my hand, once I tried swimming with a free arm and still couldn't get anywhere, growing colder and more tired, I knew I also had to let go of the canoe.

I turned onto my stomach and found some way to swing my cement arms. As long as I kicked and swam, the shoreline inched closer. When I paused to rest, I was panicked by how fast the gap between me and it widened again.

Now you'll find out, I thought. When my dad's kayaking buddy drowned, and he and Mom and I went to the funeral, which was way out in a meadow, I'd asked him if drowning was a bad way to die. Now, I thought, I'll know whether his answer was true—if drowning is just like falling asleep.

I could barely make out the canoe, could just see a sliver of it bobbing right at the surface. My dad cried pretty hard at that funeral, maybe as hard as I'd ever seen him cry. He was not alone. I tried to cry, because I thought I was supposed to, but I couldn't. At the end of everything, the man's wife and children dumped his ashes into a shallow creek that cut through the meadow while everybody else watched. My dad said that's what he wanted, too. He made Mom promise. Then there was supposed to be a moment of silence, but while we all stood there, my dad reached over and squeezed the back of my neck a little too hard and whispered about how much I meant to him.

After the funeral, there was what was called a "Life Celebration" that went late into the night. My dad drank so much that Mom had to drive us home. Dad sat in the passenger seat, half-facing Mom. He didn't even bother to talk about Mom's driving, which he was always nervous about. I sat in the back seat, slouched down where the lights from other cars didn't shine through. My dad was talking about his friend, talking about all these crazy times they'd had together. They were mostly stories about leaky tents and getting lost that generally sounded like no fun at all. But the way he was telling them—all these things were like the best things that had ever happened.

I don't know if he thought I was asleep, or that I couldn't hear him, or if maybe he even wanted me to hear. "He'd run that river a million times," my dad said. "He'd gone through that spot a million times and nothing had happened before."

"I know," my mom said.

"I hope he wasn't scared," he said. "The panic of not being

able to breathe. I hope that went away. That shouldn't be your last sensation."

"No," she said, "it shouldn't."

"I'm scared of how scared I'm going to be." My dad's head bonked against the window, and I could see he was looking up at the stars. "I'm so afraid of finding out what a coward I am."

They both got quiet after that. One time my dad told me that looking up at the sky was the best way to remember that we're human, that we're all trapped inside a body. I leaned over so I could look out the side window, and when my dad heard me moving around he said, "There's the Milky Way. That's where we live. The Way of the Milk."

"Welcome home," I said.

When I reached the shore, I had nothing left. One hand slapped into the mud, splattering some across my face. Then the other hand slapped down, and I pulled myself up on my elbows, feeling like I was about to puke up whatever was in my stomach. I crawled and struggled, and a few feet out of the water, I curled into a frozen ball.

You have to get up, I thought. The lighter, the backup matches, my dry clothes—that was all in the canoe, which was getting farther away. *Get up.*

I rolled over and faced the sun. I used to think the sun was something that was on fire, but fire is not the right word for it at all. I'm sure my dad's friend was panicked before he drowned. But I'm also sure that his panic went away, that it wasn't the last thing he felt. You feel something different.

Twenty-Three

Sometimes I think about how I might've told this story to him. I think about the things he'd want to know compared to what others keep asking about. Like the others, my dad would've wanted to know if I'd been scared, or if I'd ever gotten lonely, but he wouldn't have had to ask, because he knew that loneliness and fear were going to be part of any real adventure. Loneliness and fear and hunger and uncomfortable sleep and bug bites and butt rash. These were just givens. These were the reasons *for* going. But what he'd also really want to know about were the crazy views and the sunsets and the shooting stars and the rapids. He'd want to know about my lines, about the water that splashed in my face and peeled back my eyelids, about the improvisation with my Duffek stroke—things I couldn't explain to Roland.

I didn't think Roland was a bad person, just clueless. That's not how you're supposed to think of your therapist. He admitted he wasn't much of an outdoorsman. That's the phrasing he used. He was all dress slacks and ties. Clean, feathered hair. He said, "A picnic is about as rugged as I get."

I asked, "Shouldn't it be outdoors-*person*?"

My mom was the one who pushed it. Seeing a therapist was one of the stipulations she'd negotiated when I asked her if I could drop out of high school and get my GED instead. I didn't know why I was the only one who had to go. Mom and I got in a screaming match about it. I pointed out how Dad would've totally called her a hypocrite for it—hypocrites being one of the things he hated the most.

"You know it's true," I said.

"Like he'd be one to talk," she countered.

Roland only lasted for a couple of months. He once told me to consider not holding onto my feelings so tightly. He said, "Create room for the new feelings to come in." I thought: *I dislike you in a whole new way now.*

I actually understood what he meant. He just didn't know how to say it right. During the last Olympics, my dad let me stay up late to watch the whitewater stuff with him. The kayaking and canoeing didn't air until the middle of the night, not until all the swimming and gymnastics and track and field events were over, unless you had cable or satellite and a DVR or what-ever—then you could just watch it whenever you wanted. We never had those things.

While we were waiting, my dad made paper flags for each of us. He sat at the kitchen table and drank beers as he worked. He stapled computer paper to some barbecue skewers, colored the stars and stripes with the dried-out markers from the junk drawer. When it was almost time for the whitewater events, he made me go tell Mom, even though she was sleeping. He gave her a big smile and a flag when she came downstairs. He chanted "USA! USA!" and tried to get her to fist-pump the air.

Mom zombied across the living room, her eyes barely open, but she gave a couple of waves to the flag, which made him happy. Five minutes later, the first paddler barely under way, she was asleep in the recliner. Dad gave her a couple of pokes, but then he just adjusted the flag so that it stood in the crook of her elbow and let her be.

"Watch the racers' hands," he said to me. "Look at their pinky fingers, how lightly they're holding their paddles."

The racers plunged through a series of gates—downstream through the green ones, upstream through the red. The goal was to get through all of them as fast as you could without hitting any. Hitting a gate added a two-second penalty, and missing one added fifty seconds. The rapid was big and fast, but it wasn't even really a river they were paddling. It was more of a concrete channel with concrete blocks that could be moved around to change the features. The water got circulated via pumps, and it looked unnaturally blue, like the blue of toilet cleaners.

I told him that I didn't see what he was talking about.

"Look," he said.

"Oh, okay," I said. "And now I still don't see it."

My dad gave me his head shake, the same one he gave me when he was joking about being mad when he actually wasn't mad. What he wanted me to see was how some of them, especially the kayakers, held out their pinky fingers like they were drinking a cup of tea. That's how light their touch was.

What I noticed instead was how the muscles in their forearms flexed with each stroke, and how sometimes those muscles looked like thick, braided rope. How the racers were giving so much effort they made these ridiculous, unself-conscious faces. How at the last moment they'd contort their bodies in impossible ways and squeeze cleanly through a gate. How I would've been upside down and swimming in like a second.

"If you hold on too tightly," my dad said, "you'll be spent. All your energy gets wasted squeezing on the paddle when you should be pulling on it instead."

My dad was sitting on the edge of the couch and rolling the barbecue skewer between his fingertips. He often complained about TV, but he hardly took his eyes off it that night, not even during the commercials. He said that the holding-on thing was something he needed to remember more often, too. He was too angry sometimes, too worked up about the little things.

"Life should be a dance," he said.

The best showing for the United States that night was fifth in Men's C-1. My dad said that the countries who'd won all had longer traditions with slalom racing. Slalom racing required precision. Americans were more of approximators.

During the tandem events, my dad said something about how maybe that'd be us someday if they ever allowed mixed classes. We'd be a father-daughter Olympic team, charging hard. "Wheaties Box," he said, "here we come."

That did not sound pleasing. It sounded scary. I couldn't imagine running whitewater that big. I knew those paddlers had to do all sorts of training—that they had to get up at like five in the morning and run and lift weights and do whatever else their coaches said. They would train and train and train, and then make it to the Olympics, where they would lose by less than one second.

"Maybe," I said. "But we should be on the Fruit Loops box or something."

"How about the oatmeal box?"

"Um, no."

"Granola?"

"Nothing grosser than Cheerios."

My dad took his flag and knocked it against mine, like he wanted to sword fight with them. I whacked back. "You won't need me," he said. "You'll get on that granola box all on your own, paddling solo."

"Doesn't granola just come in bulk?"

"Your picture could be on the bins," he said. He set down his flag and grabbed for mine. I jerked it back, not giving it up right away. "Here," he said. "Put it down. Let me show you." He held out his pointer fingers in front of me, not pointed at me, but sideways.

"Pretend these are a kayak paddle," he said. "I'm going to pull, and you hold on as lightly as you can."

I grabbed his fingers, made sure my pinkies were all dainty-like. He said he'd tell me when he thought I had the pressure about right. The TV cut to one of the winners. He was chucking his paddle into the air in celebration. He grabbed his coach and threw him into the river. The paddler followed with a cannonball.

"Not yet," my dad said. "A little more. More—"

And then my grip could not hold.

"That's the breaking point," he said. "All you have to do is hold on a little tighter than that."

Twenty-Four

The canoe had washed downstream and pinned against a rock, hull first. The water wasn't super fast there, but it was strong enough that it had already started to wrinkle the hull. The silver of the kitchen box flashed just below the waterline. I could see the spare paddle tucked alongside it. My blue dry bag, its buckle straining against the front thwart, kept bobbing to the surface. Downstream, one of the bailers continued floating away.

I skidded down the loose shoreline and into the water. I had this sensation of shutting off and then turning right back on—like when there's a power surge at home and all the lights cut black for a second. That was my head.

I faced upstream, just like the mouth of the canoe, so I could brace against the current. My feet would also be less likely to get pinned under a rock that way. My left foot shuffled sideways, and then once it found solid footing, my right foot scooted over. I kept shuffling that way, moving upstream or downstream whenever I had to, one foot, then the other. The water rose to my knees. And then the middle of my thighs. The cold cut into me harder. And then it was at my waist.

Halfway there, maybe a little more—that was how far I'd made it. I knew that I needed to reach the canoe. I also knew that I wasn't going to, that this was defeat. In the kitchen box was the stove. All my other clothes were in the dry bag that was strapped to the kitchen box. Attached to that dry bag was the one with my sleeping bag. I remembered exactly how I'd rigged everything, how I'd doubled all the connections like my dad had taught me, lessening the chance that any of it would break free should I capsize.

Once I'd made it back to shore, I just kept climbing. The earth rose up at a low angle toward the rimrock, which was the color of dried blood. I walked a dozen yards or so, until I found a big flat boulder sitting in the full sun. I peeled off my clothes— took off everything—and draped them on the nearby bushes, the branches sagging from the weight.

My skin was still goose-bumped, my heart still beating too fast. The rock smelled like the dust that would burn off whenever my mom or dad would turn the heater on for the first time in fall. A droplet of water slid down my hair and onto my neck. It traced over my throat and then dripped off of me. I swear it sizzled. I reached out my left hand and pressed it flat against the rock. When I pulled away, the wet handprint evaporated instantaneously.

The rock was a kind of sandstone, forming because of the giant ocean that used to be here. The rock was the sediment, the stuff that didn't get flushed away when the water left, compacted by pressure and time. A breeze came through and my shirt fell onto the ground. I was playing with my palm print. I thought I just had to do it a few more times. A few more times and my handprint wouldn't evaporate right away. I even pulled water out of my hair. A few more times and my handprint would be a pictograph, the same kind my dad showed me earlier in the trip. He took my hand and held it up so that it matched the one on the wall, saying, "See, this was you in another life. Like a thousand years ago, this was you."

Twenty-Five

A floating blue blob, suspended in the water, shape shifting with the currents. The tarp. I had stowed it between the hull and two dry bags, but the force of the water must have pulled it free, leaving it in the eddy. The proper way would've been to store the tarp in a dry bag, but it didn't matter so much if the tarp got wet, so I'd just jammed it into its spot as far as I could. I'd even said to myself, *That's not going anywhere*—the exact thing my dad had once reassured me with when he'd packed it the very same way.

There was no way I was going to step into that river—maybe any river—ever again. I hunted down a piece of driftwood to snag the tarp with, but the first one was too skinny, and it snapped as soon as any weight started dragging on it. It took frustratingly long to find one thick enough, but finally I was able to reach out and fish in a corner. I pulled the rest in by hand, fighting the water suction, slopping the tarp in a pile by my feet.

I carried the bundle up the riverbank and spread it out in the late afternoon sun. Gravity pulled water to the seams of the tarp, and from the seams down to the corners, and from the corners the water dripped onto the soil, or seeped into the soil where the corners were already touching the ground. It was its own kind of tributary system, a watershed, just like the one the Tinto was part of, one that stretched all the way from Colorado to Mexico.

While the tarp dried, I hiked up the hillside along the river. I weaved through the sage, cutting back and forth up the slope, going slow because of my bare feet. The top of the hill rolled off to somewhere, but the closer I got to the top, the more it seemed to keep going. I paused and looked back to the river, a sparkling thread that snaked into the distance. A drop of sweat slid down my nose. Another breeze came through, and I instinctively lifted my arms a little. When the wind cut out, my skin immediately prickled with heat.

Had I really thought there'd be something once I got to the top? That I'd find a ranger station, or a road, or a trail? That there'd be a wild horse I could tame and ride home?

The horizon line of a hill is the same kind of thing as the horizon line of a rapid—where suddenly you reach a spot and can finally see what's in front of you, past the drop-off. And what I saw after the horizon line of the hill was just miles and miles of nothing. Empty brown land that rose and fell and was carved up by gullies. Only a thin band of mountains, the same mountains that my dad and I could see when we hiked up to the homesteader's cabin, separated the endless brown from the endless sky. There were no roads, no fences, not even a single cairn—nothing that would signal *humans have been here.*

My dad told me this more than once, and in more than one way: *You have to know when you've reached your limit.* He also told me about a million times that you have to push past your quitting point, that you have to go *beyond* your limits. This would have been the spot. This is where, if I were a mountain climber, I would've said, *I don't need to reach the summit.* This is where I would've turned around and gone back to base camp and gotten out the candy bar I'd stashed. Or if I was rock climbing with my dad, and we were toproping, this is where I would have asked him to lower me back to the ground. But I couldn't do any of those things. My only real option was to keep going downstream.

By the time I'd made it back down to the tarp, the sun had heated up the vinyl so much it was giving off a chemical smell. I shook the tarp out, but instead of folding it into the same square it always got folded into, I rolled it up and tied the ends together, making a loop that I wore like a sash.

"Hi, I'm from the great state of Lost-In-The-Middle-Of-Nowhere," I said aloud. "I'm Miss—"

And what went through my mind was: *Placed.*

That night the cold settled in and the fog grew thick over the river. I'd wrapped myself in the tarp, almost like a loose burrito. Despite the opening I'd left, my breath condensed on the inside, and after I'd fallen asleep for a little bit I woke up wet and freezing, instantly aware of how numb my toes were, how my teeth had actually just chattered.

I loosened the tarp and tightened into a ball, wrapping my arms across my chest, pulling my knees up close. It was the HELP position: Heat Escape Lessening Position. It did not feel like much lessening was happening, though, not of the cold, not of my worrying.

It was hours like that. Hours of stomach cramps and a knotted back. Hours of trying to understand how a part of your body can feel so frozen that it actually burns, or how you can tell a part of your body to stop shaking and it just won't. Or how the desert could be a hundred degrees during the day and then become arctic at night. Hours of whimpering like a dog.

And what I learned was that there can be a night more painful and lonely than the night your father dies in front of you. And how when you admit that to yourself, it feels so bad that you don't really want to ever admit it again. And that everyone, especially Melody Sanders and Tiffany Jenkins and all those other people in Prayer Club who prayed for the gay kids at school not to be gay anymore and stuff like that, they all had it backwards. They said hell was a place of flames and heat and endless thirst. But that's not right. Hell is dark and cold and solitary. If you are going to pray for people to be saved, you should pray they be saved from that.

Twenty-Six

Before the sun was even straight overhead, I'd already puked twice. Might have been the river water I'd drank. My ears had also started ringing, and my eyes were so dry that it hurt to blink. The colors also seemed wrong, almost like one of those old photos. Not the black-and-white ones, but the ones that looked coppery.

A wind was building upstream, blowing as hot as a hairdryer. Winds like that usually didn't come until the afternoon. The slack current would've made paddling into that wind miserable, especially by myself. My dad had planned to crank through it all in a few hours.

I went down to the river to rinse my mouth. I'd already had a couple of wipeouts, moments when my legs seemed to just stop functioning. I'd gashed my elbow and scraped my forearms, and my thumb had a deep "flapper," which is what my dad and his friends called a chunk of skin that had torn partway off. I cleaned up some of the blood that had run down my arms, then I soaked my thumb and my beat-up palms in the cool water. I thought of Magic, imagined her nudging me forward. I retied my tarp sash. When I stood up, my vision faded out. I stood there and didn't move, just tried to stay steady and hold on. My only thought: *breathe in, breathe out.*

Slowly, dizzily, from a pinpoint center outward, my sight came back.

I waited for a second to see if it was going to stay, and when it did, I started walking again.

I walked almost that entire day.

When I saw them on the other side of the river, less than twenty-five yards away, a small noise escaped me, and I thought I was maybe fainting again.

On shore, between two tents, a woman sat cross-legged in a camp chair, writing in a journal. It was early evening, and the canyon had been in shade for a while now, but the woman still had on a sunhat with a big floppy brim, one that hid her face. A cook table and a cookstove and propane tank waited behind her. Clean dishes were drying on a rack. Bobbing in the eddy was an oar raft, its metal frame squeaking as it pulled against the bowline.

For a second, the woman paused and looked up, tapping her pen against her chin. Why didn't I just scream? It seems so dumb. Opening my mouth and speaking seemed harder than squatting down and pulling a rock from the wet sand, which is what I finally did. Then I shot-putted it into the water.

Her hand went up to her chest and her posture stiffened, but then she started shaking her head at me and smiling, sitting more relaxed. She gave the kind of friendly wave people gave on the river, but I didn't return it. I had this sense to duck out of view.

Splash rings moved through the water, echoing out. I could feel what I needed to say, could feel the whole story of what had happened piling up behind me so fast and so quick.

"Gorgeous evening," she half-shouted.

One of the tent doors zipped open and a man crawled out. He was bald but had a long, scraggly brown beard. He looked a little older than my dad. He wore pants that zipped into shorts, and he stood there with only one leg zipped off. He asked the woman something, and she shrugged. He waved at me, the zipped-off piece of pant in his hand.

The woman turned back to her journal and the man busied himself with his other leg. My feet had sunk into the shoreline.

"Help," I said, weakly.

The two of them looked at me, the man still bent over. They didn't look sure about what I'd said. The man stood and held out his arms, his palms up in the way that means *What did you say?*

"Help me," I said again, this time loud enough. "There's been an accident." I meant to say it about my dad. "Please," I said instead, "I'm dead."

The man rowed. As they got close to my side of the river, the woman crawled past him to the front of the raft. She carried a red dry bag with a cross made of duct tape on it—the first-aid kit. Another man, one who'd been behind the tents, stayed back at camp. He'd filled several five-gallon buckets with river water and set them in a row. He sat down at one end of them and waited.

"Watch out, now," the woman said, even though I was out of the way. "We don't want to run you over." She'd set down the first-aid kit and was holding the coil of bowline in her hand. She could have just thrown it to me.

The raft skidded onto the sand. As the man set his oars, the woman jumped out and pulled the raft farther onto shore. As she did so, the rubber squeaked—a sound almost like a finger being dragged across the skin of an inflated balloon. It was a familiar noise, a noise my dad must have heard so many times as a guide.

She strung out the bowline and quickly wrapped it around a big rock. The man got down from his rowing perch and tossed her the dry bag. "Hey there," she said. "I'm Alex." She reached out for my arm, which I let her take. "Why don't we have you sit down?"

"Okay," I said, letting my body fall into hers.

She caught me by my armpit. My vision was dimming again. The guy rushed over and then they laid me on my back and elevated my legs, something you're supposed to do to prevent shock.

Alex, and Dan, the guy with the beard, and Kellen, the guy back at camp, were all biologists and were just finishing up a fish survey, tallying the native and nonnative species in the river. Alex explained this all to me as she checked me from head to toe—*palpate* was the term my dad used in our living-room first-aid classes. She paused when she came to my cuts and bruises and my beat-up feet, reminding me to let her know if anything hurt. This was the secondary inspection, the one you did after you first made sure the person was breathing and had a pulse and was not in immediate danger of dying. Several times, both Alex and Dan had asked if I was okay, and if I could tell them what had happened, or who I was there with, or why I was all alone, which was what I'd been trying to do, though I wasn't doing a very good job at it. *An accident. He fell. My father. It was just us.*

Dan headed a few yards upstream and scrambled onto some rocks, looking for a cell phone signal. While he was gone, Alex filled me in about the fish survey, about how this was the first trip of the year for her, and how she'd be back here in the fall, doing the whole thing over so they could track the changes. She said they captured lengths and weights, but that they were also looking at things like prey resources. Sometimes, on other trips, they would also tag the fish with transponders, or mark them by clipping their fins.

It was a relief to have Alex talk, to not have her asking questions. I guessed she was in her late twenties or something—like my mom before she became my mom. As she moved her hands along me, the bracelets on her wrist clinked together. One of them was copper, similar to the ones that a lot of my dad's buddies wore. She had on Chaco sandals, too, the footwear of choice for those same buddies. Her fingers, her hands, they weren't as big as my dad's, but they looked more like his than my mom's. I didn't have to ask to know she rock climbed.

"I've worked with Dan before," she said. "But Kellen's new. He's...interesting." She looked back across the river. "We stun the fish so they're easier to collect," she said. "We shock them with electricity. Every time he does it, he first has to say, 'Don't tase me, bro!' in this high-pitched voice that he says is his fish voice."

Kellen was still sitting next to the buckets of water. He was messing with the sand, pushing it around and making different shapes or something. The way she described him, he actually sounded kind of funny. Talking fish are just funny.

Alex looked over at him again. It was still warm out, but sometimes patches of cool, moist air washed past. She took my hand so that she could look at the cut on my thumb. "Why does a fish have to have a high voice?" she asked. "I personally think fish sound *more like this*." She finished in a deep, stuffy voice.

"Everyone knows that's how fish actually sound," I said.

She smiled back at me. "Exactly. So you see why I'm skeptical. We'll have to see how it goes." I knew that meant she liked him somehow. She squeezed my thumb a little, making me wince. "This probably could've used a stitch."

On his way back from upstream, Dan shouted over to Kellen and told him to get out the "sat phone." Kellen brushed his hands off on his shorts and headed up to the tents. Alex told me that meant satellite phone, one that could call from anywhere.

"I know," I said.

Dan squatted next to me, flashing a quick smile. Alex filled him in about my injuries.

"No calls, but I got a text out," he said. When Alex asked who, he simply said, "Bruce," and she nodded. I took that as a sign that Bruce had been a good person to text.

Dan had me sit up. I was supposed to tell him if I got dizzy again, but it didn't get bad enough that I felt like I had to say anything. Alex wanted to wait until we got back over to camp to irrigate and dress my wounds, but she also didn't want me to rub dirt into the cuts on my feet. After a couple seconds of us just sitting there, seeing if I'd pass out or spontaneously combust or something, Dan asked if I thought I could stand. I nodded yes.

Dan and Alex stood me up, and then in one smooth motion

Dan put my arm over his shoulder and grabbed me behind the knees, scooping me up so fast I squealed. I told him that I could walk on my own, but when he asked if he should set me down, I said no. "I'm just saying I could."

Alex got in the raft and helped me over the tube. "How's that? Everything good?" I sensed that things were shifting back to an ask-Emma-a-lot-of-questions phase.

"What's the name of that one kind of fish," I asked instead, trying to distract her, "the one you don't want here?"

"There's a couple," she said.

"More than a couple," Dan said, climbing up to the oars.

Alex got out and gave the raft a shove, then hopped in next to me, all in one fluid motion.

"Is one of them tilapia?" I asked.

"Yep," she said. "Do you know those?"

"They're the ones for fish tacos, right?"

Dan laughed at that. "They do make good tacos."

I told them I'd caught one upstream. "My dad showed me the markings, the bits of red on the fins."

"Did you make tacos?" Dan asked, a bit excited.

"It was too small too eat," I said. I failed to mention how I didn't really even like fish tacos anymore. Or how my dad and I had been fishing from the canoe, and instead of releasing it, my dad made me chuck the fish into the brush on shore.

"Bummer," Dan said.

"They shouldn't be in this river, anyway," my dad had said. He said some lucky bird or raccoon would be in for a treat. "Just look at it that way." *Cycle of life.* It didn't make me want to throw it any more than I had before.

Twenty-Seven

Once we got to camp, Alex directed me to the chair I'd first seen her sitting in. She pulled a sleeping bag out of her tent and draped it across my shoulders. Kellen brought over a larger first-aid kit, dropping it in front of her. "Hi," he said to me.

"Hi," I said back.

While Alex washed out my scrapes and cuts and dabbed iodine all over them, Dan unfolded a topo map out in front of me. He asked me if I could point to where I thought I'd left my father.

"Here's where we are right now," Dan said. He pointed with a sliver of wood, which he then held out for me. "And where do you think you were?"

I traced the pointer upstream along the blue line, past the spot where I thought I'd lost the canoe, past Big Sluice, around one bend, and then another, until I finally got to our camp, whose features I recognized right away. I told him I was pretty sure, even though I was positive.

"We camped there ourselves," Dan said. "Nice spot."

He made the call. The satellite phone looked like an old, huge cell phone with a really thick antenna. He'd stepped away so I couldn't hear what he was saying. While he was on the phone, Alex made a bottle of instant Gatorade. She kneeled in front of me as I drank, plopping down right where the map had been. The water bottle smelled a little musty, and the Gatorade was really diluted.

"Drink in sips," she said. I'd been chugging. I only slowed down when she reached to take the bottle from me.

"Sorry," I said, gasping.

On the outside, the water bottle was covered in stickers, most of which were gouged or scratched or smeared in some way. One was just a white oval with the letters "GCNP" printed on it, which I knew meant Grand Canyon National Park. We had the same sticker at home, plastered on the old refrigerator in the garage. Every national park we visited, we had to get a sticker.

When Dan finished on the phone, he came back over to Alex and me. Kellen had joined him during the call, but he'd split off to the kitchen, where he was boiling some water. Dan got down in front of me, wiggling himself into the sand a bit.

"First off," he said, "I just talked to some people who are very glad you found us, and who are very glad to know you're okay."

Both he and Alex smiled at that, and I could tell that I was also supposed to smile, that this would be the appropriate time for that, but I couldn't manage one. When I didn't say anything, Dan told me the rest of what he'd learned: the sheriff had already begun searching for my dad and me. My mom had called us in. She knew we wouldn't be over a day late without checking in from the road first. The deputy sheriff had actually been down to Piedra Gulch the day before, had found our van, but not us. Search parties had started working upriver. "Bruce," Dan said, as an aside to Alex, "has actually been trying to call us."

Dan went on to explain that since I wasn't critically injured, and since there was no head trauma, the thing that made the most sense was to raft me out first thing in the morning. The sheriff, the paramedics, they'd meet us downstream. "Helicopters," he said, "are really expensive."

"What if I had head trauma?"

"If that was the case," Dan said, "then we'd have to boogie to get you out of here. And you'd probably be strapped to a board right now with a c-collar around your neck and your head immobilized. That wouldn't be any fun."

I was silent, picturing it all. Picturing how far we sometimes went to save one another.

150

"Not that this *is* any fun," Alex said.

"No, I didn't mean that," Dan said.

I asked about my mom. Dan told me someone would be calling and letting her know. "If they haven't already."

"They told her?" I asked. I wondered, if she knew about me, did she know about my dad? I was hoping Dan knew what I meant.

"Probably," he said. It wasn't clear if he knew what I meant or not. It didn't really matter.

Alex and I sat around the fire. The warmth of my tea soaked through the mug and into my hands. It was still too hot to drink, so I blew on it. The steam curled up through the beam of the headlamp that Alex had lent me. She'd also given me a pair of wool socks and a fleece hoodie.

After packing some of the kitchen and the other gear, Dan had gone off to his tent to read. He and Alex had actually gotten into a small argument about taking the fire pan back out of the galley box, about making more work for the morning, but Alex said she'd make sure everything got cleaned up. She'd also gotten out the makings for s'mores, including some metal skewers, something we'd never have on a canoeing trip. Kellen was down on the raft, picking at his banjo. He was good enough to play around a campfire, but he might've just wanted to be alone. The river is always a good audience.

"Are you about ready for one of these?" Alex asked, holding up the bag of marshmallows. Only a corner-full was left. Whoever had first opened the bag had only torn a small hole into it. She shook the marshmallows down to the opening and then wiggled a few fingers through to grab one.

"I'm more of a slow roaster," she said. "What about you?"

Usually I just skipped the s'mores and ate the marshmallows uncooked. If I joined in, then I preferred to just jam the marshmallows straight into the center of the fire and burn them. The entertainment was better. "I guess I'm more of a torcher," I said.

"I thought you might be one of those. The guys are the same way." It was how my dad liked them, too.

Alex never let her marshmallow get closer than a foot from the flames. She pulled it away often, inspecting it closely, noting the changes. She'd already toasted it for about forever when she said, "I think it's starting to get there." The center was perfectly golden, the edges slightly darker. It looked like the kind of thing you'd see in a food magazine.

"You're not even close," I said. Mine had burst into flames twice and then slid off the skewer. Now it was charcoal in the bottom of the fire pan.

With one hand, Alex started snapping squares of chocolate from the bar and putting them onto a graham cracker. She asked if I wanted one and held out a chocolate. I shook my head no and she shrugged her shoulders. She popped it in her mouth.

I poked my skewer into the fire. My dad said you always had to find and make your own skewer, which is why we'd never have the kind of perfectly convenient and functional ones Alex had. Making the skewer was part of the process, and the search for the perfect stick couldn't be outsourced. It was a game, a challenge, a competition. Everything always had to be some-thing else with him.

Alex had assembled her perfect s'more and squeezed it all together. "One bite," she said to me, when I turned her offer down again. It was something my parents had been saying to Andrea a lot lately. My lips were quivering a little, and the inside of my mouth was all mucusy, so I did not feel like chewing anything.

"But thank you," I added.

The light in Dan's tent went out. Kellen seemed stuck, and he kept playing the same little part over and over, trying to get it right. Alex leaned forward and took a bite. The graham cracker broke apart and a square of chocolate fell into the dirt, which Alex blew off before eating. She ate a few more bites of s'more and offered again. When I said no, she stuffed the rest in her mouth and made a big smile as she ate, and I thought of my dad back at the put-in, his stuffed cheeks, his asking me to raise the roof.

Alex wiped her hands on the bottom of her shirt and picked up a piece of wood. Most of the fire had burned down. The embers pulsed with oranges and pinks, and she pushed them into a little mound, lifting a shower of sparks. She tossed the stick on the fire.

Kellen walked up from the raft and stood with us for a second. Alex pointed out the fixings, but he said he'd already brushed his teeth.

"Be a rebel," she said.

"Stop with the peer pressure." When I saw that he was smiling at me, I went back to watching the fire. "Anyway," he said. "No minty marshmallows for me. Bedtime."

Alex wondered if maybe we should do that, too—the bedtime thing. It was work to keep my eyes open, and the thought of getting up and standing, just the thought of it, felt like too much. Twenty-four hours ago I had been wrapped in a tarp, my stomach eating itself, and now I was in front of a warm fire, with hot tea and s'mores. I thought back on it, about how long ago it seemed, about how long ago the night before that seemed, and the one before that. I could already sense it was going to change, and that when I got home, I wasn't going to have to worry about things moving too slow, but too fast.

"I'm not really that tired," I said. I was more tired than I'd ever been in my life.

"Morning is going to come quickly. We'll get moving right away."

"I know." I almost asked her to make me one of her s'mores.

Alex set the final two pieces of wood on the fire, both of which were small. She twisted the marshmallow bag shut, then set the end of her skewer in the fire so the bits of leftover marshmallow would burn off. She went over to the galley box and grabbed an empty kitchen bucket. She told me she was going to get some water, adding that she was also going to pee. She asked if I needed to go, but I didn't. I told her I was fine.

When she came back I think she could tell. "You still okay?"

I'd had to take long, deep breaths and remind myself that I wasn't actually alone. That she was coming right back.

"I thought something was going to jump out of the dark and take me," I said. When you say it like that, people think you mean a monster or a creature or something. That wasn't what I meant.

"We would've saved you," she said. They already had.

"I think I'm ready for bed now."

"Okay," she said.

"I'm sorry."

"I don't think you need to be sorry." She asked if I wanted to put out the fire. "I always loved that when I was a kid." It suddenly struck me that she might see me that way, as a kid.

"You do it," I said.

She poured the water a little bit at a time so it wouldn't kick up much ash. Clouds of steam erupted and mixed with the smoke. The wood was drenched. She stirred the coals and poured more water, just like you were supposed to, making sure they were totally dead.

Inside the tent, we settled into our sleeping bags. Alex let me have her sleeping pad. She had set her headlamp on the floor, the beam shining up at the ceiling like a nightlight.

We were just talking. She asked if I had a brother or sister or anything, and I told her about Andrea. "We have to share a room," I said.

She told me she never had to share a room, but that she had a younger brother—Kent. She asked if Andrea and I made blanket forts, and I told her that we did, though mostly it was our dad who got us to build them.

"One time my brother and I made this fort and used every blanket and sheet in the house, even ones out of the hamper." She said it started in the living room and went up the stairs and into the upstairs hallway. "A two-story fort."

"That's awesome," I said. "What did you play?"

"What do you mean?"

"Like what else did you pretend?" I asked. "What game did you play? Was it a secret bunker, or was it like a house, or a spaceship, or what?"

"We just wanted to build a fort."

"The pretending is the whole point," I said. "The story you make up is the whole reason to play."

"Alright," she said. "If we were in a fort, what game would we play now? What would we pretend?"

I thought it was obvious. "Something not my life."

Twenty-Eight

I sensed something and woke just before Alex unzipped the door a slice. "Emma," she said, without looking in. "Emma, good morning."

I hadn't heard her get up and get dressed. Her sleeping bag, stuffed in its sack, waited near the door. Yellow light radiated through the tent walls. I recognized that light.

"Breakfast is ready whenever you are," she said. "Or I can bring you something if you want." She peeked through the opening and saw me looking back. "Hey," she said.

I groaned a hello. My body felt heavy and slushy. I pulled the sleeping bag over my head.

The door unzipped all the way. I heard her rustle inside. "I'm not a morning person, either." I felt a hand on my ankle. It squeezed gently, holding the pressure for a while. "How about I give you ten more minutes? I'll be like the snooze button." I could hear her toss her sleeping bag and pad from the tent. "I'll come back." *Zip.*

I came out before my time was up. Alex and Dan and Kellen had already broken down the rest of camp. The other tent, the stove, the propane tank, and the cooler—all of it was down by the water, waiting to be rigged on the raft. Where the kitchen once stood, a bowl of cold pancakes was sitting out for me. A half-empty jug of syrup. A fork.

I picked up the pancakes and covered them in syrup. As soon as I had, I no longer wanted them. Just the thought made my stomach turn.

I left the pancakes there and went down by the water. Right

near the river's edge, just like at our camp, a stick was poked into the sand. The water had come up a little, maybe an inch past the marker. Alex asked me if I needed to get into the tent to change or anything. I had on my own shorts, one of Alex's shirts and her fleece, the sleeves rolled up to my forearms.

"I don't know," I said.

"I'll break down the tent and all that," she said. "Your other clothes are already packed, but they're easy to get out."

Dan was in the boat. He stood up and stretched his back. He gave me a quick wave-smile and then reached for an ammo box. "You want to do a last sweep?" he asked Alex.

"Sure," she said. She had on sunglasses and a visor whose bill was frayed. She wore shorts and a thin, snap-button shirt— sleeves rolled up like mine. I could smell that she'd already put on sunscreen.

"Could I just wear this?" I asked.

"Of course."

"I already packed the sleeping bag."

"Awesome," she said. "Thanks." She told me I could hang down by the water, or if I hadn't already seen, there were some pancakes for me.

I told her I'd seen, that I still didn't feel like I could eat.

"Toilet is coming down in a couple minutes, too," Kellen said. "If that matters to you."

Ants had swarmed the syrup. Alex and I were just standing there watching them, watching the mesmerizing order to their movements, watching their numbers.

"Where do they come from?" I asked.

"Everywhere," Alex said. One was crawling on her arm. She brushed it away. "Shit," she said.

Alex grabbed the bowl and told me to start breaking down the tent. She walked over to the edge of camp and squatted down and started scraping out a hole with a rock. I pulled one of the tent stakes, but then quit and went over to watch her.

"This isn't really what you should do," she said. "You're really supposed to pack everything out."

"I know," I said.

"But sometimes I'm okay with something like this, especially when your garbage is already packed on the boat." There was a wink. She stopped digging and dumped in the pancakes, the syrup pouring out in a thick stream. She let it run until it began falling in slow drops. She pulled loose dirt back over the hole, tamping it down with a fist. She blew a few ants off her hand. She set the rock in the middle. I helped her find a couple more, stacking them on top in a pile.

"Will that do it?" I asked.

"Probably not," she said. "We probably just created a diabetic coyote." She handed me the bowl and fork and asked me to go wash them in the river.

"A coyote that hunts for pancakes," I said. "That could probably happen."

She was laughing. "Evolution."

Kellen had gone to deal with the groover. Dan was still on the raft. I scrubbed and rinsed the fork and bowl and shook the water from them. A few black ants floated in the water.

"How were they?" Dan asked, pulling a strap through one of the D-rings.

"They were good," I said.

"Good," he said. I wondered if he'd made them.

"What should I do with these?"

"Here," he said. He climbed over the rower's seat and into the front of the raft. The sun had broken over the canyon rim and the raft's rubber was already starting to get warm. He didn't have on a shirt. He was hairy and tan and had a tattoo of a lizard on his shoulder, the colors faded and washed together. He took the bowl and fork and tossed them in the cooler. "All my helpers have abandoned me," he said. "Think you can hand me that bag there?"

I grabbed the big dry bag he was pointing at and swung it onto the raft. Dan took it from there, shifting it to the back of the boat. A couple more bags sat on the beach plus a few ammo boxes. "You can just keep them coming if you want," he said. "You get them on, and I can take them from there."

I had everything stacked in the bow. He'd told me I might need help with the ammo boxes, but I didn't. There was no room for the last one, so I was resting it on top of the tube, waiting on him. I'd made sure to dip the bottom in the river to get the sand off.

"Anything else?" I asked. I'd been planning to go help Alex, even though it looked like she was almost finished.

"Do you know how to use these straps?" he asked. He lifted up an almost brand-new twelve-footer.

"We have the same kind."

"Welcome aboard," he said.

And after I'd finished—after I'd tied down all the dry bags, even the ones Alex had brought down, and after I'd strapped down the groover, which Kellen had loaded—they all looked over my work and nodded in approval and didn't correct anything, or even say anything about the food I'd wasted.

Dan rowed. When we'd left camp, he re-explained how long it'd take to get to Piedra Gulch, and how long until Upset, and that we'd probably get out to scout, just to be safe—all of which he'd first told me while I was helping him rig. "And then you'll be home," he said, even though that wasn't true. I'd be at the takeout, not home.

Kellen sat behind Dan, up on top our pyramid of dry bags. He wore a wide sunhat, the strap cinched snug to his chin, even though it wasn't windy. Alex and I were in the bow, which was upstream because of how Dan was rowing. We straddled the tubes during the flat sections, and I kept dipping in my foot and letting it drag through the water, watching the lines it made.

Dan sang for us. At first they were real songs, like fisherman chanteys and stuff, but after that he just made up tunes about Kellen or Alex or the riverside, which was just the same brown land as always. He did this variation on "Old MacDonald," replacing the farm animals with kingfishers and Kellen's hat and whatever else he saw, though thankfully he didn't include me. Alex begged him to quit, but that made him sing louder, like some opera guy. He stopped when we heard Upset.

Dan twisted and looked downstream. The canyon walls had started narrowing. He spun the boat around, and I got my leg back inside. I could already feel the harder pull of the current, could see it as the shoreline slipped more quickly. Bits of white flashed along the surface, little splashes, small waves. Dan stood up so that he could see better. Kellen didn't quite stand, but got up on his knees. Alex smiled at me, raising her eyebrows a couple of times. My hand found a strap to grab.

"Remember the line?" Kellen asked.

"Vaguely," Dan said, sitting back down. He turned the raft at a slight angle to the current and then started pulling back on the oars, ferrying us toward the river-right shore. "I'm cool with a quick look."

On the opposite side of the river—the side where I'd been hiking—a sheer rock face rose a hundred feet, which I would've had to somehow climb along to get past Upset.

Either that, or swim across.

From where Dan eddied us out, you couldn't see much past the horizon line. Alex told me that she'd hang out with me if I wanted to stay by the raft. She'd noticed my shivering. "We can have an impromptu dance party to get warm," she said, but I wanted to scout.

We stopped about halfway down, at the portage trail's highest spot. "Is that the hole?" I asked, pointing at a big white spot.

"That's it," Dan said.

"Isn't that what flips everyone, and that's why it's called Upset?"

"With the raft it's different," Alex said. "Maybe at really high water or something, but that's not a problem now."

"I'll sneak us past," Dan said, "but we could punch right through it if we wanted. Get us a big splash."

"But we'll sneak," Alex assured me.

Kellen had already started drifting back toward the boat, detouring off a little so he could pee. Dan started following. He had a throw rope with him, and he kept tossing it high up in the air and catching it as he walked.

"We're not going to scout the rest?" I asked Alex. The morning sun was hitting the water hard, the surface crackling with light. The way the river funneled down and spilled over itself, the waves surging and breaking, the way it would slap against the shore and then pull back...the same thoughts kept circling in my head...

"You feel okay about it?" Alex asked.

"I don't know," I mumbled.

Alex was standing slightly behind me, and she stepped in closer. "No?" she asked.

"I don't know," I repeated.

"Dan is a really good rower. We're in good hands. I'll make sure he doesn't splash us."

"I know," I said. As I watched the water, I kept picturing myself alone in the canoe, swept into the rapid, out of control. I could see waves breaking into the boat, could feel the panicked strokes that had no effect. The boat dropping into the hole, then flipping over quick as a blink. The plunging, the getting held under, the being unable to breathe. "I just keep getting this feeling," I said.

"We don't have to run it. You and I can walk down to the bottom and meet them if you want."

"It's not that," I said. My dad would've given me the same option about portaging, although it likely would've come with a catch, like some cranky comment later in the day, or some glint of disappointment in his eyes that I wasn't supposed to see. Upset was supposed to have been the grand finale of the trip, the hardest rapid we'd run together. And having survived it as a team, it was supposed to translate into something else—some deeper trust and closeness between us, or some confidence and wisdom and test-taking finesse that I was supposed to be able to use to dominate life in high school.

I started crying again. I tried saying, "This isn't how it's supposed to be." I'm not sure what came out.

Alex reached over and helped me sit down. She sat down next to me and then hugged me tight, pulling my head to her, rocking me a little. "I know," she said. "You're right."

My nose was running, and I was slobbering into Alex's shirt. When I tried to pull away, she wouldn't let me, but only squeezed tighter. I wanted her to squeeze me in half.

I asked her why my dad had had this idiotic idea about the Tinto in the first place, even though there was no way for her to know, and that's what she said: "I don't know." She let me sit up a bit. "I imagine he had good reasons. It doesn't seem idiotic. I like this river."

"It was totally stupid," I said.

Alex pulled down the sleeve of her shirt and wiped my face. She smiled—a gentle, genuine smile that was different from the uncomfortable nervous ones I'd get from so many people later on. She ran her finger under the rim of her sunglasses, and I realized she'd been crying, too.

"Remember Kent, my brother?"

"The fort," I said.

"I didn't say this before, but he passed away almost five years ago. It still doesn't make sense. He had to have a motorcycle, even though our dad warned him. And it won't ever make sense, because he was my little brother, and he was my parent's kid, and he was supposed to live forever. But that's the only way— you just have to accept that it'll never be understandable."

Dan walked back to find us, wondering if we were okay.

"We'll be right there," Alex said, her voice giving out a little. "Just having a quick powwow." He could tell something was up and hesitated, but then turned and left, tossing the throw rope to himself again.

"I didn't know that about your brother," I said. It was a ridiculous thing to say. Of course I didn't know. "I'm sorry."

"Don't be," she said. "You with your apologies."

Sometimes I'm not sure what I would've said to my dad. It was different in a canoe than a raft. Sometimes when I think about it, I imagine that I probably would've said portage, or that

I would've wanted to take the sneak route—options, as it turns out, that don't work so well in real life.

Other times—most times now—I see that I would've said yes. Yes, because he would've taken the time to show me the line again, tracing it down through the wave train and past the hole, picking out our markers so we wouldn't get lost once we were in it. He would've turned the big rapid into something doable, something orderly and reasonable. It was just a series of small maneuvers that would add up to something larger. That's how you had to view it.

As I sat there with Alex, it was clear that my dad and I would've been able to make it.

Maybe not dry, maybe not perfectly, but we would've been upright at the bottom, paddle high-fiving.

"Could you show me again how we're going to run it?" I asked. Alex pointed out the entrance spot, talked about the angle Dan would set, and how we'd just bop down along the waves and miss everything else. I already knew all that. "What's the other route," I asked, "the one through the hole?"

"That's the hero route," she said. "That's pretty much just point it straight downstream and charge."

"Then I want to charge," I said.

Twenty-Nine

When my dad was first telling me about the trip, he said, "There'll only be two big ones."

"Big?" I asked. He played loose with his definitions for *big*.

"Not really anything bigger than what you've done. It'll be like some of the stuff on the East Fork. But a longer trip."

"Some of those were too big."

"Well," he said. He said it in a way that seemed to imply something had been my fault.

I got quiet then and just chewed on my lip and listened to him say his spiel about the Tinto. We were in his office, kneeling on opposite sides of the topo maps he'd arranged on the floor. Mom and Andrea were in the living room. I was already starting to picture what the little blue line on the paper would translate to—wondering how it'd actually compare to that trip on the East Fork, if the rapids would be as scary, or if we'd have a problem with the stove and have to eat all our meals cold again.

He gave me the details, the "beta," like when we'd leave, and how long we'd be gone. There were gaps between his words, pauses where I could feel him wanting to tell me to stop biting my lip, or to stop picking at my cuticles, which I was also doing. He turned the conversation away from the logistics, and toward the sleeping outside under the stars part, and how the Tinto was an important stop for migratory birds, and how birders just went nuts there.

"How's that sound?"

"Birdy," I remember saying. On a different day, if we hadn't been talking about paddling, or if this whole trip wasn't somehow connected to my failings at school, I'm pretty sure he would've laughed at that.

"I mean it," he said. "I want to know. We've been talking about crossing this one off the list for a while. It's not just a quick weekend deal, though, so if you don't want to do it, I'm not going to spend a bunch of time doing all this work and putting everything together."

It was mostly him who'd been talking about the Tinto. He was the one who had the list.

"Yeah, I guess," I said. "It sounds okay."

"I'm going to need more enthusiasm than that."

On the East Fork, there was a rapid called Staircase. My dad and I didn't have any trouble running it—or he didn't have any. I wasn't much help in the bow. I got submerged by the first wave and then had water in my eyes the whole time.

At the bottom of the rapid, my dad was hooting and laughing and wanting a paddle high five. I was sobbing. We'd plowed through two more waves, the force of them wrenching my helmet back on my head, pulling the chinstrap tight against my throat. "High five," he kept saying. "High five, Em. High five."

When I turned around to show him how upset I was, he actually laughed harder. After he calmed me down enough to talk, I explained that I was crying because I hadn't wanted to run that one. He kept asking me why I didn't say anything before when we were scouting it. He'd always—ever since he'd first started taking me down rivers—told me we could portage. He kept saying that was the whole reason for us looking at Staircase that day, to make sure that everyone in the canoe was ready, that everyone wanted to run it. "I even asked," he said.

What he'd asked was, "All set?" He'd asked it about one second before turning and starting back to the canoe, before I'd even answered. In fact, I never said anything. I just followed him, which my dad later said was its own kind of answer.

There were only a few more rapids that day. At each one, my dad made sure to ask me if I wanted to run it, but the way he'd started asking made it even worse, and instead of just saying yes or no, I kept saying, "I don't know." And because I wouldn't choose, he made us portage each one.

I tried to help him carry the boat, but he didn't really bother coordinating with me in any way. I stumbled as he yanked the boat ahead, and I kept losing the grab loop. He got fed up in the middle of one portage and got back in the canoe halfway through the rapid, making me walk the rest by myself.

Back in his office, looking over the maps, he said, "I don't need to know right now, but this leaves your mom here alone with Andrea. There's Magic that needs to be taken care of. I'll need to schedule it with work. There's stuff. So I need to know that you're in."

Up to this point, the trip hadn't really seemed like it was an optional activity. I understood that it still wasn't.

"I get it," I said. "I'll think about it. It sounds good, but I'll think about it and make sure."

My dad started to put away the maps. He had all kinds in his office. He was a soils engineer, which meant that a lot of his job was telling people where they could build things and where they couldn't, and it sort of crushed him sometimes, because he often had to say yes to the same kinds of construction projects that he hated—highways, subdivisions, parking lots.

"What are the names of the big ones?" I asked. I knew he was going to tell me to look for myself, so I started scanning the remaining maps.

"Big Sluice and Upset and, depending on the level, maybe Alligator."

I found Upset. I looked closer at the blue dashes. They never tell you all of it. Blue dashes are lies.

"Did you find them?" he asked.

I started folding the map, something that had taken me a long time to learn. "Nope," I said. It was just easier that way. I'm not sure if he believed me or not, or even if he doubted me at all. He'd already started keeping the maps in a Ziploc, the same one we'd take with us on the river. He held the bag open for me, and I added mine.

"Well," he said, "they're there."

My left hand held the chicken line, and my feet were stuffed between the floor of the raft and the tube I was sitting on. The oars creaked as Dan pushed. We were still in the slack water above, moving just faster than the current, but then the gradient dropped off and the river pulled hard, flinging us ahead. "Here we go," Dan said.

The first wave hit, spraying water over the bow, drenching Alex. We pitched hard, plowing into the next wave, which is when I got hit. The inside of the raft filled with water, and it rushed past my legs. Up, then back down, the water clobbered us from the other side of the raft now and spilled over the tube. Up, then down, forcing us all to tilt hard, side to side, hooting and screaming. And then at the peak of the last wave before the hole, Dan leaned hard into the oars and yelled "Hang on!" right before all of us dropped straight down into a wall of water.

Dan let the raft spin so that the bow was facing upstream, just as my dad often did when we'd made it through a big rapid. All of us were soaked, Alex and I the most. Everything seemed electric.

"Fun one," Dan said.

We rocked through the tail end of the wave train. Alex shook her head and laughed and wrung water from her sleeves. "Not a very dry one, though."

Dan nodded at me. "Blame her."

They all wanted to know what I thought, as if my big smile and the *woo-hoo*s hadn't been clear enough. I wiped my face and squeezed some of the water from my ponytail. The hollering had all been spontaneous, which I knew was something special. I started thinking about how much my dad would've liked the run, and how he would've been *woo-hoo*ing louder than all of us, how this would've been one he talked about with his friends. Then I was on the verge of tears again.

"So?" Alex asked, pressing me for my take on the hero route.

"*Psshh*," I said, holding it in. "That was nothing."

"Yeah, girl," she said, high fiving me.

Thirty

The sheriff's department had brought in their own boat, the kind that was like a raft but also had an outboard motor and a steering wheel and a little windshield and stuff. The road down to the river was rutted and switchbacked, just like the road to the put-in, so I guess it took them forever to trailer down to the water, and by the time they'd started motoring upstream, we were already in sight of the takeout—we could see the outhouses and picnic shelters, the ambulance and trucks, and all the people standing around waiting for me.

As the sheriff's boat pulled closer, the sheriff cut back on the engine and waved. Dan, Alex, and Kellen all waved back. A paramedic was with the sheriff, holding onto a big square first-aid kit with both hands. The sheriff let his boat settle into its new speed, wobbling as its wake rolled underneath it. He pulled up to the raft at an angle and then completely cut the engine, drifting the last few feet. Even so, the two boats met hard enough that we all got bounced around.

Alex hurried and grabbed the sheriff's bow so he didn't bump away. Sheriff Mendoza introduced himself. "Who's Dan?" he asked.

"That'd be me," Dan said, still holding onto the oars.

The sheriff stepped out from behind the steering console and stood with his hands on his hips, just above his belt. He wore a pair of mirrored sunglasses and a bright orange lifejacket, the kind that inflated when you pulled a little ripcord, the same kind the paramedic had on—the kind my dad said were useless.

"And I bet this is Emma," the sheriff said to me.

I didn't say yes or no. No one did, because no one had to. I was sitting in a little hole I'd made for myself, all padded out by dry bags. I had my hands tucked into my lifejacket, my legs pulled up tight to my chest. The paramedic guy crawled over and onto our boat. He dragged the first-aid kit aboard and set it up by Dan. It opened from the middle, and as it did all these trays unfolded, too.

"Hi, Emma," he said. "I'm Patrick." He was busy putting on a pair of blue latex gloves. "What can you tell me about those bandages?"

I shrugged my shoulders.

Alex told him about my abrasions and blisters, and how I'd been eating a little and retaining fluids—that I was stable. Something about how she said "retaining fluids" and "stable" made me a little mad at her. It was that adult thing where they talk about you without looking at you, even when you're right there. Patrick explained what he was going to do before he did it, then he took my pulse and checked my pupils, shading my eyes with his hand then pulling it away so the sun hit them full bore again.

"Not sure we'll save much time having her switch boats," I heard the sheriff say.

"That's your call," Dan said. "I can get us down there pretty quick, but it's up to you."

Patrick was looking at my thumb gash. He asked me something, then Alex said something to him, and Dan and the sheriff talked to each other, but I was distracted by the last bit of the Tinto. This would've been the section where my dad would've gotten quiet and sulky, where the reality of having to go back would've messed with him. The high rocky walls that bordered Upset had fallen back, and the shore was lined once again by sage-dotted, Triscuit-colored hills. Thin clouds striped the sky. A warm breeze ruffled a pattern across the water, and despite the voices all around me, I could still hear the silence of open, empty land—a silence that would get harder and harder to know.

"Once we get you all down there," the sheriff was saying. "We'll coordinate with the recovery team."

"Sure," Dan said.

Patrick finished his assessment, giving me a gloved thumbs-up. As he refolded his kit, he told Alex that he'd assess and redress my other wounds and my feet later. He still had his gloves on when he got into the sheriff's boat.

The sheriff rotated a knob on his utility-belt walkie-talkie. He said something into the receiver thing clipped to his shoulder, then fiddled with the knob again while the voice on the other end disappeared and a bunch of loud static came through. Alex shoved the boats apart, and Dan pulled back on the oars a few times.

The engine coughed out black smoke. Gears *kunk*ed into reverse. When the boat was finally facing downstream, the sheriff pushed hard on the throttle, and as he sped off, its horrible noise echoed off the shorelines.

Dan dipped his oars into the water and leaned against them, feathering the blades out at the end of his stroke. The smell of gas and exhaust lingered. The oarlocks squeaked, and drips of water fell from the tips of the blades as he swung them forward again, dropping them in for the next stroke. No one said anything. Alex reached over and squeezed my knee. Already the sheriff was at the takeout, the whine of the engine cut silent. I watched rays of sunlight diving through the greenish water, lighting up clouds of sediment. The beams only went down a few feet before they dissolved. From here the Tinto would only get flatter, more sluggish, until finally it became Johnson Reservoir—where the bits of dirt and life that I could see suspended in the water would finally settle out.

People clapped like I'd just given a great presentation or something. Like I'd just won some award or prize. I guess my prize was that I was there, alive. Sometimes that doesn't seem like such a prize, but it is.

Dan stowed his oars, and Alex readied the bowline—just like when they'd ferried across the river to rescue me—and then we skidded to a stop on the boat ramp. Alex jumped out, splashing down in the water. The sheriff and a search-and-rescue person and some other rancher-looking guy all helped pull the raft further onshore, getting their shoes wet, even though Alex totally had it by herself.

An ambulance was parked at the top of the boat ramp, back-end first, its rear doors open. Another paramedic was in there, setting up an IV. A few people started taking off the orange safety vests they'd been wearing. Others just stood around and watched—their arms crossed, or their hands stuffed in their pockets.

The sheriff and the rancher guy wanted to link their arms together and make a little seat to lift me, but unlike when I let Dan carry me, I told them I was okay. I climbed out of the raft and started walking toward my dad's van. The sheriff's truck and the boat trailer were parked next to it. Next to the sheriff's truck was another truck, one with a horse trailer behind it.

The van was even dustier than before, but the smiley face I'd drawn on the taillight was still there. I knew where the keys were stashed, knew that there was a magnet box tucked under the front bumper, right by the license plate. Knew that inside the van there was a bag of peanut M&Ms—M&Ms that had baked in the heat and then frozen at night, cracking the shells and fading the color, which is how my dad loved them.

"How about we head over here." It was Patrick. He was taking me by the arm and directing me back toward the ambulance. "Easy steps," he said.

As Patrick guided me, it felt like I was being dragged into a quicker current again. I turned back to look for Alex, but she was still down by the raft with Dan and Kellen. When we got to the ambulance, Patrick stood next to me, waiting for me to step in. He had his arm stretched out, like *Welcome, right this way*. I thought about this time out at Peg's, when my mom and I sat on a fence railing and watched her try and trailer one of her horses— Peg inside of the trailer, pulling hard on the lead rope, her helper pushing with all his weight on the horse's rear. "That's the hard way to do it," I remember my mom saying. "With ones like that, better to walk them out and try again. Get them to think they're doing it on their own."

The other paramedic took my hand, steadying me as I stepped in. "Let's have you get all the way on the gurney," he said. The fabric on it crinkled when I sat down. All of the cabinets and drawers and shelves in the ambulance reminded me of my dad's van.

Outside, people were milling around and talking and sneaking looks at me. The sheriff was headed toward the ambulance. Alex and Dan had disappeared somewhere, and Kellen was already unrigging the raft. The second paramedic had put a little clamp on my index finger to measure my pulse. Unlike Patrick, this new guy—Scott—didn't explain every procedure as he went through it, and it made the current I was caught in seem even faster. He started swabbing the inside of my elbow, prepping it for an IV.

He asked if I had any new complaints. He meant *bodily*.

"No," I said. "Just all that stuff from before."

Thirty-One

Alex had a hand on the ambulance door. She was talking to Patrick. "I promised that I'd deliver her to her mom," she said. "You want to make me break that one?"

I never remembered hearing that promise, but maybe it was one she'd made to herself. Maybe that's why she pressed so hard.

I was reclined in the gurney, all buckled down for transport. The sheriff had already come and questioned me, asking me to explain what I'd meant when I said I'd killed him. I tried. He asked if I'd meant to kick the log, and I told him that I had, but not like that, not to make it move.

"You were just kicking it?"

"That's all I was doing," I said.

After the questions, the sheriff had explained the rest of the process—how I'd go to the hospital, how they'd get my mom and me together, how I'd have to speak with him some more. "But we don't have to worry about that right now," he'd said.

Patrick was starting to give in to Alex. The engine was running, and diesel fumes wafted our way. He looked at me for a second, and I nodded, hoping he'd see how much I needed her to come.

"I think we're going to pretend that you told me she's your relative. How's that sound?" he asked me.

"That's definitely what I told you," I said.

Parts of the road were nearly washed out, and at times the ambulance rocked so hard that Patrick and Alex reached out and

173

grabbed hold of the gurney, not to keep me in place, but to keep themselves from getting thrown around. A dust cloud trailed the ambulance, and in it I could see the flashing of our siren lights— the actual siren turned off. The sheriff's truck had its lights flashing, too, and so did the deputy sheriff's vehicle, which was pulling the boat. Behind them, spaced out in big intervals, were all the other vehicles—the search-and-rescue trucks, the truck with the horse trailer, Dan and Kellen and their rig, the tow truck carrying my dad's VW—all of them kicking up long clouds of dirt.

"Have you ever been in one of these before?" I asked Alex. She looked occupied, like maybe she was thinking about something else. She also looked a little green.

"Kind of," she said.

"Were you hurt bad?" I asked.

"No, it was for school."

"Something happened at your school?"

"*For* school," she said. "Believe it or not, at one point in my life I thought I was going to be an EMT. I was in a program at the community college where I lived. They had this old ambulance that they made us practice with. But not the medical stuff. It was for practice with backing up between traffic cones, stuff like that."

"Was it hard?"

Alex looked at Patrick before she answered. "Not that part," she said.

I thought she was going to continue and tell me which parts were hard, but she just got quiet and started greening again.

"Why didn't you become one?" I finally asked. This time Patrick looked at her.

"Actually," she said. "I did. I passed all my classes and took the exams and got certified and everything. I just never did it as a job."

"How come?"

"Yeah," Patrick stepped in, "what happened?"

"Well." She looked at Patrick for a second, then looked at me. "A lot of reasons, really. A big one being a boy that I followed around, which didn't work out so well, though he did introduce me to fly-fishing. That's how I found out there were such things as aquatic ecologists."

"Aquatic ecologists?" Patrick asked.

"That's the fancy version of my job title. It means fish counter."

"And you also fly-fish?" I asked.

"Fairly well, even."

The ambulance chucked side to side once more. When the ambulance steadied, Patrick reached up to stop the IV bag from swinging on its hook.

"And what about you?" Alex asked me. "You have your sights set on any particular profession?"

"I don't know," I said.

"Or boy?"

"Yikes."

"Good," she said.

I told Alex about the aptitude test we took last year, how it came up with things like hairstylist and administrative assistant for me. "I must not have answered the questions right or something."

She laughed out her nose. "Those things are horrible. When I took it, I think it said I should be an elevator inspector."

"Really?"

"I'm not kidding. I didn't always believe it when they said it, but what my parents always told me was that it didn't matter what you did for a living so much, the important thing was how you lived. I hate elevators."

"That must've come from a parenting book or something. I swear my parents have told me the exact same thing."

"I know, right?" Alex asked Patrick if his parents had ever said it to him, but they hadn't. She asked if he'd ever had to take those career tests in school. She and Patrick looked about the same age.

"My friends and I added extra jobs to ours," he said. "Things like stunt pilot, or lion tamer, or rock-and-roll god."

"And you wanted to be a rock god," she said.

"Maybe," he said. You could tell by his smirk that she'd been right. "I enlisted in the Army right after high school."

"My brother had his heart set on the Marines," Alex said.

"Two tours in Iraq," he said. There was something both proud and embarrassed in his tone. "How about him?"

All Alex said was, "No."

Our procession had climbed most of the way out of the river valley, and we made a slow right-hand turn onto another gravel road—this one wide and flat and recently graded. Soon we'd be all the way up on the plateau, where it'd be hard to see any trace of the Tinto at all, then we'd be back on paved roads, making other cars move out of our way so we could go faster. Except for the dead volcanoes on the horizon, the plateau seemed flat and smooth, like everything was above the surface, but that was an illusion. There were cracks and gorges and secret spots all over the place.

No one said anything for a while after Iraq was mentioned. "How'd you know he wanted to be a rock star?" I asked.

"Most boys want to be rock stars," Alex said. "People are about as predictable as fish."

"Are fish predictable?" I asked.

"Sort of. We come from fish."

"Really?" Patrick asked. I wasn't sure if he was just asking about the fish.

"For eons."

"I would've chosen lion tamer," I said.

"I know," she said.

Alex was the first one out of the ambulance. She stood in the open bay as Patrick and Scott slid me out, the legs on the gurney dropping and clicking into place. Patrick closed one of the ambulance's back doors and grabbed a clipboard from inside. He closed the other door and tucked the clipboard under his arm, nodding at Scott, who unlocked the wheels of the gurney and started pushing me inside.

I thought Alex was going to follow along, but she stayed put. "I need to get a little air," she said. "Long ride."

In front of the white building, Alex's tan looked almost neon. Her clothes stood out as dirty, her hair greasy. Other people were coming in with their own emergencies, and she tried to move out of their way.

"But don't go yet," I said. "Don't leave."

The automatic doors parted open. Air conditioning washed over me.

"I won't." She almost managed a smile.

I reached and waved, but the doors had already slid closed. They were glass, but the tint was too dark for her to see me.

Thirty-Two

I had fallen asleep waiting. I'd been in the ER for three hours—had been checked by a nurse, then a doctor, then scrubbed up and rebandaged by another nurse. Mom touched my shoulder, pulling me up through the watery layers, back into the harsh lighting. "Oh, Em," she was saying, "I'm here." When she saw that I was awake, she came in for a hug, and instead of waiting for me to sit up, she pulled me forward and wrapped her arms around me, pressing the side of her face into mine. She smelled like coffee. "I'm here," she repeated, over and over.

When I was Andrea's age, I used to get these earaches that would hurt so bad I'd squeeze my head in my hands for a weird kind of relief. My parents would give me eardrops and decongestant medicines, the kind of stuff that's also supposed to make you sleepy, but none of it really helped. After I'd been up for hours, thrashing in my bed, bawling—and after they'd been up for hours, too—my mom would carry me into the living room and sit with me in the dark, rocking me in the rocking chair, my face pressed warm to her chest, my tears soaking into her jammies. She would rock me, whispering *Sshh sshh sshh,* until somehow the pain was gone and I was asleep.

It had been a long time since she'd held me like that—since I'd let her hold me like that.

After a long cry, she clutched me at arm's length. "Look at you," she said.

"Me?" I had cried, too. "Look at both of us."

Dan and Kellen had joined Alex. The three of them were the only people in the waiting room with their backs to the TVs, and they didn't see us at first. My mom stopped to talk with the receptionist about our insurance, so I asked if I could go sit down.

"I'll try to be quick," she promised.

I walked up behind them and thought of that moment on the river, after Upset, when we were all so happy, when for some reason it felt like I'd known them forever. "Hey," I said.

They all gave me big hugs, even Kellen. He and Dan had changed into clean T-shirts and shorts, but Alex was still wearing her river clothes, like me. She asked how I was doing.

"I'm okay," I said. "Tired, mostly."

I could see that she had washed her face. Her hair had been combed through, and it was still wet in parts. I held out her fleece for her. "My mom has some clothes in the car," I said. "I can give you the other stuff in a little bit."

"Is that her?" Alex asked, looking toward my mom. "I saw her come in and thought it might be."

"Yep." She hadn't taken her top yet. "That's Mom."

"Hello, *Mom*," she said, smiling. When she noticed my goose-bumped arms, she asked if I didn't just want to keep the fleece for now. The air conditioning was insane. "It's a little small for me, anyway," she said, which I doubted was true.

If my mom had been there, I knew she'd have made me give it back.

"I'll get it some other time," Alex said. "How about that?"

Paddlers were always running into long-lost friends while on some river in the middle of nowhere, so goodbye was never goodbye, but I wasn't very confident that I'd ever see her—or any of them—again.

"It's a promise," I said.

When I introduced them to my mom, I said, "These are the people who found me."

"Technically," Alex said, "I think you found us." She gave me a poke in the shoulder.

"I guess," I said, poking her back.

"Whichever it was," my mom said, "thank you. From the bottom of my heart. A million times, thank you." The other people in the waiting room were still watching TV. The news would run a story about me later that night.

My mom wondered if there was anything she could do. "Have you eaten? Can we buy you dinner or something?"

Dan said they had to get back to Albuquerque.

"They row and do fish surveys," I added, as if that explained it all.

My mom asked Dan if he was sure. She said there was no obligation that they even had to eat with us. "I'll spring for drive-through," she said.

That didn't sway them either.

Outside, we stood near the parking lot. The night was orange and starless and warm. We'd already said our goodbyes once. "Okay," Alex said, giving me another last hug.

"Thank you," I said, hanging on.

"You're welcome," she said. "I'm just glad you're alright."

"I am." In a news conference, the sheriff would call me "alive and well."

"Take care of yourself," she said. "Be safe."

"I'll try," I said.

She was supposed to say, *Try hard enough*, but what she said was, "That's all you can do."

And then we left. The three of them started toward their rig, which they'd parked far from the door, in an empty section of the parking lot. Alex and Dan turned and waved one last time, but that was it. I just watched them walk away. My mom pointed toward her car, and then for some reason she jangled her keys at me. Miles from water and seemingly safe, I could've sworn I was drowning.

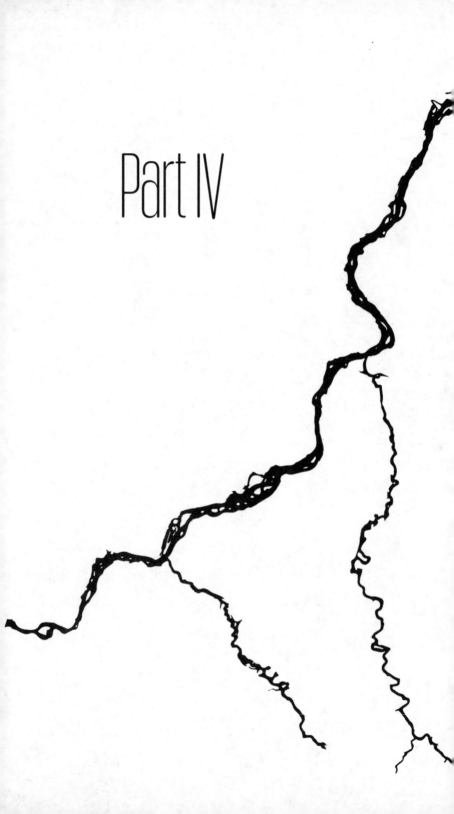

Part IV

Thirty-Three

I'd been staring into the dark for a long time before I realized I was actually awake. Except for a faint line of light slipping under the door, our bedroom was completely black. The windows had their blinds drawn. There was a ceiling, and above that, a roof. Each time Andrea exhaled, her nose whistled softly. Had I been dreaming? I remembered a tiger, and then a hyena, and then a horse wrapped up in spider silk, suspended in a leafless tree.

I snuck down the hallway and toward the bathroom. The light was coming from my parents' bedroom. The door was open, and I paused just outside of it and listened. The house creaked. I figured my mom was sitting in bed reading, or that maybe she'd been reading and had fallen asleep with the light on, which was something she often did.

When I turned the corner, the room was empty. My mom's suitcase, zipped tight, sat near the foot of the bed, the bed still made. The lamp on the nightstand was on, but there was no book. No Mom. The alarm clock read 2:57 a.m.

I found her downstairs watching TV. All the lights were off, and the room flickered with television blue. She was slouched way down on the couch, neck bent at ninety degrees, a posture she was always hounding me about. She had pulled the table close so she could stretch out her legs, and even though it wasn't cold, she had herself snuggled in a blanket, the fabric cinched tight around her neck.

She had the volume turned down low. *The Three Stooges* was on. I guess *The Three Stooges* was the kind of show where you probably didn't need to even catch the words—you just watched them hit and poke and bump into each other. And then you were supposed to laugh. My mom was just sitting there, the light flickering on her cheeks and forehead, her eyes looking as if they were focused on something a million miles away.

I cleared my throat. I'd been standing behind the couch, waiting for her to notice. Her eyes didn't move from the screen. "What is it?" she asked.

I told her it was nothing. "I saw your light on but noticed you weren't in your room."

"Andrea asleep?"

"Yes," I said. "She's nose-whistling."

On the TV, the Stooges all tried walking through the same door at the same time. "You okay?" she asked.

"I thought maybe I heard the car and that you left." That wasn't true. I just wanted her to understand that I'd felt worried.

"I wouldn't do that," she said.

"Just to the store or something is what I thought."

My mom lifted her arm out from under the blanket, and I sat down next to her. I tucked my feet up underneath me and leaned against her.

"I'm not really watching this," she said. "But I lost the remote somewhere."

"You don't like them?" I asked. "They're kind of funny."

"You know these guys?"

"Dad," I said. "He wanted me to see something classic."

"Sometimes they remind me of puppies," she said.

I thought I was going to find the remote behind one of the cushions. As I dug around, Mom wondered if it might have somehow ended up in the kitchen.

"I looked all over," she said. "It's gone."

The show went to a commercial for an all-in-one spaghetti cooker and strainer for your microwave oven. The words "NO HASSLE!" flashed across the screen, just as a colander tipped over and spilled pasta into the sink. "THAT'S NOT ALL!" I thought of the spaghetti my dad and I had eaten on the trip, how it was probably the most hassle-free meal in the world, and if you actually needed one of these gadgets you had to be the worst cook ever. I mean, if your noodles accidently got dumped in the dirt, you just rinsed them off.

The Stooges had come back on. They were on a golf course. A ball ricocheted off a tree, nailing one of the others in the head. I know one was named Curly, one Moe, but I didn't know who was who.

"I was going to sleep here," my mom said, "but I couldn't get myself to stand up and turn off the TV."

"Do you want me to?"

"I'm not sure I'll fall asleep even then."

A golf ball got stuck in a tree. The bald Stooge was shaking his fist at it. An ax came out, and he started swinging. "I'll watch for you," I said. "I'll watch, and you can sleep, and then it won't be like we're being lazy or wasting electricity or anything."

"That's not really what I was worried about," she said. After a moment, she asked about Andrea again. I repeated the complaint about her snoring.

"You should go back," my mom said. "You turn off the TV, and go back up to bed, and I'll try and get some sleep, too."

I didn't move. The Stooges were not making friends with the groundskeeper at the golf course. The groundskeeper even ran off to get the police, police who I guess were just waiting around at the clubhouse. Seeing them in their old-time uniforms made me think of Sheriff Mendoza, and I wondered if he'd ever had to arrest a golfer. I guessed he probably hadn't, but who knows?

"Let me watch for a little while," I said. "To the next set of commercials. I'll turn it off and go back to bed after that."

"There's more commercials than you think," she said. She pushed me to one end of the couch with her feet and snuggled up with the pillow. I tucked the blanket around her legs.

The episode ended with the Stooges running from the police and hopping onto a delivery truck stacked with wooden beer barrels. In the chase, one of the barrels falls off, and the Stooges stop to get it. All the beer barrels fall off then, and for the rest of the episode, it's the Stooges running after, or away from, the out-of-control barrels—barrels that hit rocks and fly into the air and nail all the Stooges in the head. The final shot has all three of them getting knocked down into a patch of wet cement.

I stayed past the first commercial break, which came at the end of the episode. Some sort of Stooges marathon was happening, and so I watched another one, and then another, and then part of another, noticing how many times they got hit in the head with something but never got knocked out. I watched until I realized that my eyes kept falling shut and I was no longer watching an episode but imagining one. Mom didn't even move when I got up and turned off the TV.

I stopped at my parents' bedroom to turn off the light, but as soon as I stepped into the room I knew why my mom had gone downstairs, and why she'd sleep down there for weeks to come. It was a presence and an absence both. Sitting atop my dad's dresser was his little pile of change, a pile that grew and shrank but never seemed to disappear. And next to the pile of change was a hand-carved wooden box that he'd gotten in Peru. In it was a picture of my mom lying down on a picnic table, her hands tucked under her cheek—just as they were tucked on the couch downstairs. The box also held a comb, a pair of cufflinks, and a little pearled pocketknife. I knew all this because I'd looked before. And hanging on the edge of the hamper, but not in it, was a pair of my dad's jeans. And inside the hamper, all his dirty clothes—his underwear, his shirts, his smelly socks. And next to my dad's side of the bed, stacked up on his nightstand, were gardening catalogs and magazines about paddling or mountain biking. Resting on top of them, a massage roller for his feet. And there on the bed was the empty spot where his pillow should be, but wasn't. He'd thrown it in the van at the last second, just in case.

Thirty-Four

Mom was taking a shower, and then she needed to make some more phone calls, and then she needed to talk with Andrea, and then maybe after that we'd go see Magic. I was upstairs, sitting on Andrea's bed with her. She had out her notebook and her markers and was flipping through the pages, looking for an empty one. When she was younger, she had a habit of quickly drawing the same picture over and over, eating through an entire notebook in minutes. She was better about it now, but Dad had also stopped buying her drawing pads because of how much paper he thought she was wasting.

Across from Andrea's bed hung a poster of a hot air balloon that was shaped to look like a panda. Black ears stuck out from the top of the balloon, and on one side there was even a small snout. The background sky was incredibly blue and dotted with other balloons, balloons as bright as Andrea's markers. Andrea went through a panda phase, right around the same time I was going through a panda phase, so Dad bought the poster and framed it for us—for us sisters to have something in common. But this was also right around the time I was going through an I-don't-want-anything-in-common-with-Andrea phase, so when my dad hung up the photo, that pretty much marked the end of me being into pandas.

I remember him standing there with his hammer, asking what we thought. Him saying to me, "What's wrong?" even though I hadn't even said anything yet.

Over by my bed, it was horses. My favorite thing was my photo of Magic—an artsy shot of me running a brush down her neck. My mom had taken it. She had also given me a blue ribbon from a dressage show she'd competed in, which I then clipped to the picture frame. My mom had told me to visualize the ribbon being mine, visualize that it was Magic and me who'd won, and that I was grooming her after the show. Sometimes I could do it, but other times, all I saw was a twenty-year-old ribbon of my mom's, nothing that belonged to me.

I noticed a picture in Andrea's notebook. "Scoot this way," I said, "I want to see one of those."

Andrea wiggled in close. "Is this it?" she asked. She was pointing to one of her drawings. She had a knack for puffy clouds.

"Turn it back," I said. "Stop. There."

The page was filled with a whole bunch of little drawings, drawings that were obviously done by different people. I could tell the page was from one of our TV-free nights—nights when Mom and Dad would make us play board games, or have us draw and paint or make things. I knew which drawings were mine, though I couldn't remember drawing them. My drawings were the horses, and Mom's were the horses that actually looked like horses, and Dad's were the goofy half-animal, half-robot monsters. Andrea's were the squiggles—her pre-cloud work. She was way better now. It had to be at least a couple of years old.

"Do you remember this?" I asked her.

"Uh-huh," she said. When I asked what she remembered, or if she could remember when it was from, she didn't say anything.

"These ones are mine," I said.

"I know." She was already turning the page.

"Wait," I said, grabbing her hand.

Heidi and Tracy and other kids at school couldn't understand why anyone would have TV-free nights, and I would always have to explain that I didn't really get it either, and that they shouldn't be thinking I was the weird one. Occasionally, the ban would get lifted, or my parents would switch it to a different night so they could watch some show they wanted to see, but that was pretty rare, and the truth of it was that I actually liked TV-free nights.

"Do you recognize Dad's?" I smiled for her when I said it.

Her eyes scanned the drawings. I shouldn't have even been bringing him up. I wanted to ask her if she understood how there weren't going to be any more of these, that these were the last of Dad's bear-robot-crocodile creatures, and that this is what it meant for something to be rare, or precious, or endangered— words that Dad was hitting us with all the time. I wanted to ask if she understood, because I wasn't sure I actually understood it myself. I took the notebook away from her. I'd thought maybe by just looking at the pictures we could somehow talk about him without actually having to speak, which was silly to think.

I tore the page carefully. When she told me to quit it, I told her that I was taking the picture for safekeeping. I told her we could even frame it and hang it up if she wanted.

"I want it in my book," she said. Her markers fell to the floor. "Leave it."

"This one is special," I said. "Let's put it somewhere else."

Andrea had grabbed the edge of her notebook. "Don't," she said.

I held tight. There was no way she was just going to pull it away. "Listen to me."

"It's mine," she said. "Em, stop." She said it loud enough that Mom would've heard if she hadn't been in the shower. Her cheeks were all puffy, and her eyebrows had this scowl to them. I could tell she knew that it was up to me, that I was big enough and strong enough to just take it. And then I realized something else: that how she would come through of all this, how she'd survive and understand it, that also was in large part up to me, a responsibility I was afraid I couldn't handle.

"This one isn't just yours," I said. "This one is all of our pictures."

"It's not. It's mine."

I grabbed her wrists and tugged the notebook from her hands. She reached and tried to get it back, screaming in my ear. I pushed her away and pinned her down on the bed. It was the same move I used during tickle wars. "I'm sorry," I said, "This is all we have of him now. We have to keep things like this safe."

Her face was turning red, and she was about to cry. I stood up and finished ripping out the rest of the page. I thought she was going to try and jump on me, so I turned my back to block her, but she just ran out of the room.

"I didn't mean to," I shouted after her. She probably thought I was talking about the picture.

Mom and Andrea talked in the living room. Mom had said I could join them, said that it would probably be nice for Andrea to have me there, but I wasn't so sure after our blowup. "Either way," she'd said, "it's up to you."

I went outside.

I went out there because I didn't want to think about it. Or that's what I thought. Because the whole time I was out on the deck, all I kept imagining was how I'd try and explain all the different parts to her—how I'd try and tell Andrea that there is this current to us, this part that has a kind of spark and electricity, and that's what makes us alive, but in Dad, because he hit his head, his brain stopped making that spark. I imagined Andrea thinking about it like she did other electrical things, and I imagined her saying that we should just fix him and plug him back in and have him here again. I tried to think about how I might explain that this kind of broken couldn't be repaired, or how I might explain that giving CPR wasn't anything like it was with the dummies.

In some versions, I imagined Andrea just nodding calmly, like she was some wise six-year-old who simply accepted all things. In others, she bawled and screamed at me and kept asking me what I meant and why I'd let him die.

When Mom invited me to be a part of the talk, I asked her how she was going to explain it. She told me that she didn't exactly know but that she was just going to try and be honest, and not make some stuff up about a better place and all that. I asked her how she'd explain the accident, and she said just like that—that it was an accident, and that accidents happen, and it's the same reason we all wear helmets when we go biking.

"You can tell her it was my fault," I said. "I want her to know."

"That's not true." She came in for a hug. "It wasn't your fault. That's not something I'm going to say."

One of the pamphlets on grief that I later read at Roland's— *Sad Isn't Bad*—advised being brief and simple, and to not overwhelm children with too many words, which was like the exact opposite of my dad's explain-it-all-very-thoroughly approach. Mom said she didn't expect this to be a onetime conversation with Andrea anyway. This was just a start. "Probably the first of many talks for all of us."

I imagined saying some of the same things to imaginary Andrea—that it was okay if she had questions, or if she felt confused, or even if she hated me. I was doing all the right things, being understandable and direct. I was not judging her reaction. Whatever she felt was okay. We would figure it out together. *This is just the start.*

And then I imagined Andrea asking the real question, the one I wanted answered, too: *When will it be over?*

The screen door startled me. I twisted around to see my mom, who looked abnormally tall. Her smile seemed drowsy. I was sitting on the stairs to the deck and she tapped me on the side with her foot. "Scooch," she said.

She walked past me, out onto the walkway. She turned her face up to the sun and closed her eyes. She had on a tank top and jeans and wasn't wearing shoes. She took a deep breath and said something like "*Oh.*"

I pulled myself up from my seat and went out into the sun with her. I closed my eyes, my face turned toward the sky like hers. All I could see was red, which I don't think was actually the red of the sun, but the blood in my eyelids.

"Is she inside?" It was obvious she was.

"She's playing in the living room," my mom said.

"You didn't tell her?"

I'd already opened my eyes. My vision was dotted. My mom

opened hers and blinked at me a bunch. "We talked," she said. "You didn't hear any of that?"

"No," I said. "What did she say? Did she not understand?"

"She understood." I could tell my mom was back in the room with Andrea for a second. "She yelled and cried and said it was the worst thing that's ever happened to her. She told me that it was my fault. Then she settled down and asked if she could play with her dinosaurs."

"Why did you tell her it was your fault?"

"I didn't. It's only because she heard it from me. She didn't mean it. It's not my fault, and it's not your fault either, so don't start with that. If it's anyone's fault—" She didn't finish, but she didn't have to.

That Andrea liked dinosaurs made my dad incredibly happy. If his life had gone differently, he easily could have ended up a paleontologist instead of a soils engineer. Some of her dinosaurs had actually been mine, and I'd actually always really liked them, but I didn't play with them the same way Andrea did, giving them names and voices and all of that, so they just sort of became hers, and it just sort of became that I was never into dinosaurs, at least according to how Dad began remembering it—like when he and Andrea and I were playing with them and he'd ask, "How come *you* never got into these things?"

I asked my mom how Andrea could be playing already. "That's kids," she said. "Playing is partly how they make sense of stuff."

"Do you think it will make sense for her?" If it could for Andrea, then maybe it could for me too.

"I don't know," she said. "Sometimes things never make sense, but making sense is also sometimes never the point." It reminded me of what Alex had told me. My mom bent over and started weeding the flowerbed, shaking out the dirt from the roots she pulled up. I'd weeded that very flowerbed myself before, several times, had listened patiently while my dad showed me (several times) how you had to dig way down to get out the long taproots—advice my mom was now ignoring. You weed, the things grow back, and then you weed again.

192

"Did she ask what happens after you die?"

"No, not really. We didn't get too far into that." My mom glanced up at me. Her forehead was already sweating. She wiped at her nose with the back of her hand, the tips of her fingers coated in dirt. "Why?"

"I just thought maybe she might wonder that."

"What would you have said?"

"I don't know." The weeds at my mom's feet had already wilted. "I guess I'd say stuff about energy, about how it doesn't ever go away but just changes shapes. I'm not sure. I guess I'd tell her what comes next is that you just have to keep going."

"Even in the afterlife?"

"Always," I said.

Thirty-Five

Magic's stable was out in Pleasant Valley, way past all the new construction. I think Peg was about the same age as Mrs. Hayes, but she looked much younger. Her skin had this shine to it, her hair just beginning to gray. Peg also owned Magic. We often just called Peg's place "the barn."

The barn had a long dirt driveway, and at the bottom of a big hill you hit a cattle guard and an entrance gate. There was an old flatbed truck that Peg always decorated for whatever holiday was next—hay and pumpkins and dried cornstalks for Halloween and Thanksgiving, a Christmas tree for Christmas, basketfuls of brightly colored plastic eggs for Easter. After Easter, the flatbed would sit empty until the Fourth of July.

When we parked, I could see that Magic was turned out in the backfield with all of Peg's other horses. The horses stood around in a loose herd in the middle of the pasture, except for Tractor and Geronimo, the two retired pack mules, who were being all aloof. A few big cottonwoods were just beginning to fill out with spring green, but there was no irrigation out there, and the field had already browned out.

Ours was the only car in the parking lot. Sometimes, like after school, it could get crowded with other boarders. Peg's truck was over at her house, which was up on the hillside. Somewhere on the property, a four-wheeler's engine was groaning. In the paddocks closer to the barn, sprinklers watered the grass. One of the joints in the irrigation pipe was leaking, and the water pooled up in a big muddy puddle right by the gate. The door to the arena stood open, and inside, one of the blue barrels had been knocked over.

Andrea kicked her legs in her booster seat, wanting someone to unbuckle her, even though she could do it herself. She'd been out to the barn a few times before, but usually it was just Mom and me who went. Once I'd brought Heidi, who said she liked it, except for the flies and how much it smelled.

I undid my seatbelt so I could turn around. We'd already given her the safety lecture, the stuff about not running, about not sneaking up from behind, about gentle touches. "Should we eject?" *Eject* was part of Dad's attempt to make the booster seat cool.

"E-ject," she said in a robot voice.

I walked down to Magic's stall and got one of her halters and a lead rope. Her water was a little low, but otherwise things weren't too much of a mess.

"We can all go grab her," Mom said, coming down the aisle. Andrea was already distracted by one of the cats.

"It'll take forever with her," I said. The cat was bumping his head into Andrea's legs and rubbing against them, and Andrea was running her hand up the cat's tail. "I don't need help."

"I know," she said. "Just be careful with the latch on that gate."

"Peg showed me."

It felt like maybe we were about to get really annoyed with each other, but then she only said, "Alright. We'll catch up."

The gate was at the far end of the pasture. A two-track road led down to it, and every week, unless it was the monsoon season, Peg, or one of her farmhands, would have to drive out a big cistern of water and refill the stock tanks. They had to drive slow so the water wouldn't start splashing too much, slow enough that I could walk and keep up.

The horses must've sensed me coming, because when I made it past the windbreak, they were all looking in my direction. Magic was standing on a high spot, tucked in between a gelding named Axle, and this Appaloosa whose name I didn't remember. Her head was up, her ears forward. She let out a long whinny, which someone else answered. As soon as I whistled my cruddy whistle, she started heading over to me, a half dozen other horses following.

Instead of going all the way to the gate, I jumped the ditch and climbed over the fence. Magic cut toward me at a harder angle, and I started across the field to meet her, grasshoppers springing ahead of me. When Magic and I got close, I stopped to let her come the rest of the way. That must have been one of the first things my mom had ever told me about horses: "Just let them come to you." Magic pulled her head back and curled her lips, showing her big teeth. They could bite a cob of corn in half like it was nothing. She shook out and whinnied again, but it sounded softer and more hesitant than before. "I know," I said.

She let me stroke her face. I ran my hand down her blaze and patted softly, stopped to feel the warmth coming out of her nostrils, her lungs. The skin on her chin reminded me of that of an old man. Maybe it was how the whiskers were so long but also so thinned out. That was the spot for her. I scratched, and her ears flicked back and forth.

Along the Tinto, I'd talked to her to keep me going. I'd imagined myself as her—with her powerful legs, with her gigantic heart. She'd even talked back. All that I could think to say now was, "Here I am."

Parts of her belly had bits of mud dried to them, and I tried brushing them out with my hand. The other horses in the field started crowding us, until I shooed them off. "I'm sorry I was gone so long," I said. I readied her halter. "It wasn't really my idea."

Magic didn't answer.

"I missed you," I said.

That didn't get anything, either.

Once her halter was on, I started leading her away from the others. She kept pulling and trying to graze, and once we were away from the herd I just let her eat. The air felt heavy and warm and still. The four-wheeler was either done or out of earshot.

Without a mounting block, I wasn't sure if I could get on. I dropped the lead rope and told her to stay put. I took a little running start and then jumped, getting on her enough that I was able to wiggle up her side and pull myself the rest of the way. Like the good horse that she was, she just stood there patiently.

I reeled in the lead rope and laid it across her shoulders. I'd forgotten a little bit what it felt like to have her under me, how she was so much wider than the canoe seats. I opened up my hips and shoulders. I reached forward to pet her neck, which was still bent toward the grass. I stretched my arm as long as it would go, seeing how far I could lean forward. She would've barely had to shy, and I would've ended up on the ground.

I repositioned myself, scooting back a little and draping my arms along each side of her. It was another thing my mom had taught me. She said it was one reason you could tell that people and horses were meant for each other—because of how people fit on top, and how you could lie down along a horse's back and it was like the perfect bed. "Just be with your horse," she'd said. Hear your horse's pulse. Feel the different muscles flexing. "You just have to be careful not to fall asleep," she warned. "Not that that's ever happened to me."

Magic stopped grazing and started moving through the field again. I stayed as I was, watching the ground pass beneath. I thought of the Tinto again, of watching my feet move but not being able to feel them anymore, and how on some nights when I tried to fall asleep, it would feel like I was still moving. You would think that riding was just about what you did with the reins, but there are so many other ways to tell your horse what you wanted. She carried me like that all the way over to the gate.

Magic was trying to walk past the crossties and out into the parking lot, where my mom was talking on her phone. I forearmed her chest and told her to stop. "Seriously," I said, leaning my weight against her. "Back it up."

I'd guessed my mom was talking to her sister, partly because Aunt Mel had already called a couple of times that morning, and partly because of how her voice sounded. Something lifted in it when she talked to Aunt Mel, though "lifted" makes it sound like she got cheery or something, which wasn't really it. The words just had a different spacing. Just by her voice, I could tell when Mom was talking to Dad on the phone, too.

I shoved my weight into Magic again, and she yielded enough that I could clip the crosstie. I took her lead rope and threw it over her neck so that it was out of the way. When I'd brought Magic over to the crossties, I made Andrea stand to the side. Besides some giddy squeals, she'd been good.

"One more minute," I said to her.

Aunt Mel lived in St. Louis. She was Mom's big sister. Mom had also already talked on the phone with both sets of grandparents. The only times I'd spent with Aunt Mel had been Christmases or Thanksgivings, but she usually made them more fun, especially when she'd come play with the kids or sit and talk with me on the couch so we wouldn't have to watch *It's A Wonderful Life.*

I'd overheard a little of my mom's earlier calls—how she assured Aunt Mel that she was eating, and how neighbors had been helping out, but how there were also all these decisions that needed to be made, all these things that had to happen. How was she supposed to make decisions when she couldn't even think?

From out in the parking lot, I heard: "I don't know. I'm trying. But I don't even know."

I ducked into the tack room to get the grooming bucket. The overhead lights flickered as they warmed up, not that I needed them. It was dusty in the tack room, and there were a million dead bugs up in those light fixtures, but the room was also totally organized, and everything always went back where it was supposed to go. Peg made sure all her boarders knew that. She reminded me of my dad in that way. I probably could've found the bucket in the dark.

Along with the dust, the room was choked with the scent of

leather. On one wall of the room hung the saddles, both English and Western. Only a few of the racks were empty. Mom's saddle was up there, a Stübben. She said you knew it was fancy because of those dots above the u. I was still just using one of Peg's loaners.

The other side of the room had hooks to hang helmets on, and a couple of racks for crops and whips to stand in. The wall on that side of the room also had rows of show ribbons hanging from it, ribbons mostly from Peg's horses, though some of them were also from other boarders who had their own horses. My mom said that when I won my own, we'd hang it from Magic's stall. That's where you were really supposed to put them.

I gave Andrea the soft brush and put her up by Magic's shoulder. That way I could be next to her, and Magic could see her better too. We'd practiced before at home on one of her stuffed animals, and I reminded her again about brushing in the same direction as Magic's hair. I put my hand on top of hers and we ran the brush over Magic a few times. "Remember?" I asked.

She wanted to do it on her own. The brush was a little big for her, but otherwise she had it. I thought of our scuffle over her notebook. Sometimes when Dad was showing me how to do stuff, when he wouldn't just let me try, he'd make me feel like I didn't even want to do it anymore. "I'll be right here," I said.

I watched Andrea for a bit and then took the currycomb to Magic's back, moving with short circular strokes and lifting the dirt out. She must've been rolling in the field, flopping, squirming, working the soil into her coat. I'd watched her do it before, the dust clouds ghosting all the way across the property. Sometimes she'd jump up quick and then tear around and buck, until she'd had enough. She'd stop and shake herself out like a dog, setting loose another cloud.

I kept brushing as Mom came to check on us. She was off the phone, but was carrying it in her hand. "Hey, you," she said to Magic, putting a hand on her neck. "And how are you doing?"

Magic nuzzled with Mom a bit, moving sideways a little. I put my hand out for Andrea so she didn't get stepped on, even though she wasn't standing that close. "And look at you," Mom said to her. "See how nice you're doing that?"

Andrea proudly held out the soft brush. I told Mom that she'd been doing awesome. "We should totally put her up on Magic later, maybe after I ride."

"That's what I was coming to talk about."

She'd said that we needed to get back home, that there wouldn't be time for anyone to ride. She wouldn't even let me take Magic back to the pasture, and we got in a tear-inducing argument about shutting Magic in her stall while all the other horses were outside. One of the other boarders arrived while we were fighting, and then Mom told me none of it was up for discussion anymore. Peg had already come down to turn off the irrigation and had overheard us. She said it'd be fine to put Magic in the turnout. She asked if I'd feel better about that, and I said yes, but mostly I just felt stupid for crying in front of her.

Now Peg was talking with Mom behind the car. Andrea was boosted in her seat. I had the window rolled down so I could listen.

"It is not a problem," Peg was saying. "Just let me know." They had been talking about switching the lease from partial to full care so that Mom and I wouldn't have to come out every other day. Mom is the one who brought it up.

My mom's phone started ringing. She looked at the number and then silenced it. She puffed up her checks and took a step toward the driver's seat.

"Let's just go ahead with it for now," she said. "That's going to make the most sense. We can always go back later."

"We don't have to set anything in stone," Peg said. "You come out anytime you want. Don't worry about what day it is."

Mom thanked her and got in the car, starting it before she even had her seatbelt on. Peg walked around the other way to say goodbye to Andrea and me, and I rolled my window all the way down. She still carried Magic's halter and lead rope. I offered to run them back, but she said she wouldn't hear of it.

Peg leaned in and waved at Andrea, who didn't really wave back as much as just hold up her empty hands. Peg had slate-colored eyes that were flecked with yellow. Her ears were pierced several times, but she didn't have any earrings in. The knees of her jeans were wet. She smiled and said she was happy to see me, something she'd already said earlier. Later, when I'd come work for her and get to know her better, Peg would tell me about some of the things that she'd lost, and then I'd feel differently about everything that happened that afternoon. I had my arm hanging partway out the window, and she gave it a little pat. "Next time you're here," she said, "I hope I get to catch you riding."

"Ha," I said. I said it like that, like a word. I sounded so much like him. I articulated it so my mom would hear. "Me too."

Thirty-Six

My mom had gotten the mirror for my bedroom when my dad started complaining that I was taking too long in the bathroom each morning. She'd also found me a stool and a little lamp, telling me how her mom had done the same thing for her when she was my age. "Do your hair and stuff here," my mom had said. "Use your bathroom time for bathroom things."

I kept looking at my face and thinking how it didn't feel right. It was supposed to be my face, and behind it—behind that skin, and those eyes, and the mouth that I could shape into all kinds of shapes—that was supposed to be me in there. But it didn't feel like me. Or it felt like me, but I didn't feel like I was in *there*, not inside that body. I wasn't sure where it felt like I was.

My sister was downstairs with Mom. Earlier, Heidi had called and asked if maybe she and Tracy could come over. She said that they both really wanted to see me. I told her I didn't know. I told her my mom probably wouldn't be cool with it since it was so late, but then my mom overheard me say that and she made a big deal of letting me know that it was fine for them to come over. If only people would just stop listening when they shouldn't. "Sure," I finally said to Heidi. "Okay."

The mirror had two drawers along the bottom. The top one held postcards and pens, old gum wrappers, and the crumpled-up start of a book report that I'd had to do for Mr. Franks last year. There was some other old homework in there too. In the other one, I kept my hairbrush and hairclips and stuff, and the little makeup I had.

I opened the makeup drawer and took out my foundation. It was the brand Tracy told me to get, even though it didn't have the little bunny on the packaging that would show it was a cruelty-free product. When I brought it home, I snuck it into my room. Then I took it into the bathroom, where I could lock the door.

The first day I ever wore makeup in front of him, my dad literally groaned. Then he had a long monologue with me about advertisers and about how I really didn't know what I wanted yet, and how it was silly for me to be covering up my beautiful face.

"I'm not going to say you can't," he said, "but I don't like it. And I'm probably not going to start liking it." But he said it was my choice. "I want you to understand that," he said. "You have to make choices."

In front of my mirror, I twisted the cap off the bottle. Instead of putting a little bit on the back of my left hand, I poured the foundation into my palm, enough that it started to leak through my fingers. I took the sponge and started painting a design on my face. A lightning bolt on each cheek. A circle around each lightning bolt. Three vertical lines on my forehead and one on my chin, the same as I gave my dad on the river.

I traced the design with more foundation. When the lines got thick and goopy, I started filling in the rest of my face. I even covered my eyebrows and lips, until I was only "buff beige," my sun freckles gone.

During his first makeup monologue to me, my dad told me that he didn't like makeup because he thought it was a mask. That makeup hid who we really were, and the whole point of life was to just be ourselves. He didn't say how he knew all this about makeup. I think he'd also forgotten that he once told me masks were necessary ("essential") parts of life. That we all wore them, we all had to, and not just on Halloween.

I looked flat and plastic. I wasn't any more unrecognizable than before, not exactly. Roland thought maybe that's why I did it, so my exterior matched the interior emotions. His idea kind of made sense, and I bought into it for a while, though I don't worry about explanations as much anymore. He thought my head was working like this: if I didn't look like me, then it would only seem more natural if I didn't exactly *feel* like me.

The doorbell rang downstairs. Footsteps across the kitchen. The front door opening, then thudding closed. My mom called up to me, "Em, your friends!"

Heidi and Tracy stood outside my doorway. "Hi," they said, in unison.

I had taken a towel out of the hamper and dragged it across my face, clearing away a swath of makeup. My chin and my forehead were still thick and goopy. Their makeup was perfect—eyebrows plucked and penciled in, eyelashes super long and dark and not clumped together at all. They were totally tan and unpimpled. They had glow. The only difference was Heidi's eyeshadow, which was dark gray. Lately, she had been alternating between grays and blacks, or else shockingly pink pinks.

"Hi," I said.

My mom was coming up the stairs behind them. "Em," she said, "Heidi and Tracy are here." She told them they could go on in, but they didn't move. She asked them if I was even in there.

"Em," my mom said again, parting her way through Heidi and Tracy, "you have guests."

I wiped at the rest of my face. My mom took in the room, her focus moving from me to the towel to the empty bottle of foundation on the desk. The mess of clothes I'd pulled out of the hamper to get the towel in the first place.

"Anything going on?" she asked.

"No," I said, "I don't think so."

She pushed out her bottom lip and frowned and started to shrink into herself. Her eyes went from concerned and confused to far away and sleepy, a look I'd come to see from her more and more, and I knew she didn't really have the energy for it. "I'm just downstairs," she said.

After my mom left, Heidi and Tracy came over and both gave me a hug at the same time, my arms pinned to my sides. Their hair smelled of coconut, which was a new thing. They were always having me smell their hair, and never before had I smelled this. There was also a faint burnt smell from a straightening iron.

"We're so sorry," they said.

"Oh my god," they said.

"I mean really," they said.

I wiggled my shoulders in hopes they'd let go. I told them that it was okay. I told them they hadn't needed to come, but that it was nice to see them. One of those things felt truer than the other, but I couldn't quite tell which one. All they'd had to do was actually study for that test.

Tracy held me at arm's length and gave me another look. She had on a T-shirt that said "Aloha" across the front, which my dad would've informed me was too tight. "Was it like they said it was on the news?" she asked.

"I don't know," I said. I hadn't watched any of the news pieces yet. "How did they say it was?"

"I don't know," Tracy said, "just that all this stuff happened."

"I guess," I said.

Heidi told her to stop talking about it, and Tracy apologized. I told them it didn't matter, that they could ask stuff, but they didn't. Heidi took my towel and threw it in the hamper, and then they dragged me into the bathroom. We stood in front of the sink, watching it fill with warm, sudsy water.

"Andy Steves got kicked out of Algebra for cursing today," Heidi said, just so there was something. "And then after, for like the rest of the period, Mrs. Willes was just a total grouch."

"She gave us extra homework," Tracy said.

There had also been an assembly about me, one where they let everyone know that I might be coming back soon. I asked why they'd said that, but neither one of them knew. There was also a reminder about the counselors who were available, and apparently people like Jackie Keifer, who never even gave me the time of day before, were going to see them because they were all distraught. Even teachers were saying how messed up the story sounded, how it was almost like a movie and stuff. There were all these different versions going around, ones where I was the one who'd gone into a coma, or ones where my dad and I went over a huge waterfall, and that's how he died. Ones where the paramedics found me naked and completely psycho, eating my own hair.

"Plus Chris Smernes keeps saying he wants to hang out with us during lunch," Heidi added, "but he's friends with Joey Olson, and he's the guy who slapped Kirstin's ass that one time in the hall, so I don't think I'm okay with that."

"That was Kenzie's ass," Tracy said.

"It was both," I said.

Tracy was holding the Noxzema container in one hand and was poking at her cell phone, which was rattling on the counter, with her other. She held the Noxzema so weakly that whenever I wanted to get some out of the tub, I had to grab the container, too. I'd wiped down my forehead and was working toward my cheeks. "It *was* both," she said. "You're right."

Heidi moved my mom's hairbrush and an uncapped toothpaste tube out of her way and set her backpack next to the sink, showing me the bottle of peppermint schnapps she'd stolen from home. She unscrewed the cap while it was still tucked inside the pack, and just before she lifted it out, she looked at the bathroom door, which she'd locked, and asked, "This is cool, right?"

Heidi and I met eyes in the mirror. I had the same feeling as before, that it wasn't me I was seeing. I shut off the water, then dipped the washcloth into the sink and swooshed it around a few times. "Sure," I said.

Heidi took a swig and then scrunched up her face a little. She took another quick drink and wiped her mouth. Her eyes were watering a bit. She smiled. Tracy kept texting.

"Is it bad?" I asked.

"It's just super minty," Heidi said, "kinda like mouthwash." She leaned over and gently breathed on me.

"I guess so." I thought of Kellen and his minty marshmallows.

"You can get drunk off of that, too," Tracy butted in. "Mouthwash, you can totally get buzzed off that." She had put down her phone and was holding out her free hand for the bottle. I took the Noxzema from her. Tracy drank a few times, wincing as badly as Heidi. Then she held the schnapps out for me. "Have some," she said. Her phone vibrated with a new text.

Behind us, the bathtub was full of toys from Andrea's bath. One end of the shower curtain was flopped over, pulled from the rings. A mound of dirty towels covered the bathmat. There were more towels, two or three deep, hanging on all the hooks, including my dad's hook. The red towel that was on top was probably from the shower he took the morning we left.

Heidi and Tracy had asked me to drink with them before. I'd even watched Heidi smoke pot once. What I'd always told them (and what was true, and what they knew was true) was that I didn't like the taste, so I wasn't really interested. If I changed my mind, I'd tell them. Also: my dad would've killed me if he found out. They said it was the same for them, that their parents would've murdered them if they got caught, but it wasn't the same, because their parents *had* found out, a couple of times, yet here they were—Heidi and Tracy, unmurdered in my bathroom. I'd told them they just didn't get it.

It was something in her tone, something about the way she shoved the bottle at me so she could answer her text, as if she was saying, *Now there's no way he can find out!*

I think Heidi knew I was about to have some. "Here," she said. She took the bottle from Tracy and capped it and put it back in her backpack, all without taking a drink herself. She took the Noxzema and the washcloth from me, smeared some cleanser onto the washcloth and began scrubbing my jaw with small, gentle circles.

"Oh my god," Tracy blurted out, "Hayden is such a dork."

Heidi and I were supposed to ask what, or why, or something, but we didn't. Heidi took a piece of my hair and tucked it behind my ear. She rubbed tenderly, and I felt like I should close my eyes like when I was getting my hair washed at the hairdresser's. Before spring break, she'd told me how she'd been feeling anxious and depressed, so she took all these online tests about herself, and they all rated her as *clinically* anxious and depressed, information that made her feel a thousand times worse.

"Thank you," I said. She'd resoaked the washcloth, and it was nice and warm.

"Sure," she said. "Your freckles came out. Your skin is so pretty like that." I was mostly bug bites and pimples and sunburn.

The words *skin* and *pretty* caught Tracy's attention. "What is?" she asked, still texting.

"Nothing," Heidi said, working on my chin.

"Who?" Tracy asked. She didn't look up from her phone.

"Just some person," Heidi said, which was enough for Tracy. Heidi and I smiled at that, a little secret between us, but then she told me to quit because I was moving too much.

"Thank you," I said again.

"Quit."

I'd told them that I might not be feeling well. That puking was a possibility. Heidi had finished cleaning my face, and I'd even run water through my hair, but then it had become clear that there wasn't anything else to do. Watch Tracy text more. Go back to my room and talk. Get drunk and blow up the universe. It all seemed equally dumb.

We were standing in the hallway by the bathroom. Tracy handed me a white paper bag. "We got something for you. We spent a whole afternoon shopping for it."

I unfolded the bag and slid out the necklace. It was made of big brown wooden beads.

"At first we were going to just get you a bracelet like ours," she said, holding up her hand so I could see, "but then we thought you'd probably like this better."

"It's made of nuts," Heidi snorted.

"Like all my jewelry," I said.

Tracy took the necklace and unfastened it for me. I let her clasp it around my neck, let her place her hands on my shoulders and turn me so that she could see. "It's totally perfect," she said. Her smile didn't feel quite right.

"Is it?" I asked.

"Yes," she said. "Go look in the mirror."

"Alright," I said, trying to fight pep with pep.

I locked the door behind me. I said that maybe it was food poisoning, or maybe something from the water on the trip. I told them I was sorry and that I totally loved the necklace. I thanked them for getting it for me. Told them how thoughtful it was. I wasn't even really looking at it anymore.

I was remembering that day my dad and I had played in the mud while on the Tinto, and how quickly the mood had shifted, and how quickly it had shifted again.

Heidi wanted to know if they should maybe get my mom for me.

"That's okay," I said, "I'll be alright. You guys just go. Tell her I'm in my room if she asks."

"I hope you don't puke," Heidi said.

"Me, too," I said. "I probably won't. I'll call you later or something."

"Did you mean it?" Tracy asked before leaving. "Do you really like the necklace?"

"I do," I said, even though I knew I'd probably never even wear it. That made me feel so guilty I had to sit down on the floor. "I love it," I said.

"I was right," Tracy said. "I totally knew it was your style."

What Heidi said was, "Just feel better."

Thirty-Seven

Mom and I headed to the airport to pick up Aunt Mel. Mom had wanted me to stay behind and help Mrs. Hayes watch Andrea and clean the house and get ready for the service. She didn't use the word service, just cut things off at "get ready."

Part of the drive was the same as it was to school, except that instead of turning left onto Silver Road, you went straight, onto the expressway. Most mornings, Dad drove. Mom usually picked up. Depending on his stress level, or on how much sleep he'd actually gotten, the drive would either be silent, with him swearing under his breath at the other drivers or about how he was already out of coffee, or it'd be loud and jokey and fun, with both of us making wisecracks about the overly exuberant radio commercials, or making up stories about the people in the cars next to us. It wasn't just him, though. If I had a big test that day, or a project was due, or if I just felt crappy and kind of tired and didn't want to have to deal, then I'd initiate the silence. Recently, there'd been a lot of quips from him like, "If you'd gotten your permit, *you* could be driving *me* for a change."

When he'd drop me off at school, he'd tell me what kind of day to have, changing it each time:

"Have a great day."

"Have a perfectly average day."

"Have a 93 percent awesome day."

Once, it was just, "Have a day."

At home after school, when he'd ask me how my day had gone, I almost always just answered: "Good." He'd ask me what that meant—"What does *good* mean?"—and I'd tell him I didn't know.

He'd get mad because he thought my answer was generic, that it wasn't special and specific, like each day was supposed to be. He thought it was some kind of automatic response. Sometimes he'd tell me that he couldn't wait for the day when I answered with something like, "It sucked!"

Well, here it was: sucking.

Our airport wasn't much, was only like three gates, but every day there was a morning flight to Phoenix, and an afternoon return flight, which my Aunt Mel was coming in on. We were a little early, but instead of getting a parking spot, my mom just pulled up to the curb by the arrivals door and told me to wait inside in case anyone came and wanted us to move.

"What if they think I'm a terrorist?"

My mom pulled the keys from the ignition. "I'm sure that's really what they're going to think."

"I feel pretty suspicious," I said.

Her purse sat in her lap, its mouth open. She reached over and pulled my head toward her and then kissed the top of it. "Let's make this easy," she said. She locked the doors when she left.

The entire front of the terminal was mirrored glass. Except for an old guy in a cowboy hat standing in the smoking area but not smoking, no one else seemed to be around. The old guy had one of those wheel-along suitcases sitting next to him, a black one, and it looked a little bit like a dog heeling next to its master. Wordless music played over a loudspeaker. After every other song, the same announcement played, reminding us that the front of the terminal was for passenger loading and drop-off only, and that due to security risks, unoccupied vehicles would be towed.

After about ten minutes, I unlocked the car and got out. It was like that night Alex made marshmallows, when I worried

I was alone again. The air smelled like heat and tires. Past the edge of the building, I could see part of the runway. Most of the planes were across the parking lot, and they were all little single-prop ones, some with dust covers over them. They were the kinds of planes that flew low enough to read the signs I'd made on the river.

Two brothers or college buddies or something plowed through the front door, slapping each other high five, as if making it out of the airport was some kind of accomplishment for them. "Yeah, bro!" I caught a brief glimpse inside, saw the rounded corner of a baggage carousel. Mom and Mel came out next.

"Come here," Aunt Mel said. She held out her arms for me. One of my front teeth hit a button on her shirt. "Emma Wilson."

Mom and Aunt Mel looked a lot alike, though my aunt's hair had started to lighten. A few years ago she had been treated for thyroid cancer. Ever since then, her face also appeared bony, though I actually think that was just an illusion created by all her smile wrinkles, which had become enormous.

I was sure my mom was going to be pissed at me for getting out of the car, but she didn't say anything. Aunt Mel quit hugging, and we both just sort of looked at each other. Her head had a slight side-to-side motion. Her eyebrows were arched, her eyes puppy-dog big. What did this expression mean? I saw it from so many people for a while. I took it as pity, which is something you're not supposed to want, but which is something everyone still seems to want to hand out.

"I'm so happy to see you," she said, "even though I wish it wasn't like this."

"It's okay," I said. "I'm happy to see you, too."

She asked me how I was holding up. I replied that it was mostly due to my skeletal system. "Anatomy and such."

That brought out a laugh. "So your bones are good?" she asked.

"Solid." I rapped on my skull. And then I couldn't believe I'd done that. I was worthless.

Mel didn't seem to catch it. "I take calcium supplements," she said, still kind of chuckling. "They're supposed to help us old ladies."

Mom had already put Mel's bag in the trunk. She was standing at the driver's door, waiting. "What are you two even talking about?" she asked.

"I don't remember," I said, which wasn't true.

When Mel had her thyroid surgery, Mom flew out and stayed with her, while Dad stayed home with us. Andrea was still in diapers then. I remember nights when my mom would call home, and how she would first talk to Dad for a long time, and then me and Andrea, and how I could tell if she was upset by the way she'd say, "I'll talk with you tomorrow." One of those nights, later, when my dad was tucking me in, he said that Aunt Mel wasn't very good at accepting help from people. "She's kind of like your mother that way," he said. Kind of like him, really.

As Mom drove us home, Aunt Mel kept telling her that we hadn't needed to come and pick her up, that she could've rented a car. Worry about us, not her.

"Let me worry about what I want to," Mom said.

Aunt Mel apologized. She was here to help. "I'm not meaning to be bossy," she said. "I just want you to know that it's alright to take care of yourself."

Mom and Mel exchanged small smiles. "And that another car might have been good."

"Yes," Mel said. Both their smiles got bigger. "And that."

Out by the airport, there was this place that sold corrugated steel pipes, some of them almost big enough for a car to drive through. As we passed, we were at a right angle to the stacks, and I could see down the length of them. The pipes were stacked in big piles, with smaller pipes stored inside larger pipes, all these circles inside of circles.

"Everyone wants to help," Mom was saying. "They ask me to tell them what I need. But I don't know what I need, or how they are supposed to help me. I don't want to be treated like I have the flu or something, or like I've sprained my knee and need help getting around."

"I'm not trying to treat you that way."

"Please promise not to start."

I thought of what Mom had said back at the airport: "What were we even talking about?"

The pipes. The way the circles seemed to spread outward, almost like splash rings.

"Aren't those beautiful?" I said.

Aunt Mel turned her head a little, but then looked back at my mom. "I have no real idea how this feels for you," she said, "but I don't imagine much of it feels very good at all."

A sound came out of my mom. It went something like *nnnnn*.

"I've been through some things," Aunt Mel said, "and so have you. So you know that the situation will get better, but you're the one who has to get through it. Emma, too. I'm here because I'm your sister, and Emma's aunt, and Andrea's, and that's what I'm supposed to do."

Aunt Mel turned around and draped an arm over the seatback. "Right?" she said to me.

Behind us, the circles were receding. "Right what?" I asked.

"That I'm your aunt, and that I should do what an aunt is supposed to do."

"But not the other stuff, like about the car?" Mom and Mel both cracked up at that. I told her she was right, that she was my aunt and therefore should do aunt stuff. I asked her if she'd seen all the pipes, and she gave another half glance in their direction.

"What do you think they do with all those?" she asked.

Sometimes my dad would just be sitting in his office and watching videos of floods on YouTube. Not videos of kayakers or rafters, but just floods. He'd watch them for hours, clicking one after another, mesmerized. It was the way they could tear apart everything in a matter of seconds, the way they rewrote the earth.

The way they liquefied it. If it was a really big flood, with roads and cars getting washed away, or even whole houses floating off, sometimes he'd bring his computer out into the living room and want us to watch, but sometimes there were dead bodies and stuff and he'd tell us cover our eyes for a second.

"They're for all the water," I said to Mel. "So the water has a place to go."

Thirty-Eight

The bathwater had turned lukewarm. I thought about draining some off and then refilling the tub with hot water, but I'd done that once already, and I could hear my dad's voice in my head, could hear him reminding me about conservation and how there was a finite amount of fresh water on the planet, and how even though it just spent its life shifting from solid to liquid to gas, once it was polluted, it couldn't just shift back to clean. We used biodegradable soaps, and sometimes, if the bathwater wasn't too soapy, he even made us haul it outside and water the landscaping with it. Then he'd tell us the lawn statistic: That 50 percent of the water used by American households goes to watering their precious lawns. That another 49 percent was used for showers and toilets and washing machines. That we only drank like 1 percent. That we were running out.

My hands had become pale and pruned, as had the bottoms of my feet. My hard crimson scabs had turned mushy and gray. I'd planned on shaving my legs but didn't. It was my dad's voice again, a story of how when he was in college he had a bumper sticker that read, "A WOMAN WITHOUT HAIR ON HER LEGS IS LIKE A DAY WITHOUT SUNSHINE."

"Don't conform to some manufactured standard of beauty," the voice went. "Corporations shall not rule."

On another occasion, just after my mom had shaved, and when he had forgotten I was in the room or something, he ran his hand way up her leg and the voice went, "*Oooh...nice.*"

I sunk down into the water again, just to where my ears were below the surface. I could hear the droning noise of the TV downstairs. Aunt Mel and Mom were parked in front of it, splitting a bottle of wine. Earlier, Mom had told Mel about getting the call from the sheriff, about how he'd asked her to find a safe spot and pull over. Andrea was over playing with a friend. Mom was out by the Walgreens, on that section of Gordon where it is more like a country highway than just a street. She was running errands, trying to keep up routine, because routine seemed like a kind of glue that might hold things together. She signaled, slowed down, and eased onto the shoulder, telling the sheriff exactly what she was doing as she was doing it. "I'm stopped," she'd said to him.

She wasn't sure how long she sat there. She'd already known, known in her heart, but she was just so relieved to hear I was alive. She broke down crying, pounding and pulling on the steering wheel, and it felt like her head was filling up with water. She'd thrown her phone at the passenger-side door, cracking the screen. She'd chucked it when the sheriff asked if there was someone he could call. "My someone to call," she said to Mel, "was always supposed to be Parker."

I took a breath and went all the way under, eyes open. My knees jutted into the air and goosebumps rose on my skin. I could see ceiling, the rest of the bathroom, all of it warped. The sensation was something familiar and strange all at once, like maybe this really was how we used to live, back when we were fish, before we crawled up onto land. I tried to stay down, but had to come back up after only like a minute.

I dipped my right hand and let the drops fall as they did between each paddle stroke. *Dripdripdripdrip*. I pictured my view from the front of the canoe: my legs, a wedge of boat, river all around. A memory came back. My father and I on the third day, miles upstream of our layover camp. We were passing through a flat section, the shorelines choked with those view-blocking reeds. Our paddles bumped softly against the gunwales. My dad had wanted to "enjoy the quiet," and so we weren't talking, which was fine, because I didn't really have anything I wanted to talk about then anyway. *Dripdripdripdrip*.

My dad suddenly put in a backstroke, leaning on it hard. "Stop," he said. "Backpaddle."

We turned around and then ferried back upriver. We crawled our way along the shoreline to a little side channel. "In here."

The channel was only about ten feet wide, and it became shallow quickly. When it was too shallow to take a full stroke, we choked up and took half strokes, or used the paddles to push off the bottom. I asked him what we were doing, and he said exploring, which felt like one of the automatic answers he always accused me of giving.

As we moved down the channel, the breeze cut out and the air grew humid. A cloud of mosquitoes settled over us. When I complained about getting bit, he told me too bad. "I have a hunch about something," he said.

I was sure we were going to get stuck. *Grounded*. Sometimes the paddles made big sucking sounds as we struggled to yank them free. The muck smelled like rotten eggs.

And then, after pushing through a last tough part, the channel got deep again. The water's color became different—clear, yet almost brown from certain angles. I watched the muck dissolve off my blade as we paddled. We went around a curve, and then the channel started to widen. And there, another fifty yards out, was a little lake.

The lake was dotted with egrets, their white feathers bright against the vegetation. Some of them waded in the shallows, looking for minnows. Others stepped along the shore, their necks stretched long, or they stood perched upon a piece of deadfall. You could tell they were snowy egrets and not greats, my dad said, because of their black bills. He thought it was a little early for breeding season, but then he pointed out the long delicate plumes coming off their heads and backs, and he said he must be wrong.

218

Of course, I'd seen egrets before. They're not rare. And I'd even seen that many birds together before—I'd seen clouds and clouds of starlings, once—it was just that I'd never seen so many *big* birds together before, and seeing that many, seeing that many hidden like that, it awed me almost like a magic trick.

"How'd you know they'd be here?"

"I saw two different ones fly in," he said. "Plus you usually find neat things down side channels, so I figured why not. It was a guess."

We'd stopped paddling and the canoe drifted sideways a bit in the lake. Besides the egrets, there were also a number of red-winged blackbirds, some grebes and ibis, a blue heron, and even a cormorant that was holding out its wings so they'd dry in the sun. I shifted in my seat, accidentally clunking my paddle against the boat. An egret lifted off, its wingspan as wide as Andrea was tall. It made a wide, gliding turn and then landed in one of the nearby cottonwoods.

"How many are there?" he asked.

"Counting that one?" I asked.

"Including that one."

He came to thirty. I got thirty-one. Thirty-one big white birds. And the two of us.

There was a knock on the bathroom door.

"I just really had to pee," Aunt Mel said. I could tell as much by listening to her go. I'd slunk down into the water again and crossed my arms. She said that she'd close her eyes if I wanted, or that I could pull shut the shower curtain, but I told her it was fine. She'd changed my diapers before, had wiped my butt, and we'd both been skinny-dipping together, even though that had been in the dark.

She had a half-drunk glass of white wine with her. She set it on the floor by the tub. Before, they'd been drinking red. I noticed how sweaty the glass was, how sweaty all the surfaces in the room were. When she was done, she stood and pulled up her pants. Then she closed the toilet lid and sat back down.

"*Gracias*," she said.

"Sure." I stuck the plunger thingy from the faucet between my toes. I was going to wait for her to leave before I pulled it and got out.

"I always like to have candles," she said. "Turn the lights down. I have these giant teabags that are filled with lavender and eucalyptus. Makes your skin all silky." She took a sip from her wine, her eyes scanning the room. All the lights were on. You could see everything—Andrea's toys dumped on the floor, the piles of towels, the scum between the tiling. Most people wouldn't have called it mood lighting—or they'd have described it as setting a mood of *not* relaxed—but when it was night, when outside it was dark, I liked a room with all its lights on.

"I didn't mean to take so long in here," I said.

"What about a bubble bath?" she asked. I noticed her glance at my body, my bruises and scabs. She was thinking something. "You ever take those?"

"Sometimes," I said. "Not this time, I guess."

She finished her drink. I was going to ask if she and Mom were getting crazy downstairs, but then Mel confessed that she would've waited except she'd wanted to check on me. "Sorry," she said.

"It's okay," I said. "It makes sense. But I haven't drowned yet." She didn't seem to appreciate the *yet*.

She got down off the toilet seat and sat with her back to the bathtub. She played with the stem of her wine glass for bit. I took my toes off the faucet, let my foot splash back in the water.

"At least for a while here," she said, "a lot of people are probably going to try and come check on you, which can be hard. *Is there anything I can do? Are you doing okay?* Maybe they won't say it to you as much as to your mom."

"Will it always happen in the bathroom?" I asked.

"Well, this is all I'll say about that. Here's what I really want you to know. Some of these people will be asking more for themselves than for you. They will ask if they can give, but they'll be taking. They'll probably also offer lots of advice. And for them, it's not horrible to just tell them what they want to hear, even if it's not the truth. But there will be others, and I want you to understand that I am one of them, who are asking for you. Because we love you and support you."

She paused and turned her head, looking back toward me. She seemed to be waiting for me.

"I know," I said.

"If you ever need to talk—about this, or about your mom, or about whatever—I'll listen."

"I know," I said again.

She lifted her wine glass to her mouth, tilted it up. She looked at it as if she was surprised nothing came out. Maybe it wasn't surprise, but something else. "I'm going to tell you something for me now," she said. "I think this totally sucks. This should not have happened. It's rotten and unfair, and it's bullshit. It's total bullshit."

I started to tell her that it was okay, but she told me to stop. "You don't have to say that," she said. "Don't feel like you have to say that."

She started telling me about when she was going through the thing with her thyroid, she hated how people kept telling her that they were sorry. "And now that's all I want to say to you."

I thought about telling her about how I'd made the log move. About how I wanted to say *I'm sorry*, too.

"It was an accident," I said.

"I know," she said. "It's still bullshit."

I'd eventually tell lots of people all the details, would explain it again to my mom and Roland and others, including Mel. They would tell me it wasn't my fault. They would tell me that it was helpful to talk, to let go, to be forgiving.

Aunt Mel got up from the floor. I must have looked cold, because she reached down to test the water. It was cool enough for the landscaping.

"Can I get you a towel?" she asked.

"Mine's that red one," I said, pointing to my dad's.

She set the towel on the edge of the tub. "Thanks for indulging me," she said.

I sat up, one arm crossed over my chest. She asked if I needed anything else. "Yes," I said. "It's just one thing."

"Okay." She waited to hear what.

"Please don't ever tell me that accidents just happen."

"That's it?"

"Yes."

"What if that's true, though, that they do just happen?"

"Don't care," I said.

"Emma—"

"Say it to whoever else you want, but just not me."

"So if you overhear me say it to someone, or something like that, that doesn't count. You can't hold it against me. That's just a conversation happening."

"Agreed." I pulled the plug on the drain.

"I can do that," she said. "Absolutely."

Thirty-Nine

The service took place in our backyard. Aunt Mel had pressed Mom about having it at the funeral home, where my dad had been cremated, but my mom insisted that he wouldn't have wanted it that way, which was true. "Outside," my mom had said. "It has to be outside."

People were already arriving as I helped Mr. Hayes set up chairs. Mr. Hayes said that it was nice of me, but that I didn't have to, and that he could do it. I told him I wanted to. But then one of the other neighbor dads was helping Mr. Hayes, and then some other guy came over to help, saying, "Here, let me," trying to take my chairs, though I wouldn't let him.

We dragged chairs over from the deck, pulled the kitchen chairs out of the house. I grabbed the extra camp chairs from the garage. Mr. Hayes brought over a bunch of folding chairs, all of which were the color of pea soup. He also brought a folding table, which he and Mr. Here-Let-Me set up under my dad's Siberian elm.

Aunt Mel covered the table with a Guatemalan tablecloth. She set a vase of sunflowers, one of my dad's favorites, right in the center of it. She disappeared into the house and returned with a framed photo of my dad, a photo of him from before I was even born. Mom had picked it out. In the photo my dad's wearing a rucksack, and he has a big grin on his face, and his ears are sticking out because of the tie-dyed headband he's wearing. He's standing in a grove of yellowing aspen. The trees appear to go on forever. My mom was the one behind the camera. It was their honeymoon. For their honeymoon, they went back-packing. No fancy resort. No aquamarine water. They went on a long walk and slept under the stars.

Aunt Mel had to lean the picture against the vase because the frame didn't have one of those kickstands. From where I was standing, the sunflowers looked to be sprouting from my dad's head. Next to the picture would go the urn, which arrived from the funeral home with a piece of blue tape securing the lid.

My mom greeted most people right at the front door. She had on the black dress that she sometimes wore for parties, or when she and Dad had a special date night. She'd told me I could wear whatever I felt most comfortable in, but I wore the skirt and blouse I'd gotten last year for Dress for Success Day—a day, my dad told me to remember, that was really based on a very "narrow and capitalistically slanted definition of success." He told me this on the way home from the mall, the shopping bag right next to my feet. The skirt was dark enough blue that I could almost pretend it was black.

I sort of attached myself to Aunt Mel, and then when she said that I needed to stay in the living room with my mom, I sort of attached myself to various pieces of empty furniture. I didn't sit down, but stood next to them. If someone *did* sit down in one of them, then I tried to slide away before they'd even gotten their butt on the cushion.

I recognized most people. Mrs. Dugan, from down the street, came to the door holding an already crumpled tissue, which she dabbed her eyes with. She wasn't the only one like that. For the most part, my mom kept herself collected, and she didn't cry until later, when Grammy and Gramps, my dad's parents, arrived. People would say things like "I'm so sorry for your loss," or "Please accept our condolences," and then my mom would simply reach out and shake their hands, or she'd open up her arms and give them a hug. She'd thank them and invite them inside, point-ing down the hallway, which is how you got to the backyard.

A lot of my dad's kayaking and rafting buddies came, includ-ing his best friend, Ron. He gave me a big hug, something he'd stopped doing a couple years ago. "I don't know what I can tell you," he said. That was just about perfect.

The river rats were easy to spot. They drove in from rivers all over—California, Utah, Idaho, Oregon. A group of them had even chartered a plane down from Durango. The river rats were the ones who had graying dreadlocks, or who were wearing flip-flops and Hawaiian shirts, or who sported polarized two-hundred-dollar sunglasses. Those of them who had girlfriends, or who were married, they seemed to try and dress up a bit, but most of their dress-up clothes looked unnatural on them, like they hadn't been worn in a long time.

Peg came. She squeezed my hand so tightly it hurt. Mrs. Meyers and her husband came. Mr. Leverson, who was the principal. Partners from Dad's work. Our old neighbors. Ann, who my mom had volunteered with at the library, came. The bagel shop guy, the one who my dad always joked around with. The whole Diarssi clan, including Tracy. They all had to come over to my zone of furniture to tell me how sorry they were. Mrs. Diarssi went on about how she almost considered me one of her own kids, and Mr. Diarssi said that was true for him, too, and I thanked them for that—even though the last time I'd slept over there, Mrs. Diarssi had literally screamed at Tracy and her brother for like four hours straight and I didn't want to be one of the Diarssi kids at all.

While the rest of her family went outside, Tracy stayed with me. "Is this really horrible?" she asked. She was wearing a white sundress that was dotted with little pink flowers. She had two braids in her hair, which crossed in back. Her eyebrows were perfect again. Her eyelashes so long. "This must be horrible right now."

"This is," I said. I had meant speaking to her. I thought I should feel bad about thinking it, but I didn't.

"Heidi is sick," she said. She had both thumbs bapping on her phone and was texting her. "She doesn't think she's going to make it. What do you want me to tell her?"

"Tell her it's okay," I said. Later, I'd find out she was actually hungover. "It's fine."

"She's sorry," Tracy said.

"I know." Everyone was.

"She texted a sad face, too. I told her to get better."

"Okay," I said.

"She's going back to bed."

"Okay," I said.

When she was done texting, Tracy just kind of played with her phone for a while. Out of the corner of my eye, I could see pictures scrolling by. Every once in a while she would pause at one of the photos, and eventually she stopped on one of them long enough that I could see what she was looking at.

"Look," she said. There was a picture of a kitten, reaching out its paw to me. Maybe she was just trying to cheer me up?

"I have to stay with my mom," I said, "but you can go hang out if you want. There are refreshments and stuff."

"That's alright. I can stay with you."

"It's just that this might be a while. We have to welcome everyone. It's kind of this formal thing, I guess." I was trying to talk quietly so my mom wouldn't actually hear. She'd already told me to go outside and mingle. "Really," I said, "you totally can go. I don't mind."

"You're okay?"

"My mom wants me to stay," I said. "But you should go. It's super nice out there."

Tracy gave me a one-second hug. "Thank you," she said.

Aunt Mel went around telling people it was time to start. Others began to pass the word as well. Seats slowly began to fill. Some of my dad's friends seemed reluctant to sit. People mostly looked straight ahead and spoke in hushed voices, waiting. Grammy and Gramps were already in the front row with Andrea, saving seats for Mom, Mel, and me.

It was what he would have called a bluebird afternoon—no clouds, but not too hot, not even in the sun. Exactly the kind of day my dad had built the deck for. A breeze played through the

226

wind chimes that were hung in the different parts of the yard. Those were my dad's creations, too. We needed reminders, he said. Without reminders like wind chimes, we started to forget about the mystery in the world. The music. Somewhere else in the neighborhood, someone was running a leaf blower.

I walked out and sat next to Andrea, keeping my head down the whole time. I could feel everyone watching me. Andrea said my name so loud I had to *ssshhh* her. Grammy put her arm around her and whispered something. Andrea looked over at me like she was going to say something more, but I put a finger up to my lips.

"Emma—"

"Not now."

Andrea started to say something, but Grammy leaned over again and whispered something more. Grammy smiled at me, and then Andrea gave me a look, and then I gave her one back, and then she snuggled up to Grammy, who put her arm around her again. Andrea couldn't see, but Grammy reached over and gave my shoulder a little squeeze.

After that, like almost everyone else, I just stared straight ahead. They put blinders on horses so they didn't panic, and I guess that's what it was like for us. The urn had been set out, the tape removed. Inside of it were my father's remains. It felt like a strange word. What remained of my father was six pounds of ashes the same color as kitty litter. Because the urn wasn't permanently sealed, my father's ashes had to also be in a plastic bag, which seemed about the stupidest thing ever, even stupider than the blue tape—my dad, in a plastic bag, a twisty tie to keep it closed. The guy in the picture would've been flipping out.

I didn't have a watch, but I knew it had been a pretty long time, because other people had started checking their watches, and they'd begun to speak in louder and more concerned voices, turning in their seats and looking to see where my mom was. I spotted Aunt Mel talking to Mrs. Hayes by the screen door. Aunt

Mel ducked inside, and even though Grammy told me to just sit and be patient, I got up and rushed down the aisle to follow.

While Aunt Mel was looking upstairs, I found Mom in the laundry room, sitting on top of the dryer. When I asked what was going on, she said she'd just been thinking.

"About what?"

"I was trying to remember something," she said.

"Was it about him?"

My mom nodded. "It was."

There were more people in the house now. I could hear their footsteps upstairs, down the halls. I slowly slid the door closed.

"Was it something good?"

"No," she said, "not particularly."

"Don't think about bad memories," I said.

"I don't think any of the memories are bad anymore."

"None?"

"There won't be any new ones," she said. "They're precious now. Isn't that the same thing you were telling Andrea about the drawing?" Andrea had tattled on me before Mom even finished her shower.

It was the same thing, sort of. But there were also still a bunch of memories that I thought I wanted to forget. "What did you remember?" I asked.

She asked me if I could see that spot on the wall where the plaster looked different, a little smoother. I told her I could. I'd noticed it for a long time, but didn't know it wasn't supposed to be there, that it wasn't part of the original construction.

"That's where your father punched a hole," my mom said. "It's smooth like that from him patching it."

"Dad punched a hole in the wall?"

"I was standing right there." She pointed toward the utility sink, a few feet away.

I wanted to know why he'd do that. I asked if he was drunk or something. "Wait," I said, the thought suddenly jumping into my mind, "was he going to hit you?"

"What I was trying to remember is what I'd said to him. He

wasn't going to hit me. He never once did anything like that. But when you know someone really well, you know what things you can say to them, the things they're most ashamed of, or most sensitive about. It was something like that," she said. "We were arguing, and I said something, something probably very cruel."

"He punched the wall because you called him a name?"

"Not a name. Something about the kind of person he was, or about the way he treated me. I'm pretty sure that I accused him of loving you girls more than he loved me."

I asked her if that was true.

"I think that's how it went."

"No, about him loving us more than you."

"I don't know," she said. "He loved both of you. He loved me. How can you possibly measure something like that? What's the point of it even?"

"I guess," I said.

"He probably did, at times. We only have so much attention we can spread. The more his went to you both, the less it went to me."

Someone was headed toward the laundry room. Mom reached out a hand so I could help her off the dryer. She was wearing low heels, and it took a second for her to steady herself.

"We don't have to go yet," I said. "We can take some time."

"They're waiting. You shouldn't make people wait."

I was about to open the door when she reached out and stopped me. She drew me in for a hug, telling me she loved me. I told her I knew, because I did, because as much as I understood anyone, which was not very much, I understood her.

She held me for a long time, and after she let go, she smoothed out her dress. I looked at the spot in the plaster. What if he had loved us more than Mom? What if I had loved one of them more than the other? She'd said it couldn't be measured. But love felt different—with different people, at different times—and wasn't feeling something a kind of measurement?

"I think that it was actually me I was talking about," she said. "I accused him, but I think it was me who didn't have enough. He had enough love for all of us."

It took me a second, but then I asked if she really believed that.

"About him, or me?" she asked.

"You."

She wouldn't look at me. "Yes," she said.

Aunt Mel had found us, and she slid open the door. She'd heard me saying "—wrong."

"What's wrong?" she asked.

My mom took my arm and folded it around hers. She was back to the composed person she was earlier, when she was greeting everyone. She started walking me out of the laundry room, causing Mel to have to move aside. "I had this idea about someone," my mom said, "but someone just helped me see that it was wrong."

Forty

There was no priest or anything like that. Instead, Ron just went up by the urn and the picture of my dad and welcomed everyone and thanked them for coming. It brought him joy, he said, to see everybody there. He knew that it also meant a lot to Mom and me and Andrea. I'd never said that to him, but he was right.

Ron led us in the reading of a poem, one that my mom had pulled from a journal of my dad's. It was actually just part of an old hymn that he'd jotted down during a multiday river trip in the High Sierras, on a day he was stranded in camp because the river was too high with runoff and there were no real hike-out options. Aunt Mel had gone to the copy store and made copies on nice pieces of paper so that everyone could have one.

> Shall we gather at the river
> Where bright angel feet have trod;
> With its crystal tide forever
> Flowing by the throne of God?
>
> Yes, we'll gather at the river,
> The beautiful, the beautiful river—
> Gather with the saints at the river
> That flows by the throne of God.

Ron started his eulogy. He said what he wanted to do was just tell stories, so he started in on some—the first about the High Sierra trip the poem had come from, how Ron was so scared that he was puking, but my dad was just sitting around transcribing hymns. The next was about college, about how he and my dad ended up stuck on top of a train they'd hopped for a quick trip across town.

"Nine hours later," Ron said, "freezing all night, trying to share some flimsy jean jacket between us while hanging on at the same time, we were in Needles, almost two hundred miles from home, watching one of the most gorgeous sunrises I've ever seen."

In Needles, the two of them wandered around trying to figure out what to do. No cash. The days before ATMs were everywhere. Before everyone had a cell phone. Ron hinted at hangovers, which made people laugh.

Eventually, they passed a church whose landscaping irrigation was on. My dad reached down and pulled a sprinkler head all the way out of the wet ground, twisting the top off, and making a faucet.

"That was him," Ron said. "Resourceful. Straight ahead." He said that after the train ride, instead of having someone come get them, or even instead of hitchhiking back, it was my dad's idea to hop another train home, which is what they did. "The thing about that night," Ron said, "or even that morning, while I was mostly moaning about what bad luck the whole thing was, Parker was pointing out constellations, and talking about mythologies and dreams, and wondering about other destinations. If he had fresh air, if he was moving, he was the happiest man alive."

I presumed that most people were thinking about the *he*, but for me it was the *if*, and how conditional everything was.

Ron turned toward the urn. You could've mistaken it for some fancy food storage jar if you didn't know. The photo of my dad was looking out at us. "Parker, man—" Ron was choking up. He bit at his lower lip. His trying to hold it together made my mom break apart. She bent forward, face in her hands to muffle the sobs. Aunt Mel rubbed her back, but Mom's shoulders kept shaking. "I'm so proud to have called you my friend," Ron said. "I miss you already."

Others were invited up to speak. There was a quiet moment—broken only by someone blowing their nose—where it seemed like maybe no one else was going to step forward, but then Mr. Hayes got up and got things going and said what a wonderful neighbor my dad was, and what a lovely wife my mom was, and what sweet girls we were. Gramps came forward and started with something about Dad and skiing and winters, but the story quickly went unintelligible with tears. One of my cousins had to help him back to his seat. Some of my dad's other paddling buddies came forward and remembered more adventures and said how trustworthy he was. Said that on the river you had to be able to count on the people you were with, and my dad could always be counted on, they never had to worry about that. These two women he once guided rafts with read this thing they called a poem-song, which was addressed to the "Great Spirit." They did not sing it, and it did not rhyme, but it had lots of stuff about seasons changing, and caterpillars becoming butterflies, and fallen trees becoming mother logs. They pressed their palms together and bowed toward the picture when they finished.

It kept going like that for an hour, with people I knew, and people I didn't know, all talking about him—describing the dad I knew, but also didn't.

Ron asked a last time. "Is there anyone else?"

My mom hadn't spoken, nor had Aunt Mel. Mom's cheeks were red, her eyes glistening. Throughout the tributes, in between the tears, or sometimes during the tears, she'd been breaking into smiles. She smiled again, and Ron smiled back at her, and then my mom looked over at Andrea and me. She smiled at Andrea, and then smiled at me, and then asked if either of us wanted to say something.

"Are you going to?" I asked.

"No, my job today is to just witness."

I didn't know what she meant by that, because it seemed like she should say something, something for us, something *from* us, as a family. That seemed like her job.

No one else had come forward. I could feel this thing

between my ribcage, this thing that was telling me maybe I did want to go up and say something, though what that something was, I wasn't quite sure. Had no clue, really. I thought maybe if I took long enough, Ron would declare the ceremony over and would invite everyone to stay for food and drinks and conversation, but then I noticed that Ron was looking at me with the same kind of go-ahead expression my mom had. He shuffled to the side a little and gestured toward that spot where everyone else had spoken from.

"It can be anything," my mom said.

The most messed-up part? The most messed-up part was that when I went up people clapped for me again, just like they had on the river.

Everyone watching, waiting. I said "Hi," and a few of them said "Hi" back. I couldn't quite look at the crowd directly, so my eyes went all over. Tracy motioned to me, hand held low in her lap, just her fingertips wiggling. Grammy and Gramps leaned on one another, like two sides of a triangle. Some old guy in a black blazer and bolo tie, some person I don't think I'd ever met before, fanned himself with a copy of Dad's poem. Standing near the back, bald head gleaming in the sun: it was Dan.

"I guess what I want to say—"

You could just tell them. You could explain it to them. *This might be what happened. But this almost might be what happened.*

"I want to—"

A flicker swooped out of a tree and then over into another. They're a kind of woodpecker, and for some reason when they fly they remind me of penguins gliding through water, which is, if you're the right species, its own kind of air.

The flicker dropped again and skimmed just above the sunflowers on the table and then landed behind me. The two women who'd read the poem-song later informed me that it was my dad's spirit signaling to me. I told them it was just a bird.

"What I want you to know is—"

He often told me that if you weren't sure, it was better to think about it first, to find the best words, and then when you were ready, then you speak. But I wasn't convinced that I was actually thinking while I was standing up there, or that my brain was actually working, because the only thing running through my mind were jumbled images of my dad:

The Christmas he dressed up as Santa and waited by the tree, just long enough so that when I was coming down the stairs I'd catch a glimpse before he dashed off into the garage and changed his clothes, him going "I knew it! I knew he was real!" after I'd told him what I'd seen.

Him taking me to the Desert Museum in Tucson, the reptile exhibit. Him lifting a cuddly rattlesnake toy out of the gift shop bag and telling me he'd bought it so that I'd learn how most things that people said were scary weren't really that scary at all.

There was him raking leaves. Him showing me how to hold the rake, how to pull everything into a pile.

Him cooking meatballs while wearing Mom's Wonder Woman apron.

Him riding the tandem bicycle that he'd got for Mom and him, riding it around the neighborhood all by himself, ringing the bell on the handlebars, waving to whomever he passed.

The time he yelled at me for dropping a gallon of milk in the store, even though the clerk assured him it was no big deal, and how he marched me across the parking lot and then drove home way too fast, swearing at all the idiot drivers.

The time, during the first full day on the Tinto, when he said that in just a couple of years I'd be headed off to college. That soon I'd probably feel like I couldn't get away from home fast enough. That I probably *already* felt that way. Wanting to tell him that he was right. Grateful now that I didn't.

"Nothing I can say will bring him back," I began, "so it almost feels like there's no point in saying anything at all. I guess I know that isn't true, that it matters to say something. Thank you for saying all those nice things about him. Some of the things I hadn't heard before. It was fun to hear those." People laughed at that. "What I guess I want to say is just that I loved him, and that he was my dad, and that I am sorry, and that I don't know what else there is."

I went and sat back down and felt like I was going to start bawling, though nothing came out. There was more clapping. Mom leaned over and kissed me on the forehead.

Ron was emotional again, but he was reminding everyone to please sign the guestbook before they left—and that there were also markers and pieces of cloth somewhere, and that people were invited to leave prayers or pictures or messages on them, all of which would be made into a prayer flag.

People began standing up and moving out of the aisles. "I didn't know what to say," I said.

"That was great," Mom said. "Perfect." She reached out for Andrea and hugged all three of us together. I squeezed back tightly. Mom told us both we were perfect, too.

"You are, too," I said. The truth is that none of us always are. But you don't always have to be perfect. It just has to be when you need it.

Forty-One

I stood in the side doorway of the garage, watching a few of my dad's friends build a fire in the fire pit. The sky was inky, and behind me the garage had gotten so dark you could barely see the things inside—the tool bench and the lawn mower and the bikes, all of them were just dull gray shapes. I'd spent much of the afternoon in various doorways, which were the safest places. In a doorway, you had options about staying or going, and that seemed important. For the whole reception, people kept telling me what a wonderful job I'd done talking about my dad. How heartfelt it seemed. How composed I was. How right about him. Talking about my speech was a way for us to talk about him without really having to talk about him, and I understood that. A few people, especially after the drinks had been going for a while, forgot they'd already complimented me and complimented me all over again.

The table that my dad's urn had sat on during the ceremony was folded up and leaning against the deck, along with the rest of Mr. Hayes's chairs. The urn itself was inside, centered on the hearth. The flowers were up on the mantel, along with a whole bunch of other flowers that people had brought. All afternoon there had been food and stories and guitars and singing. Someone had put together a slideshow on their laptop, which they set up in the living room, playing on repeat, until the battery ran out. More food and more stories and more music and singing. More doorways.

I'd talked to Dan at first from the doorway of the living room.

My mom had invited him, had invited all three of them. Dan told me that Alex was already on another survey and that Kellen was doing something else. He wasn't exactly sure what. But he knew that Alex had really wanted to make it. She had made him promise to say that.

"Tell her thank you," I said.

"It was important for me to come, too." He said that I might not have sensed it while it was happening, but finding me shook him up quite a bit. I thought of the argument he and Alex had over the fire pan, but I also thought about how calm he seemed. "My plan had been to skip that camp," he said. "I wanted to push on to Piedra Gulch and be on the road that night, but those guys finally talked me out of it."

I thought about another night out there, about whether or not I would have made it. I think maybe Dan knew the answer to that question, too.

"I'm glad you listened to them," I said.

"And I almost didn't."

I heard someone peeing around the corner. I could tell it was a guy. Whoever it was must have walked the other way around the house, instead of past me. Many of my dad's out-of-town friends would be spending the night, and their tents already dotted the backyard. Others had camper shells on their pickups, or pop-up vans like us. It was too much for our one bathroom, so the shrubbery as toilet wasn't unexpected.

As Dan turned the corner, he was zipping his fly while also trying not to spill his beer. He spilled worse when he noticed me.

"Oh, hey."

"Hey," I said back.

He sucked beer off the edge of his hands. "Just hanging out in the shadows scaring people?"

"I guess." I'd already spent an hour in my dad's office with Andrea and all the other little kids watching old Disney cartoons, had already been run out of the kitchen by Mrs. Hayes and all the other women who were trying to clean it up. I didn't ask him if he was just hanging out in the shadows peeing.

Dan took a sip from his cup. "I was going to check out your fire pit," he said. "You want to give me the tour?"

"A tour of the fire pit?"

He tried again: "I'm going to go to the fire pit. Would you like to come?"

Ron was over by the fire, along with a couple other of my dad's friends that I actually knew, like Steve Ho and Billy. But there were also a lot of people I didn't know. Someone had pulled one of the benches from the picnic table over, and three women sat on it. Aunt Mel was pouring herself a beer from someone's keg of homebrew. I still didn't see Mom.

"What about a tour of the neighborhood?" I asked. "I'd do that."

"Like the whole neighborhood?" he asked.

"How about just the street?"

Our road didn't really have streetlights, so we walked along the sidewalk in darkness, Dan with his beer. I pointed out the Norlands' house, and the Dugans', and the Wilkersons', whom my dad didn't care for a whole lot. I pointed out Heidi's old house, said that the people who moved in after her were the Carrolls, and that after that came someone else, but I didn't know their name. As we walked past the Greenbergs' house, I had us pause and listen to the howling. "That's Charlie, the beagle," I said. "We sometimes can hear him from home."

We kept going, headed toward the one light on the corner. I pointed out the purple house, though it just looked black in the dark.

"I noticed that one on the way in," he said.

"I don't know her name, but the lady who lives there even has purple hair."

Just past the purple house there was a big cottonwood, and the roots had pushed up the sidewalk, bulging it like a ripe zit.

"You're supposed to run and jump off the top of this and kick your heels in the air or something. Some little trick." My dad did it all the time, like every time he crossed it, and sometimes he could get all of us to do it when we were out on a walk—Mom, me, even Andrea, though she mostly just ran over it because she couldn't really jump yet. We'd give each other scores, like the Olympics.

Dan asked if I was going to show him how, but I told him I didn't really feel like it, and that it was too dark anyway. "But you go right ahead."

Dan took a last gulp of beer and set down his cup. He gave himself some starting room, and I stepped out of the way. His feet slapped hard on the concrete as he ran. He went up the rise and jumped, and did something in the air that I couldn't really see. He stumbled when he landed and then veered off to the side, crashing in the lawn, laughing.

"How was that?" he asked, getting up.

"Like a six," I said. "Maybe six-point-five."

"That landing," he said.

"Your landing needs work."

When we got to the corner, we stopped. Dan gave an approving nod and told me I had a pretty nice street. I wanted to keep going, wanted to go up past Hillcrest and Jacob Lane and maybe even cut over to the park, but I could see that he was somewhat concerned about his empty beer.

I sat down on the curb, just out of reach from the streetlight. It was the exact spot I kissed Sean Scardino in fifth grade, which had seemed like such a big deal when it happened, but now just seemed kind of silly. A car left our house and came up the road. It slowed as it passed, and for a second I thought it might stop, but it was only slowing for the intersection.

"You don't have to stay here," I said. I felt like I was back in the living room with Tracy, and I think that came through in my voice somehow. "I'm just not ready to go back yet."

He came over and sat a few feet away and told me not to worry. He asked if there were any other points of interest he should know about. I could've told him about Sean Scardino.

"Not really," I said.

Except for the electric hum of the streetlight, the night was quiet. Or as quiet as it could be around here.

After a few minutes, he said, "He sounded like a good person. I wish I could've met him, maybe gone boating with him. What you said when you got up and—"

"You don't have to say that," I said.

He'd stopped, but I could tell he wanted to keep going with something.

"I'm sorry," I said. "It's just a lot of people have talked to me about that today, and I think a lot of them were just saying stuff they didn't really mean."

"I would mean it," he said.

"I know," I said. "I believe that."

I sat back, leaning on my elbows, my legs straight out into the street. Bugs circled the streetlight. Across from us, a porch light snapped to life. I looked at the section of sky above my house, though I wasn't quite sure what I was looking for.

"I could be ready to go back," I said, changing my mind. "It's fine."

"Only if you want to," he said. "I'm happy to sit here. It's nice out."

We sat there not speaking for a few more minutes, watched a few more cars leave.

"When I was hiking out," I finally said, "before I found you guys, but even after that, like when I was with you, all I could think about was getting back here. Getting back home, to my room, and my horse, and my stuff. I would think about it, and I'd imagine getting here, and I was so sure of how it was going to be. And the way I'd imagined it, it felt a certain way, but it wasn't like this, like how it actually feels now."

"No?"

"No."

"And how does it actually feel now?

"It was supposed to be like it was in all my memories, but it's not anymore. It's not the same place. It's all distorted."

"The same river twice," he said.

"What's that?" I asked, even though I knew.

"You can never step into the same river twice. A river might look the same, but it's always in constant flux. It's fluid and dynamic. You are always meeting the present."

I didn't want to hear it, so I stood up. Dan held out his hand for some help. I had to pull back hard to counteract his weight.

"This isn't a river," I said, once he was up.

"It's not?" he asked.

"No."

He shrugged his shoulders. "If you say so."

Forty-Two

The bonfire was more of what had been going on all evening—
stories and laughing and acoustic guitar. My mom had changed
into a pair of jeans and a sweatshirt. She had a blanket wrapped
around her shoulders, and when she saw me she spread open
the blanket and invited me to come sit on her lap, which I did.
She asked where I'd been. She smelled a little like cigarettes.

"Around," I said.

My mom had been talking to one of her friends from her
running club. I put my head against her chest and let them talk
again. I listened to her heartbeat with one ear, while with the
other I tried listening to all the conversations around me. No
one was really talking about my dad anymore. My mom's friend
was talking about a new apartment building being constructed
by her house, how some of the units would look right down
into her backyard. Ron and Mike and those guys, they were now
spinning their own tales about their own adventures—routes
they'd climbed, peaks they'd bagged, rapids they'd been trashed
in—getting louder with each telling. They talked of places: the
Darién Gap, Patagonia, Siberia, China. Of last chances to run
rivers before they were dammed. Of the latest greatest piece
of gear. They complained about having to go back to work on
Monday, and they contemplated driving the long way back
home. They spoke of *reentry*, which is what they called going
back to that other world—as if the adjustment from backcountry to frontcountry was as dramatic as a spaceship hurtling back
to Earth, burning through the sky. Sometimes those ships broke

apart with explosions that looked like fireworks, and no one survived.

Somebody howled like a wolf.

I was still in Mom's lap when she woke me up.

When I asked, she said I'd only been sleeping for a few minutes. More logs had been dropped on the fire. I didn't even remember falling asleep. "You started breathing loud," she said. The woman next to us stifled a laugh.

I dragged myself upstairs. The lights in our room were on. Andrea was in her bed, but not sleeping. "I think your eyes are supposed to be closed," I said.

Andrea quickly shut her eyes. She was on her back and had the bedspread pulled up to her chin. Her fingers clutched the edge of the fabric.

"Nice try."

I sat down on my bed and took off my shoes. Andrea was looking over at me. I couldn't understand how she was even still awake, or what kind of sense this was all making to her. I wanted to ask her what had been going through her head when she drew an eight-legged cat on her square of the prayer flag. Instead, I asked her why the light was still on.

"I wanted Mom to tuck me in. Aunt Mel said she was getting her."

"Did Aunt Mel put you in bed?"

"She told me to try and lie still, and that Mom would come up in a little bit. I turned the lights back on so she would be able to see."

I started changing into my pajamas. There had been other kids Andrea's age at the house, and instead of having awkward conversations with adults in random doorways, she mostly just hung out with the other kids and laughed and played—chasing each other through the house until they got kicked outside, or later watching those old Disney DVDs in Dad's office. The only time there was any real crying from one of them, it was about someone falling down and scraping a knee, or someone stealing someone else's spot on the couch. None of it was about Dad.

That was gone now. Her eyelids looked heavy, and her cheeks a little puffy. I wondered if she'd really been up this whole time, or if she'd woken as I was headed up the steps. Out of all of us, she'd be the one who'd have the most trouble sleeping again—even after Mom had moved back upstairs.

"How about I be Mom for now?" I said.

"She's coming," Andrea said. She sounded like she might cry.

"Who do you want to be? You can be me, I guess."

"I want to be Mom," she said.

"And who should I be? Does that mean I get to be you?"

"You be me," she said. Her tone had shifted. I suddenly realized that she could've assigned me the role of Dad.

"Good. I'm you." I got close to her and made the brattiest face I could. "*Ugh*," I said.

"Em, stop."

I tickled her until she was all giggles. "Emma's my big sister," I said. "She's awesome."

Andrea got out of her bed and made me get in. She went over to her shelves. "I will read you exactly one book," she said, in an almost perfect imitation of Mom.

She picked Martha Blah Blah. She only read a few parts, and mostly improvised by describing the pictures, which was better anyway. When she got to the last page, she slapped the cover closed and said, "*Thhheee* end!" She pulled the blanket up so that it was tight to my chin, just like it had been for her when I came in. I puckered my lips and she bent forward and pecked me a kiss.

She walked over to the switch and turned out the lights. "Bedtime," she said. "I mean it."

The nightlight in the hallway was on, and I could see her standing just outside the doorway. She stood there for a few seconds, and then came back to her bed.

"Emma?"

I didn't answer. I was sure she could see, even in the dark, that my eyes were open and that I was smiling.

"Andrea?" she asked.

"Yes."

"Do I have to sleep in their bed now?"

Dad could hold a straight face forever, making it so you never knew if he was joking or not. "If you're Mom," I said, "that's where Mom sleeps." What I should've said was, *Of course you don't.*

"Does she have to?" I thought I heard her snuffling. "Can she maybe sleep in this one, for only tonight? Because Andrea likes it when Mom does that."

"She does?"

"Yes," she said.

"Okay." I pulled back the covers and scooted over. "But get a pillow from Emma's bed first."

Andrea half-skipped over and grabbed my pillow.

"And no hogging the sheets," I said, as she climbed in. "Mom has a tendency to do that."

"She won't."

For a long time we both just lay on our backs. The last time I'd been with her like that had been the night when I'd heard Mom and Dad talking on the deck, when I told her to come snuggle, and I put my arm around her and tried to imagine what it would be like if Dad actually left—if we were finally going to have different rooms, or if there were going to be weekends where the two of us wouldn't get to be together, or where one of us would have to go stay at Dad's, while the other stayed with Mom. I never told Andrea anything about what I'd overheard. I almost did once, when I got really mad at her and was going to say that she was the reason they were having problems, but something stopped me.

She fell asleep quickly. I wasn't far behind. Her breath was warm and smelled like mushrooms, so I rolled over. Sounds drifted up from the backyard—wood crackling in the fire, someone having a coughing fit, and then a bunch of laughing.

The absence wasn't anything to imagine now. It was real, and I realized how wrong I'd been about it. That night I'd last snuggled with Andrea, I'd been sad and worried and anxious, but there was also something else that had maybe felt exciting about him leaving, about the idea of having a different life.

There had maybe even been a part of me that had wanted it to happen.

Forty-Three

Andrea was sleeping over in my bed when I woke up the next morning. I put on some shorts and went downstairs and found the kitchen filled with dudes. One was at the stove, where all four burners were filled with pans of eggs and potatoes and bacon. Another was chopping fruit. A duo was blending smoothies. Someone else was on toast duty. There was the whisking of pancake batter. The gurgle of the coffee pot. One guy was wearing my mom's Wonder Woman apron.

My mom was sitting on the deck with Aunt Mel, both of them in sunglasses. Mom had a wine glass of fresh orange juice in one hand, and her feet were propped up on a chair. She took them down so I could sit. "Good morning," she said.

"Is Dan still here?" The fire pit was heaped with charred wood and ashes.

"I haven't seen him, but I don't know. Andrea up?" I told her she was still asleep. "And you slept okay?" she asked.

"Like a rock," I said.

Dan had left a note. I found it after breakfast, after the kitchen had been cleaned and cleared of people. It was over by the basket of markers and the prayer flag. The note simply said that he'd wanted to say goodbye but that he'd had to leave early in order to get back in time. He said he was sorry. He told me to stay strong. "Stay fluid." He'd left his email address. "Anytime you want to go count fish. You can count, right?"

I went and found the guestbook to see if he'd written anything there, but he'd only left his name. I remembered him doing something for the prayer flag, but when I looked through all the squares—all the prayers and poems and inspirational quotes, the hearts and peace signs and eight-legged cats—I didn't find any with his name on it, and I couldn't tell which was his.

It was after three by the time everyone had gone. Mom and Aunt Mel both went and took naps. I wasn't exactly sure where Andrea was. Mr. Hayes had come to get his chairs. His truck was backed up at an angle in the driveway, the tailgate hanging open.

Mr. Hayes carried the chairs one in each hand. He'd take two, and then come back for two more. He didn't stop as I wrestled the stepladder out of the garage and over to the elm, but I noticed him look my way a couple of times. I set the ladder against the trunk, and then went to get the prayer flag.

I untangled it outside, by the tree. You're not supposed to let them touch the ground, but this wasn't a real one anyway. I tested the ladder and reset it when it went cockeyed. Mr. Hayes just kept marching back and forth, shrinking down the stack of chairs. I began climbing, one end of the rope gripped in my teeth.

The closer I got to the top, the less steady the ladder became. I could see I wasn't going to be able to reach the first branch, but I raised the flag to check anyhow. My free hand gripped a thick ridge of bark. I was short at least two feet. I looked at the hard ground below me. I could climb up maybe one more rung. I raised my arm to check again and held it like that, trying to think.

"Wishing your arm was longer?" Mr. Hayes asked. He'd steered away from the path he'd been trampling into the lawn and now stood behind me.

I checked the distance one more time. "I need to hang this from here."

"Come on down," he said. He held the ladder so it wouldn't wobble and took the end of the flag from me. "Now tell me exactly what you're trying to do."

I told him I was trying to string the flag from the tree to the corner of the deck, where the trellis was.

"Your mom wants it like that?"

I nodded.

He seemed to be considering it. "Here," he finally said. He handed me the other end of the flag. "Go run this over there." He meant by the deck. "Let's see if this will even reach."

The line reached—I'd pulled it so taut that it slipped out of Mr. Hayes's hand—but there wasn't enough length to tie it around anything.

"We're going to have to make it longer," he said. "Come on back." He asked me to hunt down some twine or string while he went home and got a different ladder. "Give me ten minutes," he said.

My dad had coils and coils of different thicknesses of rope near his workbench: three mil, six mil, eight. *Mil* meant millimeter. He also had coils and coils of webbing. He even had an electric cutter for the ropes and webbing that kept the ends from fraying, one that didn't so much cut the material as melt through it, creating little black clouds of toxic smoke. I grabbed a bundle of red three mil.

When Mr. Hayes got back, I helped him carry the ladder from his truck. It wasn't a stepladder like my dad's but an aluminum extension ladder, and it rattled and pinged as we carried it to the tree. He had me set down my end first, and then he walked the ladder upright. He pivoted it so that it was parallel to the trunk and pulled on the cord so that the rungs extended almost all the way up to the first branch.

I told Mr. Hayes about my dad's cutter, but he said it was fine. He pulled a small folding knife from his front pocket, flicked it open, and then cut off two long pieces of rope and handed them to me—ends frayed, as poofy as dandelions gone to seed.

My dad would've used a double fisherman's, but Mr. Hayes just used a square knot. Once he had both extenders tied on, we went over to the deck and hung that side first. Back at the ladder, I picked up the rope and handed it to him. He climbed up a few rungs and then instructed me on how he wanted me to steady the ladder.

When he'd gotten to the branch, he asked, "What do you think?" He pulled the flag tighter, so that it was almost a straight line. "Like this? Or do you want it with a little more slack, so there's a dip in it, like this?" I didn't say anything, and he pulled the line tight again.

"The other way," I said.

He wrapped the rope around the branch twice before tying it off. Even so, a long tail hung down and he got out his knife again and cut it off. Back on the ground, he stood the ladder up and lowered the top part, the catches rattling on the way down. He walked that end out and then laid the ladder on the grass. He came and stood next to me and we looked at the flag.

"Did you make a square?" I asked.

"Bonnie signed our names for us. I believe she also drew a cross."

The air was calm and the squares just hung there. I started looking for Mr. and Mrs. Hayes's.

"Tell me how this is supposed to work again?" he asked. "These are prayers?"

"They're more like wishes or blessings," I said. "They get spread by the wind. That's why you're supposed to hang them up high. They put them at the highest peaks in Tibet and Nepal. And then because they're up so high and there's lots of wind, the blessings can get spread all over the world."

"Hmmm," Mr. Hayes said. "That sounds kind of nice. It's generous. What do you think?"

"You're supposed to let the sun and wind and rain destroy them. It's to represent the cycles of things and letting go. Like when the flag has disintegrated, then it's time for moving on." I wasn't sure if that last part was true or not.

He pointed at the ladder, and we bent down to pick it up. "What did you do for your square?" he asked.

On traditional prayer flags, the square in the very center usually had a wind horse on it, a mythical creature that was as strong as a horse and as swift as the wind. With its power and speed, the wind horse was supposed to help transport the blessings. The square in the middle of our flag simply had my dad's name on it.

The truth was that I hadn't been able to bring myself to make one. "I drew some waves," I lied. They'd been a common choice. "So he could surf."

"Oh," Mr. Hayes said, "good idea."

"Yeah?"

"It's creative."

"Thanks," I said. "I wasn't very sure what to do. I didn't think anything would be good enough for him."

Forty-Four

Aunt Mel stayed until the following Monday. Even with her there, the house seemed empty and quiet and too big. Mom pretty much either stayed pajama-bottomed and inside, or she went out for these super long runs and then crashed. Andrea had become obsessed with Aunt Mel's iPad, which Mel let her play with, something that would've freaked out Dad to no end. I mostly hung out in the backyard and observed the air currents and tried not to think about how much I wanted to go to the barn. Sometimes I texted Heidi and Tracy, though I wasn't sure why I was even texting Tracy anymore. Days were fed by leftovers.

On the Sunday before she left, Aunt Mel announced that we were going to have a pizza party and then set off cleaning the kitchen and the fridge, chucking the dried-out meats and grayed salads and stale desserts. She took out the bulging trash and washed all the Tupperware and even wiped down the inside of the fridge. She grabbed her purse and the keys for Mom's car.

"Now is the time for requests," she said. "Name it. Anything from the store, or anything you want on your pizza."

None of us seemed to take the bait of her enthusiasm. I asked for whole-grain cereal.

An hour later, she returned with two bags of groceries and a large pepperoni from Cal's. She'd gotten me whole-grain Cheerios. She'd also gotten milk and coffee, and root beer. Two bottles of wine. Bread and cheese, and stuff for making sandwiches. Boxes of frozen enchiladas and lasagnas. So there wouldn't be much cleanup, she'd bought paper napkins and disposable plastic plates that said "It's a Party!" on them—another Dad freaker.

We ate at the kitchen table. For the first slice or two, everyone was pretty quiet. I had school the next day, which was not a happy prospect. Andrea was getting to stay home. But then Mom and Aunt Mel had gone through a couple of glasses of wine, and Andrea through a couple of cups of soda, and the bouncing and the goofiness started coming out of them. Aunt Mel made an impromptu party hat from one of the napkins, and then Andrea insisted she get one, too, and then we all were wearing them, trying not to move our heads too much so they wouldn't fall off. The pizza was so good and warm and greasy it was hard to stop eating, which hadn't been the case for me since coming home. We went through napkin after napkin, wiping the almost iodine-orange mess from our fingers, piling the used and crumpled napkins on the lid of the pizza box, which was also soaked with grease. I had to use both hands because of how slippery my cup had become.

The belch was more of an eruption. It had been unexpected, and I moaned from how good it felt. "Excuse me."

Andrea cracked up, and right away she tried making herself do it. She wasn't very good at it, though. A small forced one came out, which she thought was hilarious.

"Don't," I said to her. "It's gross."

"You started it," she said. The corners of her mouth were orange. She tried to swallow more air.

"Mine was genuine. There's a difference." I could tell she wasn't going to listen.

Mom's had the bellow of a walrus. She actually said *buuuuuuuuuurrrrppp*. It almost had an echo. For a second, we were all, maybe even her, stunned.

And then at once, all of us together, we were laughing as a family. And it almost felt okay.

Aunt Mel drove me to school. Her flight didn't leave until two. She said she wanted to get in some more time with me, joked about how she and Mom and Andrea would be sitting around watching morning talk shows while I was at school studying. "Actually," she confessed, "I still have all my packing to do."

She switched lanes without signaling to pass some kind of delivery van. We were along the stretch of Jefferson where the businesses started popping up—the payday loan place, the bowling alley, the used-appliance store with the sun-faded sailboat for sale in its parking lot. I'd already watched those places streak past like a million times, would have to watch them streak past like a million more before I graduated.

The panic—how quickly it peaked and barreled and then broke over me.

"I don't want to go," I said. It didn't sound as urgent as it was supposed to.

"I don't want to go, either," she said. We weren't even talking about the same things.

I asked her how I was supposed to do math, how I was supposed to retain things about history and English. "They're all going to ask about it," I said. "Or they won't, which is kind of worse, and no matter how I explain it, I'm going to hear some version later in the day that is completely wrong, and people are going to say all sorts of things about me, and it's just going to suck."

"There's a chance," she said.

We were getting close. I was telling Aunt Mel about how I didn't think I could sit at a desk all day. I wanted to explain about wandering into the junipers at the rest stop, how that feeling of wanting to move was coming back. We'd stopped at a light, and there, on the corner, stood a guy holding a sign for a furniture store. The sign was shaped like an arrow, and the guy was taking the sign and spinning it and flipping it, all the while doing some dance moves. He wore fingerless gloves and mirrored sunglasses. Very white socks.

"I want to be that guy," I said. "Outside. I want to be in the sun riding my horse."

"You don't want to be that guy," she said.

The light had turned green. She was waiting for the car in front of us. The sign guy did a three-sixty spin, the sign held above his head so that you couldn't see what it said. I'd never been to that furniture store before. I couldn't even recall if I'd ever been to *any* furniture store. We started moving. The sign guy waved and smiled, but because of his glasses I couldn't tell if it was to me. I wanted to know if signs like his even worked. I mean, did they actually attract customers, or was he just out there dancing for nothing?

"Please," I said. I meant, *Please, can we just go back home?*

"How long would it take?" she asked. When she saw my confusion, she clarified herself: "With your horse."

Mel could spare two hours. I told her it'd take fifteen minutes to get out to the barn, even though I knew we'd have to backtrack across town. I thought the expressway would be faster, but at some spots the traffic was all hard braking and we just crawled. It took a half hour to get to Stanton, the turnoff for Peg's.

Magic was in her stall, eating her grain. I didn't see her around, but Peg must've just come through and done the feeding. A few other boarders were out. One was with the farrier and the other riding in the arena, working on half halts.

"This is her," I said. I tried getting Magic to keep her head up, but she was more interested in eating than letting Mel see her. I reached into her bucket and grabbed a handful of pellets. I had Mel hold out her hand and I poured some into her palm. I thought of my dad and the tarantula. "Make sure you keep it flat," I said. I didn't need to tell her that. She hadn't ridden like my mom had, but she'd been around horses before.

As Magic lipped the grain out of her hand, Mel shivered a little. "Their teeth," she said. "I always forget how big they are."

"It's not like they're fangs or something." Magic was sticking out her chin so I could rub it. I reached up to get her forelock out of her eyes.

"Have you been bit yet?" she asked. I told her I hadn't, which was the truth. They always bit each other harder than they bit us anyway. "A horse got me on the shoulder once and the bruise lasted for weeks," she said. She reached over and used her hand to get me.

Peg walked in from the far end of the aisle. She must have seen Mel first and not recognized her from the service. "Can I help you?" she asked. Her voice sounded firm, but when I stepped into view, it softened. "Emma," she said. "Well, I didn't expect to see you."

Mel reintroduced herself when Peg came over. "I have to leave today, so I just wanted a chance to see Emma's horse and where she rides and what it's like out here."

"Of course," Peg said. She told us to look around, told me to show the place off. "This one is also getting her feet trimmed today, otherwise I'd let you turn her out." She patted Magic's neck a couple of times. "That's right," she said to Magic. "When Lenn is done with Flash, it's your turn. And you're not going to be a knucklehead about it, are you?"

Magic seemed to understand Peg was talking about her, and nickered. I knew that Magic behaved with the farrier, that she just stood there and lifted her foot when you asked. Mom and I had watched Lenn a couple of times before, and he even said to us how easy she was. One time Peg had even let me hold Magic's lead rope while Lenn was working on her, and she only pulled against it once, barely.

"She's not a knucklehead," I said.

"No," Peg said. "She's a good horse. A very good horse." She said it in a way so that Magic was supposed to know she'd been kidding. "There's actually another young girl coming out later who's thinking about picking up another partial lease on her."

Aunt Mel was looking at her watch then. My legs felt as weak and tingling as they had on the Tinto, when I'd first spotted Alex. While I'd be at home, some other girl would be out here riding Magic. "If you want to show me around," Aunt Mel was saying to me. "We'll have to make it quick. We're starting to run out of time."

Forty-Five

We parked in the visitor's parking lot, and Aunt Mel walked me to the office. Because the school didn't have enough money and staffing, and because there weren't enough classes for everyone, the school had begun using students to replace office workers, and Suzie Snider, who was in my grade, was behind the reception desk. She asked us how she could help.

Aunt Mel explained who I was, and how she was my aunt, and how she wanted to make sure I didn't get marked tardy or absent or anything like that. "Okay," Suzie said to Mel, and then quickly to me, "Hi."

"Hi," I said back.

Suzie pushed her chair away from the desk. "I have to go get a real person to change attendance on the computer," she said. She went into Mrs. Conway's office. There was another person in there, but I couldn't see who it was, and Mrs. Conway was talking to them. Suzie just waited.

"What class are you supposed to be in right now?" Aunt Mel asked. She was holding her left wrist and staring hard at her watch again.

"I'm not sure," I said. It was either Spanish or study hall. I looked at the clock on the wall. A cage covered it. We had long passed Mel's two hours. "Study hall," I said. "Then lunch."

Suzie finally talked with Mrs. Conway. She came back and sat in her chair and then looked at Aunt Mel and me. "She'll be right here," Suzie said. "She's just finishing up." She told me I didn't have to wait and could go to class if I wanted.

"I don't mind waiting," I said. Aunt Mel didn't like that.

"That's cool," Suzie said. We stared at each other for a bit longer. Then she asked me how things were going.

"You know," I said. Suzie and I weren't really friends, but we also weren't strangers, which pretty much summed up my relationship with most of my classmates, so I never felt quite sure how to act around them. "Pretty good, I guess. Not too bad." I figured wide latitude was a good idea.

"Cool," she said.

"Yeah, awesome."

I had been in study hall for like two minutes before Mrs. Meyers came and got me. She took me out into the hall, and she made sure we were standing so that everyone in the classroom could still see us through the door window, and then she put her hand on my shoulder and told me how sorry she was for my loss, and that she was glad I was safe, and that the whole school—everybody—was ready to support me.

She didn't say anything about the email she'd sent my parents those weeks ago, the one my dad had replied to, thanking her.

I glanced into the classroom. This kid, Seth Tripp, was raising his hand with some question, and Cindy Carrol was poking this other girl in the back, almost right in her armpit, and Duncan Miller was staring and sticking out his tongue at me, and then Mrs. Meyers was saying how she hoped that maybe I wanted to go talk with Mr. Kluge, the counselor.

"We want to make sure you have a smooth transition," she said. "Academically, of course, but also emotionally."

One time, freshman year, I'd seen Mr. Kluge in the hallway, walking with the side of his head pressed against the wall, his eyes down, his hands in his pockets. People were laughing and mimicking, but he didn't seem to notice or care at all. He often had that faraway look. The joke was that our counselor needed a counselor himself. I'd laughed with them, too. It just seemed so weird. Now I thought that maybe I got it, that everyone else was weird for *not* moving through high school that way.

"You mean reentry," I said.

"Reentry?"

The temperatures during reentry, when those astronauts are hurtling home, reach thousands of degrees. In order to survive, you needed some sort of vehicle that can dissipate all that. You needed to come in at the right speed and the right angle and have the right pitch—angle, momentum, lean. For my dad and his friends, those vehicles became all sorts of things—a reentry burger at McDonald's, setting up a slack line in the backyard, an enthusiasm for microbrew beer. The ones who knew they couldn't handle it, they just stayed out there forever, adventuring from one wilderness to the next.

"Instead of transition," I said, "call it reentry."

Mrs. Meyers was amused. She thought I was talking about coming back to school, but I meant more than that. "That's clever." She tried it out: "Well, we want to make sure you have a smooth…reentry." She asked again about Mr. Kluge. "How about we go say hi?"

I looked into the classroom again. Duncan Miller was writing in his notebook and seemed to have forgotten about me. No one else spied on me, either. I thought maybe it was going to be that easy to be left alone.

"I'll go during lunch," I said, "I'll be sure to. I know I need it. I know that it helps." I actually didn't know those things, not in any clear way, but it was something I'd heard people say.

"Wonderful," she said. "You can go whenever you want to. Don't even worry about getting a hall pass."

Heidi and Tracy wanted to sit with me during lunch. I was at our regular table in the corner, waiting while they paid for their food. At the table next to me, some freshman was having a hard time keeping his hamburger together. Music was leaking out of his headphones, and it sounded like it was heavy metal or hard techno or something like that—something unrelenting—and I thought about how loud it must be for him if I could hear it so well. I used to do the same thing, but now I couldn't imagine how he could stand it, how he could stand so much noise in his head.

Nearby, this girl who was in English with me dropped her fork. It bounced into the aisle just as this senior, Milt Brandt, was walking through. Milt stopped in front of it, his tray held aloft. I thought he was going to pick it up for her. A couple of his friends stood behind him, crowding in to see. He actually waited for her to start reaching for it before he kicked it across the room.

"Oh my god," Tracy said, sliding in across from me. She was totally laughing. "Did that just happen?"

"That was horrible," Heidi said. She was laughing too. She set down her tray and waited for Tracy to move over.

The girl had sat back up and was just staring down at her food and shaking her head. The look of shock had given way to something more wounded. There were a few other girls at the table with her, and all of them leaned in close, asking her things I couldn't hear. Every once in a while, one of them would look over and scowl at Milt and his buddies, but they were all busy laughing and punching each other in the shoulder and not even caring.

"Is she from English?" Heidi asked. She and I had it together second period.

"Yes." I couldn't remember her name, only that she was really good when we had to act out lines from Shakespeare.

"Look at her," Tracy said. The girl had declined a fork from her friend and was just eating her salad with her hands, dipping each piece of lettuce into a little cup of ranch dressing.

"She's nice," I said. "That was so cruel of him."

Tracy tried to hold in her glee. "I know," she said. She'd gotten us all a plate of nachos to share, and was digging out the first chip. "The timing was so perfect, though."

Heidi smiled in agreement. She nudged the nachos my way. They were drowning in yellow cheese, which I used to love.

"Everyone is talking about you," Tracy said. "You are the most popular person here."

"People in line were just asking us things," Heidi added. "I told them you were a hero."

The kicked fork had come to rest under a table at the end of the aisle. A kid was half stepping on it, his foot bouncing restlessly. I thought the thing to do would be to go and pick it up and give it to Milt. Tell him to return it and apologize and not be such a jerk. Make him say it in front of everyone. Tell anyone who'd laughed along that they should apologize, too. I wanted to be the kind of person who would do that.

"Don't say that," I said. I swung my legs over the bench and stood up. I grabbed a chip that was doused in yellow, thinking I could drop it on Milt's head. "It's not even true." I threw the chip back on the pile, where it stuck as if glued. "If you're going to talk about me, at least say things that are true. At least tell them what really happened."

"What should we say?" Tracy asked.

"Tell them what I did," I said. "Tell them I killed him." I slid my hand under the plate and lifted it up. "And that I did this." That's when I smashed the nachos onto the tray, globs of cheese spraying all three of us.

Mr. Kluge wasn't in, so I sat in the career room, hoping Heidi and Tracy wouldn't find me. The career room was really just the waiting room outside Mr. Kluge's office, and its main feature was a bulletin board with all sorts of fliers for scholarships pinned to it. There were also posters for universities and faraway colleges, posters that had little tear-off reply cards for requesting information, hardly any of which had been taken.

Mr. Kluge came back right after the first bell. He had on a robe sweater, the belt tied tight. He carried a Ziploc bag with some carrot and celery sticks in it.

"Ms. Wilson," he said. "*Hola.*"

"Fourth is about to start. I should get to class."

"Not an issue," he said. He pulled a ring of keys out of the big pocket on his big sweater and unlocked his door. As he did so, without a hint of irony, he said his office was always open. "I do have someone who might be coming in for an appointment, but until she gets here, let's chat."

Mr. Kluge put his baggie of vegetables in his desk drawer. He pointed to the chair I was standing next to and told me to sit. I noticed another spot of cheese on my jeans and scratched at it with a fingernail. I hadn't really wanted to talk as much as just flat out tell him that I wasn't ready for school yet, that I needed to be outside and working with Magic or something, and that he needed to call my mom and make her be cool with all of it. It was too noisy and too crowded, and something about it reminded me of being held under again. Before I'd even spoken, the second bell rang. Just after that, Jenny Weaver popped up in his doorway. I don't know how many months pregnant she was, but she was beach-ball big.

Mr. Kluge asked Jenny if she could wait a few minutes, but I interrupted before she had a chance to answer. "You already scheduled this," I said, pulling out the chair for her. "I'll come back later."

Mr. Kluge told me to at least wait so he could give me a hall pass, but I told him how Mrs. Meyers said I didn't need one. The truth was that I didn't need one because I knew I wasn't going to actually go to Global Perspectives.

"Please come back," he said. "I'm glad you came."

"I will. Me too."

I left his office and went all the way down past the art room, took a right by Mr. Chang's metal shop, and then went out the double doors that lead to the back of the school. A few smokers were out there, and a few other kids were hurrying in tardy. I crossed the parking lot and walked through a gap in the fencing, then skidded my way down a little hill. I followed the gully until I was past all the ultra-green sports fields and then found a mesquite tree to hide under.

When Mom picked me up after school that day, she asked

how things had gone. Mel hadn't told her about the barn. My shoes were covered in dust, my bangs wetted with sweat from hiking back through the gully, my clothes stained. Teenagers were swarming all around the car.

"Good," I said.

"Yeah?" She seemed to be forcing her smile. "That's good, right?"

"It is," I said, forcing one back.

"Well, okay," she said. "First one is always the hardest."

Forty-Six

The next morning, we were right back to where I didn't want to be. I'd explained away the automated your-child-has-been-absent call from school by saying that I'd been with Mr. Kluge, which my mom took as a healthy sign. Healthy would've been if I'd just told her the truth right away about how I actually felt.

My mom pulled to the curb and put the car in park. She just sort of spaced out on the gearshift then, thinking about something. In front of us, Julie Haverson stepped out of her mom's BMW and picked at her crotch, unwedging her short shorts. If my dad had been there, he probably would have shaken his head and said something like, *Oh, Jesus Christ…*

I lifted my backpack into my lap and reached for the door handle. "Alright," I said, "have a nice day."

It took a second to register, but then she looked over at me. "I will," she said. "You too. I love you."

I opened the door and got out. I put on my backpack and tugged down the back of my T-shirt. I gave her a wave and joined the stream of students heading inside. I looked back once, but only right before the front entrance, just to make sure she'd left.

In the mornings, all the other doors were locked from the outside, and the front entrance was the only way in, which meant the front hallway was always insane. I pushed my way through, and then down over to my locker, where I dumped the books I didn't need. As part of my school supplies, my dad had gotten me a water bottle, which he made me keep there, arguing that a brain needs water to function well. I was supposed to fill it up every day, drink the whole thing. I'd used it after gym class a couple of times, and there was still some water in it from whenever that was, water that now smelled of mildew. I took the bottle off the shelf, dropped it in my backpack, and then kicked the locker closed.

I went the same way I had the day before, past the art room, past Mr. Chang's. In the flood of all those bodies, I hadn't seen Heidi and Tracy yet. Even though the front doors were the only way in each morning, you could exit whichever way you wanted.

I wasn't alone. There were other kids fleeing, some of them on skateboards, some in their cars. I cut through the fence again and down the hillside. I walked along the gully, past the sports fields, until I was finally forced out in a residential area full of big, close-together houses. The streets kept branching off, dead-ending in culs-de-sacs, and I couldn't find a way through. By the time I had finally gotten to a place I recognized, my shirt was soaked through with sweat and my water was gone.

I didn't get any offers for rides until I was out of town. The first was at the Quick Mart, where I was sitting outside in the shade, drinking the Gatorade I'd bought. Heat ripples were rising from the blacktop parking lot. An older-looking man whose station wagon was stuffed with clear garbage bags full of soda cans had come out of the store and told me that he appreciated what I did for him. Anywhere I wanted to go, he said. I told him my dad was right there in the bathroom. The guy let his look linger, so I stood up and started pounding on the bathroom door, telling my dad to come out, even though I knew nobody was inside.

The second offer came about a mile later on the side of the highway, from a woman who was about my mom's age.

"I just don't think you should be out here," she said. I could see that there was a child seat in the back of her minivan.

"No," I tried to explain, "I've walked like this before. I can do it."

"This is a dangerous road. People drive crazy out here."

A semitruck flew by, its wind shaking us. "I'll be alright," I said.

"Can I call someone for you?" When I said there was nobody, she said, "Please don't make me call the police."

"I'm almost there anyway. It's just a little bit further."

"How far?"

"It's just that next road." I had no idea where the road I was pointing to actually led. It wasn't my road. The road I wanted—the road to the barn—I wasn't even halfway there.

"It'll take a second in the van," she said. "Please."

When she dropped me off, I thanked her for the ride. I didn't say it to her, but sitting down, just for that little bit, felt good.

"Rethink this next time," she said.

"I will." I tried to sound as sorry as I could. We waved, and then I started walking down the road, the opposite direction from Peg's. The woman waited a bit before she pulled back onto the highway. As soon as she was gone, I turned around.

Peg backed her pickup along the shoulder, the truck's brake lights lit the whole time. I was making it down the last stretch of highway. When she got close, she stopped and turned on her hazard lights. As I walked alongside her truck, she leaned over to roll down the passenger-side window.

"I thought that was you," she said.

"Yep," I said, "it's me."

"Everything alright? Car troubles?"

"No," I said. "I just walked."

Next to Peg, on the bench seat, was a new toilet float, still in the package. "I have a leaky toilet," she said, when she saw me looking. "Hopefully this one works. Hate driving into town more than I have to." I nodded like I understood. "And what about you?" she asked. "You're walking a long ways from nowhere. I assume you have a destination."

I looked through the cab, past Peg. On the other side of the road, the hills looked like a row of knuckles. Beyond them was another row, and then another, and then tucked in a little valley was her place. I started explaining about Milt and the fork. And that I'd heard someone in the hall call Kevin Kelly a retarded whale, which was really bad because he was actually autistic. And that I didn't really see the value of schoolwork, because so far it had done a pretty lousy job of preparing me for what I was going through. And that adults just did what they wanted to do without even asking anyway, like climbing up stupid logs, or changing horse leases, so what was even the point?

I told her how the school had probably called home already, and that my mom was probably going crazy, which I actually felt really crappy about. "But I guess not crappy enough," I said, about to cry. "Because here I am."

Peg leaned over again and opened the door for me. "Come on," she said. She cleared some room on the seat. "Hop up."

I set my backpack next to the toilet float. "She's not going to understand," I said.

"She might not," she said. "But she also might surprise you."

"I doubt it. I know my mom. People are as predictable as fish."

"People are predictable until they're not," she said. "Like horses."

Peg turned on her signal and waited for a car to pass. I wasn't sure if she was going to do a U-turn or if she was going to take me to the barn.

"Please don't take me back to school," I said.

Peg drove slowly until she had all four wheels on the pavement and then got up to highway speed. I leaned my head toward the open window, relieved by the wind, even though it was warm. The receipt from the hardware store took off and swirled around the cab until Peg batted it down. She told me how her cell phone was in the glove box, and how she was going to pretend that it wasn't, which meant that we'd have to drive to her house, where we were going to use the landline to call my mom, so that she at least knew where I was, because I owed her that much. And then Peg told me how after that, there were afternoon feedings to get done, which I was going to help with, and if my mom still hadn't gotten to Peg's, then there were probably some stalls to clean. If she still hadn't arrived, then Peg said we'd figure it out from there.

"We'll get as far as we can get," she said, "and then we'll figure it out from there."

Forty-Seven

My dad sometimes told me how he thought the word *river* should also be a verb. He thought it should mean to move or act as a river. There was the verb *rive*, which meant to wrench open, or split off, or tear apart, but that didn't work for him. Rivers could tear apart the earth and split off pieces of rock, of course, but my dad didn't just mean those qualities. To river was to act with grace, to bend, to flow. A balance between power and gentleness, depth and shallows. It was to dance. To catch the light of the sun.

We had stopped to eat lunch at the bottom of a small rapid. We were floating in the eddy and getting ready to leave. I asked my dad how much energy he had.

"Why?"

"That wave over there." I spun my paddle over my head, much like a helicopter's blades. "Isn't this how you do it?" My dad called it the helicopter stroke. It was a show-off move. The trick was to get on a wave, find its sweet spot—the spot where it would just hold you, no need for even a rudder—and then you spun your paddle and flew.

The wave wasn't a thrasher. It was flat and wide and almost glassy. We had to climb to the top of the eddy to get to it, where the shallow water made it harder to get in a good stroke. We'd switched positions at lunch. I was in the stern. Up front, Dad could help with the momentum and lean parts, but it was now up to me to set our angle.

The first couple of tries, I couldn't pry hard enough as we crossed the eddy line, and instead of skimming onto the wave, we flew out into the current and were swept downstream, where my dad would plant his big forward strokes and almost single-handedly get us back into the eddy so we could try again.

"Watch how the water is actually pouring off the shoreline," he said. "See how it's directed this way?" He held up his arm to mirror the current. He was showing me how to translate it, how to begin to understand water as a kind of language. "That means we want the boat to be more like this." He held up his paddle to show the angle I wanted to keep us at.

"That's enough?" I asked.

"That's how I'd do it."

We backed up in the eddy, giving ourselves a little more room. He held up his paddle one more time to show me the angle I wanted. I switched paddling hands and moved the stern into position. I switched hands again, shouting for him to go. When the bow hit the eddy line, I was already pulling. I could feel it through the hull, could hear my dad shouting, "Yes!"

Water peeled off the canoe as we dipped into the trough. Because he was so heavy, just by leaning forward or back, my dad could change our position on the wave, either pushing the bow further down and building the spray, or letting it slip back into the perfect pocket. Once we'd found our spot, all I had to do was play with my blade angle, carving us one way along the face, and then back the other, all that water rushing past.

"Helicopter stroke!" I shouted.

My dad began spinning his paddle over his head. When I hooted for him, he twisted around to check on me. "Come on," he said. "You, too!"

I centered my weight, pretending I was galloping on Magic, something I'd only done a few times. I lifted my paddle out of the water, just testing things. The canoe kept tracking, holding its place. If it started to drift, I just had to shift my knees.

"Come on!" he shouted. "Get it up there!"

I spun my paddle over my head. My dad kept yelling for us to spin faster, claiming that he could feel us lifting off. I spun as hard as I could, knowing it wouldn't work, but also not caring, because that wasn't the point.

After the helicoptering, my dad switched to tossing his paddle up in the air and catching it, and then after that, after he almost lost it and I had to save us with a high draw, he switched to using it as an air guitar. His finale was to balance it on his chin.

He'd gone through all his tricks. He was just sitting there, paddle across his lap, watching the water. The sky streaked past in silver reflection. We were flying. I could've kept us there forever.

"Headstand," I said.

He'd gotten his hands positioned on the gunwales. He planted his head on the seat, then brought up his knees and steadied them on his elbows. He'd warned me we might get swamped, or that we might end up swimming. As long as I was cool with that, he'd said.

His sunglasses fell down over his forehead. He was just beginning to stretch his legs skyward. He'd been focused on the bottom of the boat, trying to keep his balance point, but then he looked up and met my eyes. I saw the goofy grin, and I knew.

"Don't!" I screamed, both of us cracking up. "Don't!"

In one last grand move, he thrust his legs straight into the air. He held it for a moment—legs together, toes pointed. It was perfect for a moment, and then he toppled over, flipping us upside down.

Forty-Eight

I was hauling a wheelbarrow of manure when my mom arrived at Peg's. I took the wheelbarrow over to the pile and dumped it, shaking out the last few bits of dirty bedding. Every couple of weeks, Peg would take her tractor and move the pile. It'd get tilled into the pastures once the ground softened up with some rain.

There were still a few more stalls to muck, but I put the wheelbarrow away, leaning it against the barn wall. I'd heard two car doors close and the screen door to Peg's creak open and thwack shut. I looked down the aisle, the other end an unbroken square of light. I hung the pitchfork in its place, put the gloves Peg had lent me back on the shelf she'd pulled them from. My hands and arms and legs were sore in a way that felt good. I checked again, but no one was coming yet.

Magic was turned out in the far pasture. I walked over to her stall and looked in, leaning against the door. She had so much space out there, and so little in here, but I guess it was enough. I'd filled her water and spread out fresh shavings. That was about all I could do for her, but I was proud that I did it. It was something.

Andrea came running down the aisle. "Panda-bean," I said, scooping her up.

"I think you're in trouble," she said. It was hard to tell if she was happy about it or worried.

"Do you think?"

It wasn't until a few days later that Peg would come up with her proposal—where instead of going to school, I could come help her at the barn, and she'd offer me a kind of informal work-study position, and that if need be, part of it could even include time to study for my GED. She'd actually done something very similar with her own daughter. I only had to spend about one night talking my mom into it, and at first it was just going to be short-term, and with stipulations, though that changed pretty quick. My mom said it was something that Peg had said to her in the parking lot that really convinced her.

"She was mentioning all these things that happened," Peg said. "At school, and with friends, and they were all supposed to explain how she'd ended up on the side of my road, but you could see it in her eyes. How she wanted to do right, how worried she was." Peg said it was a look she recognized. "You see it in green horses. It's not that they're meaning to misbehave," she said. "It's that they're unsure of what's being asked of them, and they're confused, and they're just trying things to see what'll work. You know that you have to give a horse one thing at a time to build it up. She's trying to figure out what was being asked of her."

I knelt down so Andrea could crawl onto my back. She was still so light. I carried her around and showed her the few horses in their stalls. She liked finding pieces of straw to feed them. I even let her pretend feed some to me. When there were no more horses to see, I started toward the arena. I was going to gallop her around for as long as she wanted.

Mom stood at the far end of the aisle, silhouetted by the sunlight. She asked if we were ready to go. Only as I got closer could I really make out her expression, which mostly looked exhausted. I had Andrea hop down. Mom grabbed the top of her head and gave it a playful shake. She tilted Andrea's face up and then leaned down to give her a kiss.

"Why don't you run to the car?"

"Time me," Andrea said.

Mom hit a few buttons on her watch, gave a ready-set-go, and then Lil' Ripper was off.

It was just Mom and me and a couple of old horses. She reached out for a side hug, and I couldn't stop myself from sliding into it. "Hi," she said.

Maybe I did want her to yell at me, to get as worked up as Dad sometimes got. Maybe it wasn't so much about the action as the reaction. That was something Roland once suggested. Occasionally, the guy had his moments.

"Listen," she said. "All I'm going to say is that from now on, at least for a good solid bit here, please just tell me where you are and where you're going to be. That's it. Okay?"

I nodded. "I'm sorry," I said. "I didn't mean to—"

She squeezed my shoulder. Her head rested gently against mine. "I didn't mean to, either," she said.

"What?" I asked.

"Whatever I did to hurt you."

"You didn't," I said.

"That's not how it feels."

Dad's van was still chained to the bed of the tow truck. The driver had parked on the street, right in front of our house. As we pulled into the driveway, he had his seat kicked back, his ball cap pulled down over his face. Mom had to knock on his window to wake him up.

I couldn't tell if he was the same guy from Piedra Gulch, but it was the same towing company. Andrea and I watched from the yard as the guy worked the controls—slowly extending the ramps, slowly raising the platform, slowly lowering the van. Mom stood in the driveway, her arms crossed, holding the invoice in one of her hands. The sky was cooling off. A bat arched away from a chimney. The smell of lighter fluid drifted in from somewhere. Out in the street, the Dunlap twins, still not freed from training wheels, rode around in circles. Across the street, Mr. Dunlap paused from edging a flowerbed. Down the road, Charlie was howling.

Once the van was unloaded, the guy went through the same slow process as before—putting the platform in place, stowing the ramps, securing chains. I picked at the scab on my thumb, peeling back part of it, stopping when a bright red dot oozed out.

Last thing was the keys. A new bright green tag hung from the ring, right next to the one from the shuttle service. The driver handed them to Mom. "That should do it," he said.

After he left, we all sat on the porch, Mom and I just staring at the van. "Wow," she said. "It's so dirty. Those must have been some roads."

"They were," I said.

"He'd be out washing it right now," she said. Whenever he came home from a trip, unless it was super late at night, Dad always wanted everything unpacked and cleaned up and put away.

"I know," I said. "I'd have to do the vacuuming."

"That ratty old sponge of his."

"I know."

She unfolded the invoice, looked at it quickly, and then folded it back. She folded it in half once more. She made a fist around Dad's keys.

"We could wash it," I said. "There's time before dinner. I'm not that hungry. We could even just go to one of the drive-through places." Andrea loved doing that. "What do you say," I asked her. "Do you want to go through the spray wash?"

"Not one of those places," Mom said, cutting off Andrea's response. "We should do it here. But let's do it tomorrow. That'll be the reason for tomorrow."

"Tomorrow sounds good," I said.

Mom and Andrea went inside, but I sat on the porch for a bit more, alone like the first night I'd come home. The front door was still open. Mr. Dunlap had gone back to edging, and the twins had gone back to racing one another. Andrea had requested mac and cheese and peas, and I could hear banging pots in the kitchen as Mom searched for the one she needed.

A few days after the funeral, a postcard from Alex arrived in the mail. It was displayed on the fridge now, stuck there with a magnet that had been holding up one of the sheriff's business cards, a card I'd thrown in the recycling. Unlike the postcards my dad sometimes sent, ones where he wrote in super tiny letters and used every bit of space, cramming so much in that you sometimes couldn't even read the words, Alex's was brief.

On the one side, a double rainbow stretched over the Grand Canyon. On the other it said: "Just about to put on the river again and wanted to tell you something. Last time I saw you I told you to be safe. But I should've also added this: be wild."

I got up and walked to the van. You could barely see the smiley face under the new layer of dirt, blasted on from miles of travel. I grabbed the bottom of my shirt and was about to erase it. I decided to redraw instead.

Epilogue

I'd tried getting us all the way to Pinedale, but my eyes had gotten too heavy, so I stopped at a rest area about fifty miles outside of town. Mom and Andrea were already asleep in the back, and instead of climbing in with them, I unrolled the sleeping pad and got out my new bag and slept on the floor. The drive could be done in fourteen hours, but so far we'd stretched it into a three-day journey, stopping for a day in Zion and later taking a long side trip to visit the Topaz Internment Camp, which is one of the places they forced Japanese Americans to go during World War II. Mom bought a postcard. We were supposed to make sure we sent one to Peg.

As soon as it was first light, I got out of my bag and slid into the driver's seat, pumping the gas as quietly as I could to set the choke. Once the van started, Mom poked her head up and asked where we were.

"Close."

"Did you sleep?"

"On and off," I said.

"Do you want me to switch with you?"

I'd driven almost the entire way, even when we hit snow outside Salt Lake and Mom and I about froze our fingers off while trying to put on the chains. "I'm good."

When we got there, it was still early. Except for the gas station on the edge of town, everything else in Pinedale appeared closed. At the end of Main Street, a jagged row of backlit mountains stretched the horizon. We passed a restaurant whose sign read

279

"OPEN AT 7:00," so I circled around the block and parked nearby on the street. I pulled the curtain across the front window, tilted my seat, and grabbed my bag from the floor, unzipping it and using it blanket-style. Mom woke up again, and I told her we'd made it. Andrea squirmed, and I thought she might wake up too, but she didn't.

"There's a diner," I said. "We can get some coffee in an hour."

"You were right," Mom said to the waitress as she came to clear our plates. She had tried to warn us. All three of us had ordered the pancakes, Andrea's with chocolate chips. Actually, we'd each just ordered *one* pancake. None of us had even come close to finishing ours.

"As long as you stopped because you were full," the waitress said, "and not because you didn't like them."

"No," my mom said, "they were delicious."

"Seriously," I said.

The waitress, arms filled with plates, asked if we wanted any more coffee, winking at me for some reason. Both Mom and I answered no. "Back with the check," she said.

We'd been the first customers that morning, coming through the door right after the waitress had flipped the sign to "Open." The diner was still mostly empty. A few guys with cowboy hats and faded jeans sat at the counter and shoveled hash browns and eggs into their mouths. Closer to us, an elderly couple split a gigantic cinnamon roll. It seemed like the kind of thing the couple did often, and I wondered how long they'd been coming, because the building seemed like it'd been there for centuries. They sat by the big windows, just a few tables away, the light spilling in orange and heavy but cool. The windows stretched almost all the way to the ceiling, and the glass was so old it had turned wavy. On the walls hung several pieces of dusty taxidermy—elk heads with huge antlers, antelope, a black bear with snarling teeth, a stringer of nice-sized trout. Next to the trout hung a neon Coors sign, with the second "o" brighter than all the other letters.

The waitress returned with the bill, and my mom got out her purse. While Mom dug for her wallet, the waitress took a little standing break, letting her gaze drift to the street. She asked about our van, the Arizona license plates. "Long way from home," she said.

My mom put her debit card in the bill holder and handed it back. She said we'd been hearing about Pinedale, Wyoming, for a long time. "Call it an unconventional spring break."

The waitress slid the billfold into her apron and grabbed Andrea's empty glass of orange juice. "People around here usually seem to head your direction for spring break," she said. "Arizona. California. Maybe Mexico."

"Hawaii," I added. Tracy was there again this year. Heidi was in Flagstaff, at the treatment facility her parents had sent her to after she'd gotten caught with vodka at school again. I didn't really talk to either of them anymore—just texted with them once in a while, and we'd all say that we missed each other, and then we'd do nothing about trying to hang out.

"Or Hawaii," the waitress agreed.

After breakfast, we walked Main Street, pausing to look into some of the shop windows. At a fly-fishing place, a faceless mannequin in neoprene waders stood near the window, and I stared at it for a long time, thinking of Alex, picturing her knee-deep in some mountain stream, casting. Months ago, just after New Year's, she'd visited me at Peg's, and we took out Magic and another horse and rode along the back ridge to an overview, where we watched a flooding Rio Verde and talked about the lines we'd take. Afterwards, we exchanged a few emails, and even started talking about meeting again, but then she went on a trip to the Yukon, and I just kind of stopped hearing from her.

We'd walked up one side of the street and back down the other. "Well," Mom said, when we had reached the van again. Andrea was pulling on the sliding door to get in, even though it was locked. "What do you think?"

I took the keys out of my pocket. "I think so," I said.

The bridge was another twenty miles north of town. Rangeland stretched out in all directions. Parts were still yellowed from winter, though others were beginning to turn green. In the distance, the black mountains of the early morning were now in clear view—towering, knife-like ridges sugared with snow. No one was speaking. Mom sat in the passenger seat, the plastic bag of ashes in her lap. Andrea wouldn't meet my eyes in the rearview mirror.

It was an old steel bridge, with a sign warning about the low clearance of the trestlework. I slowed down as we crossed it, stopping right in the middle. The river was wide and shallow, but swift. Leafless dogwoods speckled one shoreline with their bright red bark. The other had been trampled to dirt by cattle.

"I think this is it."

"Over there," Mom said, pointing to a gravel turnout across the bridge.

From the turnout, a little trail led down to the water. We walked downstream a ways to escape some bits of trash, an old sock, empty beer cans. Even though the river technically started far up in those snowy mountains, draining out of a small alpine lake, this was the first put-in where it was deep enough to float a loaded down kayak. This was where he'd planned to start. This was the trip he'd always wanted to do: the Colorado River, from source to sea.

The water ran clear blue, and all three of us squatted down to test its iciness. Across the river, a merganser made its way against the current. Mom stood up and took a deep breath. I thought of grabbing Andrea and acting like I was going to push her in, something Dad would've joked about doing, but she didn't play like that much anymore. Instead, I picked up a piece of bulrush and tossed it toward the river, where it fluttered down and got stuck on an eddy line.

We had Andrea go first. We'd decided it would be up to each person if they wanted to say something or not. She didn't even really want to hold the bag, let alone say anything, and when it looked like she might spill the whole thing, Mom helped her. The ashes spread across the water's surface, floating downstream, not really sinking at first. "He's off," Mom said. "There he goes, see?" She'd meant it to be comforting, but it made Andrea cry. Mom pulled her in for a hug, and then I was joining them, too, my arms around them both.

From there, the river headed south, collecting tributaries on its way to Fontanelle Reservoir. After that, on the border with Utah, it reached Flaming Gorge Reservoir and its dramatic red cliffs. It would've taken my dad days to paddle across the reservoir, and then after Flaming Gorge came Dinosaur National Monument and the Gates of Lodore, those two massive stone buttresses that signaled the start of Lodore Canyon. Then Desolation Canyon, which was almost a mile deep, and then Labyrinth and Stillwater Canyons, where the river cut several giant oxbows and you could paddle right up alongside the sheer rock walls. After that the Green River joined the Colorado, and from there it was Cataract Canyon, where you hit the first big whitewater—though some of the biggest rapids, really, the ones at the end of the canyon, were buried under Lake Powell. Powell next. Like Flaming Gorge, it also would've taken him days to paddle across. He would've stopped at Rainbow Bridge, even if it meant dealing with a bunch of motorboats and houseboats, just so he could pay tribute to all the sandstone arches that were now, like the rapids, buried underwater. After Glen Canyon Dam, it was Lee's Ferry, which was the put-in for the Grand Canyon. He would've slowed down in the canyon, stopping for plenty of layovers, exploring the more hidden spots like Silver Grotto and the milky turquoise pools at Mooney Falls.

Past the canyon was Lake Mead, with its white bathtub ring from where the water has come down so much lately. At the other end of Lake Mead was the Hoover Dam and the electric glow of Las Vegas, and following Vegas it was Lake Mohave and Laughlin, and finally—after dams in Wyoming, and Utah, and Colorado, after dams in Arizona and Nevada—the river reached its first Californian dam: Lake Havasu. At Havasu, diversion canals would start sucking out millions of gallons of water, sending some of it east to Phoenix and Tucson, the rest of it west to LA and San Diego, shrinking the river back down to a shallow stream, much like how it was where we were standing. Next came Imperial Dam, which was also a desilting facility, and then it was more diversion canals, splitting off at right angles until it was hard to tell which was river and which was canal. At the border with Mexico, the Morelos Dam funneled what was left of the water through a big sieve, and then after that, the river was mostly turned into lettuce for the US. What was left became toxic agricultural runoff, moving through more canals, until it reached an intertidal dead zone. Where there used to be three thousand square miles of delta, now there was just a giant mud-flat that you couldn't cross in any kind of boat, and then—after miles of land that shouldn't be land—somewhere out there was the Sea of Cortez.

Mom thought she might as well go next, since she already had the bag. She told Dad she loved him, said that she always had and always would. She held the bag close to the water to keep the dust down. Small splashes of bone shook out. "Paddle hard," she said. A cloud bloomed in the water, and a few minnows darted over and nibbled at it.

Next, it was me. I kneeled down at the water's edge. Mom had rolled down the top of the bag so that it was easier for me to pour. She had mentioned something earlier in the trip about maybe keeping some of the ashes, about maybe wanting to have some for the urn back home, so that the urn was actually holding something.

"Do you want me to save some?" I asked.

Andrea was leaning against Mom, and Mom was stroking Andrea's hair. Both of them were standing. I thought of the prayer flag back home and how it had almost worn through. "No," she said, "let's leave him all here."

One of the reasons I think my dad never attempted a source-to-sea trip was because he didn't want to see what the Colorado had become. As I poured out the remaining ashes, what I silently wished for was that he would still never have to—that his ashes would travel far, that they'd run through all the beautiful canyons and whitewater, and then maybe into the belly of a coyote, or a mule deer, or even an oarsman, but not all the way to those ugly canals.

After most of the ashes had been carried away, I turned the bag inside out and rinsed it, stirring up the water one last time. I sat on my heels and watched. Gradually, as everything settled, the water turned clear and blue again. Mom had said to take as long as I needed, but I was ready. I'd been trying to tell which parts of the sediment were made of him, and which parts had been there before, but they were indistinguishable now. There was no separation. It was all just river.

Acknowledgements

No book is written alone, and I am deeply grateful to the following individuals and organizations for their help with this one: Thank you Per Henningsgaard, Abbey Gaterud, and everyone at Ooligan Press. Thank you Tenaya Mulvihill, Sabrina Parys, Stephanie Podmore, Alexandra Haehneart, Ellie Piper, Katey Trnka, and the rest of the team—you helped shape this manuscript in so many beautiful and important ways. Thank you Rachel Pass for that critical and encouraging first read. Thank you Oregon Arts Commission for the numerous ways you've supported Oregon artists, including me. Many thanks to PLAYA for the generous residency you provided: it was overlooking Summer Lake that much of this book was written. Thank you to the Fishtrap Gathering of Writers, Fishtrap, Inc., and the Rose E. Tucker Trust. Thank you Ann Powers, Mike Midlo, and Charles Finn. Thank you Cindy and Luis Urrea. Thank you Chelsea Jennings and Alex Carr Johnson. Thank you Mark Bailey, Kirsten Johanna Allen, and Laura Stanfill. Thank you Traci Glass, Virginia Harness, Tyler McMahon, Liesl Schwabe, and Karen Shepard. Thank you Margo Crane. Thank you everyone who is part of the Prescott College tribe. Thank you to the Wisconsin Library Association and librarians everywhere. Thank you Bill and Donna Kallner, Craig Reidner, Jamee Peters, and anyone who has ever taken me down a river. Thank you Melanie Bishop, mentor and friend. Thank you Manbuddies. Thank you Stripes. Thank you Mom and Dad, and the rest of the BLT family. And most of all, thank you Shannon and Josephine, my hearts.

About the Author

Eliot Treichel is a native of Wisconsin who now lives in Oregon. His first book, *Close Is Fine*, is the winner of the Wisconsin Library Association Literary Award. His fiction and creative non-fiction have appeared in *Beloit Fiction Journal, CutBank, Passages North, Southern Indiana Review,* and *Hawai'i Pacific Review.* He's also written for *Canoe & Kayak, Paddler,* and *Eugene Magazine.* For more information, visit his website at www.eliottreichel.com.

Ooligan Press

Ooligan Press is a general trade publisher rooted in the rich literary tradition of the Pacific Northwest. Ooligan strives to discover works that reflect the diverse values and rich cultures that inspire so many to call the region their home. Founded in 2001, the press is a vibrant and integral part of Portland's publishing community, operating within the Department of English at Portland State University. Ooligan Press is staffed by graduate students working under the guidance of a core faculty of publishing professionals.

Project Managers
Stephanie Podmore
Alyssa Gnall

Acquisitions
Tenaya Mulvihill (manager)
Sabrina Parys (manager)
Zach Eggemeyer
Alexandra Haehnert
Molly K.B. Hunt
Gloria Mulvihill
Margo Pecha
Ellie Piper
Brandon Sanford

Editing
Katey Trnka (manager)
Olenka Burgess (manager)
Megan Doyle
Alex Fus
Alyssa Gnall
Alexandra Haehnert

Molly K.B. Hunt
Margo Pecha
Ellie Piper
Stephanie Podmore

Design
Erika Schnatz (manager)
Ryan W. Brewer (manager)
Stephanie Podmore
Jessica Weber

Marketing
Ari Vives (manager)
Dory Athey (manager)
Megan Doyle
Alex Fus
Alyssa Gnall

Digital
Meaghan Corwin (manager)
Cora Wigen (manager)
Molly K.B. Hunt